summer island
A PRINCE IN PERIL

summer island Books
by Robin Russell

A Prince in Peril

A Jail for Justice *

* to be released May 2010

summer island
A PRINCE IN PERIL

ARVON BOOKS

Summer Island — A Prince in Peril / by Robin Russell
Summary: When a group of children gather to spend the summer on
an island, their vacation turns into a series of dangerous
entanglements as they strive to save a prince in peril.

ISBN 978-0-9841884-0-6

Printed in USA

For Aunts

Acknowledgements

This novel has been a long time in the making and there are some special people I'd like to thank:

Ngoc, a writer's most devoted assistant, for her late nights editing and her relentless commitment to this project.

My students, for pestering me to publish and promising to read the book.

Dennis, for his meticulously wielded fine-toothed comb.

Carol, for making sure I never 'feel badly' again.

My beautiful family — Maria, Stephanie, Mario and Giovanna — for their staunch support, their zeal and for bearing with my frequent absences.

My sisters, Kelly and Shawnee, for sharing and spurring my love of adventure.

Seymour and Zoë, for rejuvenating me with their unbridled enthusiasm.

And most importantly, my mother, Jennifer, for her genetically predetermined penchant for article-clipping.

❧ C o n t e n t s ❧

summer island
A PRINCE IN PERIL

1

❧ The Invitation ❦

Greta hated summer vacation with all her heart. She knew this wasn't normal. She knew every other kid she'd ever met loved summer vacation. They couldn't wait until that bell rang and they were free for ten whole weeks. *Well, they don't have to spend the summer at Poor Camp*, thought Greta. That is really what she hated: Poor Camp. The concrete, the hoop without a net, the snacks made with government cheese and stale crackers. It would be her sixth year and she just couldn't bear it. *No*, she thought, *that isn't the right word. I am dreading it. I am filled with morbid consternation. I am morose.* As Greta started to think of even more words to perfectly match her feelings, she was reminded of what it was that made Poor Camp so deplorable. Sure the concrete was bad, the kids were exceedingly big — and mean — but she could have survived it if she had been able to go unnoticed.

You wouldn't think to look at her that anyone would notice Greta. She was small for her age and very thin. She was black, but so were most of the kids at her school. And all the girls wore the same dreary, blue uniform. No, Greta wouldn't stand out one bit, if she didn't know quite so many words. Expansive. That is what Principal Jones called it.

"You have an expansive vocabulary, Greta. You should be very proud. It is good for a girl your age to excel at something all her own."

Greta could not care less about excelling. In fact, if she had her choice, she would prefer not to excel. Then she wouldn't be noticed. She didn't like people looking at her, thinking about her, making assumptions, thinking they knew her, knew her family, knew everything about her. It was presumptuous. What Greta did care about, had always cared about for as long as she could remember, was rightness. The perfect fit. The "click" she felt in her gut when she found just the right word to express a situation or person or feeling. She loved it. It was like solving a puzzle and it made her so happy that she couldn't help smiling at the beauty of it. Of course, that didn't help at all.

"What're you smilin' at?" one of the biggest girls from Poor Camp had asked her last year. "You think you're so smart, 'cuz you know all those fancy words, huh?"

"No," Greta had said softly.

"Yes, you do. You think you're smarter than me. You probably think you're smarter than every kid here, don't you?" the girl had demanded as she started to shove her.

Greta had looked around, hoping to find a counselor. She saw a sea of children but no adult in sight. *They were probably smoking cigarettes in the break room*, she had thought.

Greta shuddered with the memory. She looked at the clock. Eleven minutes left. Eleven minutes of school, of structure, of reliability, of all the things Greta treasured. But she wouldn't have them for long. In just a few minutes, now only eight, she would be immersed in the frenzied chaos of hot concrete, terrifying children and horrible food. Greta was miserable.

A rustling of feet brought her mind back from her daydream. The bell had rung and kids all around her were racing to get out of the classroom. They were laughing and talking and pushing. They seemed so thrilled. Greta didn't know what their summer plans were, but she was almost certain that none of her happy, carefree classmates would be joining her at Poor Camp.

Greta grabbed her book bag and slowly walked through the door and out into the hallway. As she made her way to the bus, all she heard were pieces of excited conversations. Plans for family vacations: horseback riding, swimming, hiking, sailing and camping. Each adventure sounded even better than the one before and just made her more melancholy. If these kids were riding horses, she'd be riding one of the four bikes at Poor Camp without a flat tire. They'd be swimming in lakes and she'd be swimming in her own sweat!

By the time Greta got off the bus, she could not have been in a worse mood. She walked the two and a half blocks down Carver Avenue until she reached The Ocean Vista Apartments. *That's a joke*, Greta thought to herself. *I've lived here my whole life and I haven't seen one single drop of an ocean.* She climbed the stairs to the third floor and opened the door of number 317, the apartment she shared with her mother.

"Greta!" her mother yelled happily. "I have wonderful news! Come in, sit down, let me get that for you." Mrs. Washington took Greta's bag and hung it by the door. "What's with the long face, sugar? I thought kids your age were delighted when summer vacation came. Or has that gone out of style?"

Greta didn't say anything. She hated arguing with her mother. They had gotten into some big fights about Poor Camp but it hadn't changed her mother's mind. Actually, that wasn't fair. It wasn't…accurate, that would be a better word. In fact, her mother sympathized with her. She knew Greta hated the place, and Greta knew how much it bothered her mother that she dreaded going there. Still, it was either that or stay home and there was no way Mrs. Washington would ever allow that, even if Greta was eleven-years-old. She had begged not to go.

"I'm sorry, honey. I know how much you hate this. If I could make it better I would, but we just don't have the money."

"Please just let me stay here. Please. I'll do anything. I'll do all the cleaning. I'll wash clothes. I'll get a job, anything!"

"Baby, we've talked about this. You get your say but when I make a decision, that's it. There is no more discussion."

"But Mama —" Greta had started.

"Greta Lynn Washington! What did I say?" Her mother rarely used that tone and Greta dropped the subject.

"Yes ma'am," she had said sorrowfully.

That night, her mother had made Greta's favorite, spaghetti with meatballs, for dinner. After that Greta tried to stop moping around as much. She knew how hard it was for her mother. She was going to school and working and being a parent too. Plus, it wasn't as if she was deciding this to be mean. For her, it must be like Greta begging for the moon. She could relate to her daughter's wanting something but it just wasn't possible. Since then things had been better. They had struck an unspoken compromise. Greta tried not to show her mother how disappointed she was and her mother didn't put on a façade and pretend it was going to be a great summer.

At least not until now.

Mrs. Washington was grinning from ear to ear. Poor Camp was bad enough. Greta shouldn't have to be happy about it too.

"Now, let me see...." said her mother. "What is the one thing that you want most in the whole, wide world?"

"What?" Greta asked. This was...unexpected.

"I'm not talking like 'a promotion for my mom' or 'world peace' or anything like that. I'm talking just about you, the thing *you* want more than anything." She waited expectantly.

Greta was afraid to speak. What if she told the truth and her mother said, "Greta, I've told you for the last time, you are going whether you like it or not. Now guess something else!"?

"Come on," Mrs. Washington said eagerly. "Say it!"

"Not...to..." Greta began slowly, "...go to..."

"Poor Camp!" her mother nearly screamed it. "Exactly — although you know how I feel about calling it that. Still — yes, yes, yes!" Her mother grabbed her and gave such a squeeze, Greta wondered if she was in her right mind.

"Mama," Greta began hesitantly. "What exactly is going on?"

"Only this," her mother replied as she casually tossed a thick envelope onto Greta's lap.

She picked it up. It was on lavender stationery and addressed to "Miss Greta L. Washington". Greta noticed the seal wasn't broken. "It's not even opened. How do you know — ?"

"I guess I just do," she said coyly. "Now open it, open it!" Mrs. Washington was acting like a little kid on Christmas morning.

Greta stuck her finger below the flap and used it to break the edge free. She pulled out a wad of paper surrounded by a lavender note card. She looked at her mother.

"Oh, honey, I am so happy. I thought maybe this year, but when it didn't come I figured.... Oh, never mind — see what's inside."

Greta opened the card. The first thing she noticed was a blue airplane on a folded envelope. She picked it up and peered inside. It was a plane ticket. "I don't understand," Greta said.

"Read the note," her mom said softly, taking the ticket and placing it on the coffee table.

Greta looked down to read the note and was distracted by a bright, crisp bill. She picked it up. It was twenty dollars. "What is this?"

"Wow," her mother said. "When I got mine, it was only five. I guess that's inflation for you."

Greta wasn't sure exactly what that was supposed to mean but she surmised her mother wasn't planning to volunteer any more information.

She read the note.

Greta,

I do hope you will be able to join us on The Island for the holiday. Enclosed are your ticket and money to help with traveling expenses.

Dinora will meet your plane in Boston and take you from there. I am very much looking forward to meeting you.

Give my love to your mother, Tia

2

❧ The Airport ❧

Mario carefully added sulfur dioxide to the test tube. Immediately, the liquid inside turned from fuchsia to lime green. He placed it gently in the centrifuge just as his sister barged through the door, causing his equipment to rattle dangerously.

"Dinora!" he snapped.

"Oh!" Dinora glanced at the closely averted catastrophe and tried to look contrite. "I'm sorry."

"Yeah," Mario said skeptically.

"Truly I am, but Mario, we need to get going! Papi has gone to get the car and you're still fooling around in here. If we miss the plane in Mexico City, there won't be another until tomorrow. Already, we don't know for sure if it will connect in time with the one in Miami and Tia asked me to meet Greta and I told her I would and that's a big job and what if I'm not there and —"

"*Tranquila*, Dinora," Mario told his little sister. "We'll make it in plenty of time."

"Aargh," Dinora growled, rolling her eyes. She would never understand him. He was just like their father, always in the lab with the bottles and plastic glasses. Not to mention those chemicals that stank up the whole house.

Mario shut off the centrifuge and turned to face his frenzied sister. "Okay," he said calmly, "no more chemistry." He shifted easily from Spanish to English, "You said Father is getting the car?"

"Yes. Are you going to bring anything? I put my bag in the car last night. I wanted to be sure to remember it because if I forgot it, not that it is the most important thing, but still…. I'm ready whenever you are," Dinora rambled, also in English.

They were probably not even conscious they did so, but each summer, before they got on the plane, they found themselves conversing more and more in the language they would use over the summer.

"Little sister, I may be running late but you are running too *early*," he teased her as he nodded his head towards a small leather bag in the corner.

She grabbed it and ran out of the room. Mario made some quick notes before abandoning his experiment. After cleaning up, he took one last look around the lab to make sure everything was in place. He smiled wistfully before closing the door.

Greta gripped the arms of her seat as the plane descended. The stewardess had given her a piece of gum to chew so her ears wouldn't hurt with the change in pressure. Greta chewed it with all her might. She was so focused on this job that she didn't even look out the window until the lady next to her pointed out Boston Harbor, one thousand meters below them. Minutes later, it looked like they were about to drop right in. Then the wheels of the plane skipped along the runway and they were on the ground. It was the successful completion of her first plane ride. Greta breathed a deep sigh of relief and almost inhaled the gum which she had forgotten was still in her mouth.

"Miss Washington, will there be someone here to meet you or would you like me to escort you to your next flight?" the stewardess asked her sweetly.

"No, thank you," Greta answered quietly. "I mean, yes, someone is meeting me. I'm fine."

The stewardess smiled and progressed down the aisle. It seemed like no time at all had passed when Greta found herself disembarking with her small bag in tow. Her mother had told her she wouldn't need much, just some comfortable shoes and her underclothes. That seemed strange but her mother assured her it had always been like that at Tia's. Of course Greta had asked her mother nearly a hundred questions about her summers spent at Tia's. Who was Tia? How did she know her? What was "The Island" like? Why wouldn't she need anything? But Mrs. Washington was elusive in her answers, rendering Greta even more curious. As it turned out, the invitation had arrived just in time. The plane was scheduled to depart on Sunday morning, leaving little over a day to prepare.

Greta tried to clear her mind of all her suspicions and worries. She pulled her shoulders back and held her head high as she stepped out into the airport. No one was there. Well, not "no one". She should be more precise. There was a janitor sweeping the wide corridor and a father holding his son up to one of the large windows so he could see the planes. Greta looked out over the vast waiting area, scanning carefully for the woman who was supposed to be meeting her. Still — no one. She began to feel panic creeping into her lungs. The family behind her pushed by and Greta managed to move her legs over to one of the seats lined up in rows.

She sat down and tried to catch her breath. "Everything is going to be fine," she whispered to herself. "I'm not stranded. I'm not stranded." She repeated it a few more times until she felt her pulse slow down. A *million little things could have happened,* she told herself, trying to grasp the situation as best she was able. *Traffic,* she thought. *People complain about it all the time. Her car could have gotten a flat tire. She could be a minute away, a second even. Everything was going to be fine. Just —*

"Greta?" a voice above her asked hesitantly.

Greta looked up into the cheerful face of a girl her own age.

"Oh, good, I found you! I was so worried. I ran all the way here from my plane because we came in late and well, okay, not *straight.* I didn't come straight here but the thing is — I just love these pretzels." She held up a large soft pretzel covered in mustard. "We have them in Mexico but I just like these better. They're just so — oh, I don't know — good, I guess. And I can only get them here. And when I knew our plane was running late, I just hoped and hoped that even if we were very, very late we wouldn't be so late that I wouldn't be able to get a pretzel before I went to meet you. I'm Dinora by the way." She shoved a chubby hand into Greta's and shook it vigorously as she continued. "Then, when we landed I had to race to the doors and I had barely eight minutes and I knew it would be just enough so that if I could find out your gate quickly, and if it wasn't too far from mine, and if it was past the pretzel stand then I would be able to get you *and* the pretzel." Dinora took a deep breath to replenish her lungs. Greta just stared at her.

"Well, of course, I didn't! I mean I didn't get you — at least not in time and I'm terribly sorry. There was a man in front of me at the stand and it actually wasn't *exactly* on the way here and well…. Would you like some?" Dinora offered the pretzel.

Greta continued to stare, dumbfounded. She'd assumed Tia would send an adult to meet her. Dinora was a child — and not much older than she, if at all. Greta tried to stay calm. She looked at the pretzel, then back at the girl. Greta smiled weakly and shook her head.

"Well, you don't want to hear all about that anyway. It doesn't have anything to do with anything." She reached down and picked up Greta's bag and started walking towards the main corridor before confirming, "This is yours, right? I guess someone told you that you wouldn't need a whole lot. Tia has everything. Was it your mom who came?"

Greta didn't respond as she struggled to keep up with Dinora who, for a plump girl, was exceptionally fast.

"Greta?" Dinora turned around to face her while still plowing straight ahead.

"Huh?" Greta sped up even more so Dinora wouldn't accidentally smack into a pole trying to talk to her.

"Was it your mother who came when she was little?"

"Oh — yes, my mom," said Greta.

"It was our dad. Kind of weird, huh — spending the summer where our parents spent theirs? Anyway, we better hurry. I told Mario I'd arrange the next flight while he met Seymour's plane."

"Who's Mario?" Greta asked as she and Dinora dodged some passersby.

"My brother. He apologizes, by the way. He would have come with me to meet your plane but then Seymour's plane was delayed so he couldn't. Well, I guess he still could have, technically, but then Seymour wouldn't have known where to meet the rest of us and then we would have wasted time and Tia prefers we arrive before dark. Otherwise she worries and as it is we'll probably just make it…."

There was so much activity around them, Greta found it difficult to concentrate on what Dinora was saying. Adding to this confusion was the girl's tendency to prattle. *Yes*, thought Greta, who was quickly developing an affinity for her new companion. *That is it exactly. Dinora doesn't just talk. She prattles.* Greta's attention was dragged back as Dinora pulled her quickly out of the path of a small vehicle making its way down the hall.

Dinora deftly sidestepped a group of businessmen and next thing Greta knew, she was heading down an escalator. It dawned on Greta that from the moment she'd met her, Dinora had not stopped talking. Her mother had taught her it was rude to interrupt someone but Greta decided if she was ever going to get a word in edgewise this is exactly what she would have to do.

"... and that's what made the flight so boring —"

"Dinora?" Greta blurted.

"Yeah?"

Greta had a million questions in her head, all scrambling to be asked first. She had no idea where to start but she was smart enough to know that if she didn't ask something quickly, she would lose the opportunity. And although it wasn't the most pressing, she asked the one which came most easily.

"Who will be at Tia's?"

Dinora didn't break her stride as she adjusted easily to the new topic. "Well, you, of course. You're the youngest. Usually Tia invites you when you turn eleven. I got to come two years ago, when I was ten but that was because Mario was there so I guess Tia felt like there would be someone to look after me. He's seventeen," she said proudly.

"And who else?" Greta hoped to keep Dinora on track as much as possible.

"Then Seymour and Zoë. They're cousins. They've been coming forever. That's it — five. Sometimes there are more. Last summer it was just the four of us. I'm awfully glad you came this year. Seymour and Zoë are fourteen, and even though everyone is loads of fun, it is nice to have someone my own age — especially a girl. Oh!" Dinora pointed to a sign that read *Charter Flights* and made a sharp turn towards it.

The lady at the counter looked as if she could imagine plenty of other things she'd rather be doing than working there.

"Excuse me?" Dinora said, in an authoritative voice. This was a whole new side to this seemingly featherbrained girl. Greta had underestimated her.

"Whaddya want?" the lady replied, not even looking up from her crossword.

"I'd like to book a flight for five to Deer Isle, Maine."

"That'll be forty for the flight and one passenger, then five for each additional passenger. Burt can take you in half an hour. Meet him on the landing outside of gate 6C." The woman sounded almost like a recording.

"Fine," said Dinora succinctly, opening a wallet she had taken out of her pocket. She placed three twenty-dollar bills on the counter.

The woman took the money, put it in a drawer, pulled out a receipt book and scribbled something on it. She passed it to Dinora with a half-hearted, "Have a nice trip," all without looking at them once.

"She's always like that," Dinora told Greta as they left the counter. "Mario said she was like that even when he was our age. Oh! Look at the time. We'd better get going."

Dinora darted off and this time Greta was prepared. She went right along with her and did a much better job of dodging, squeezing through and keeping up. Greta was so focused on her task of not getting hit in the head with a big carry-on bag that she didn't see the boys until they were right in front of her.

"Has the plane landed?" Dinora asked excitedly. "We got the flight. It's out of 6C, but it's Burt again. Zoë's not going to like that, but it's not as if I had a choice. I mean, who you get is who you get and the lady said half an hour, so as soon as —"

Dinora's yammering was stopped as one of the boys pulled her into a huge hug.

"Oh, Dinora, how I've missed you," Seymour said dramatically. "The peace and quiet has been too much to bear." He was laughing as he released her.

Greta liked Seymour immediately. She couldn't quite place it but there was something about him. He was immense for one thing — taller than Mario, even though he was three years younger, and just big all around — like a football player. But he seemed so gentle too, like a peaceful giant. *No*, Greta thought, *that wasn't the right description.* She looked again at his head topped with golden curls. Whatever the word, it encompassed strong and gentle and kind and…

"You must be Greta," Seymour said.

"Yes." Greta didn't stray from her shy demeanor. This was all a *lot* to take in.

"I'm Seymour and this is Mario," he said, pointing to the tall, thin boy with glasses standing next to him. Greta had no problem finding the right words to describe Mario. They came to her immediately. Serious. Intelligent. Reserved. In a way he kind of reminded her of Spock from Star Trek.

"And pretty soon my cousin, Zoë, will be walking off that plane and we can get going. How does that sound to you, Dinora?"

"Fine, fine. All I was saying —"

"Excellent," said Seymour decidedly. And then Greta saw his whole face change. Now it looked almost sad but in a distracted kind of way. Greta followed the direction of his eyes and saw them meet a young girl stepping off the plane. Greta couldn't help but stare. The girl was gorgeous. Her clothes were crumpled and her long black hair was messy. She also looked tired from what must have been an exhausting flight, judging from her fellow passengers. Despite all of this, she was beautiful — more than beautiful. The girl was stunning. Her gaze connected with Seymour and she pushed her way through a crowd of people to run towards him. It looked as if she was starting to cry.

"Come on, Dinora," Mario said softly, putting his hand on his sister's shoulder and guiding her away. "Let's give them a little time while we make our way to the plane."

"But if we don't hurry —" Dinora began.

"They know, Dinora," Mario said calmly. "They'll be right behind us. Come on."

Dinora appeared as if she was about to say something but then seemed to think better of it. She looked back. Seymour had dropped his bag to embrace his cousin. Something in that seemed to change Dinora's mind. "Yeah, you're right. It's still so sad how people can do that to kids."

Greta kept waiting for Dinora to explain herself. It seemed strange that the girl could go on forever about the most boring thing in the world, and now that she had what sounded like a very interesting topic, she didn't want to talk. The three of them made their way back down the hall to the same escalator. Greta looked back at one point and saw Seymour and Zoë lagging behind, talking as if they hadn't seen each other in years.

They exited through the door marked 6C. Before them was the smallest plane Greta had ever seen. It looked to be just barely big enough to fit all of them. Good thing they hadn't brought much luggage.

The pilot reached for Zoë's bag.

"You?" she screamed. Immediately, Seymour and Mario moved between Zoë and the pilot. It was the first thing Greta heard Zoë say and it instantly forced her to alter her initial assessment of the girl. "You mind getting us there in one piece this time?" Greta thought that despite her small stature, Zoë acted as if she was as big as Seymour.

"Listen, young lady," Burt replied angrily. "If you don't keep your saucy mouth shut, you and your friends will be lucky to get there at all."

He grabbed her bag and threw it carelessly into the plane. Greta hoped it didn't contain anything breakable. Zoë pushed Seymour aside and stepped right up to Burt's face, except that she came to his shoulder. This seemed to make no difference to her. She took her finger and began poking his chest like she was trying to pick a fight. Seymour pulled her away as Zoë struggled mightily to get free. Mario put his arm around Burt and steered him towards the front of the plane. The soothing tone in his voice must have worked because Burt got into the rickety contraption and began buckling himself in.

Greta sat in the seat next to Dinora. There were eight seats total in two rows.

"We had a little mishap last year," Dinora whispered quietly.

"What do you mean?" Greta asked, matching Dinora's volume. The engine had started now and she could barely hear herself.

"Burt had a heart attack while flying and Zoë had to crash-land the plane."

Greta thought her eyes were going to pop out of her head. "What?" she yelled.

"Shh," Dinora said quickly. "She's very sensitive about it — scared her half to death."

3

∂ The Island ᔥ

The ocean was dazzling. Greta had seen it as her plane landed at Logan Airport but what sprawled beneath her now seemed so different. This was…. She searched for the perfect word. Spectacular. It had been nearly two hours so far and Burt appeared to still be healthy enough to fly. Greta was becoming more amazed by her companions each minute. She longed to ask Zoë about the crash but it was very clear the girl was in no mood for talking. She had given Greta a curt, "Nice to meet you", when Dinora had introduced them. Since then she had sat with Seymour in the very front of the plane. Zoë had not once taken her eyes off the controls.

"Okay, kids," Burt called. "That's The Island to your left. We should be landing in about five minutes."

Zoë muttered something and Burt shouted, "I heard that, young lady!" Zoë was about to shout back when Seymour subtly moved his hand to her forearm. She pushed it away but seemed to reconsider aggravating their pilot.

"Why's he so mad at her?" Greta asked Dinora across the aisle. "Didn't she save his life?"

"Sure. She saved his life but she also destroyed his livelihood."

"The plane?"

"The plane," Dinora confirmed.

Suddenly Greta felt everything fall beneath her, even her own seat. She fell a second later and her stomach a second after that. Her initial response would have been panic except the others gave no indication this was anything out of the ordinary. Then, just as quickly, the plane lurched forward and caught her. This happened two more times, neither of which was any more pleasant, although at least they weren't unexpected. Greta looked out her window as they made their way down. She felt as if she were about to vomit and was grateful the feeling didn't last. A few short, terrifying minutes later, the plane touched ground and came clumsily to a stop. Greta made sure she was the first person to get off.

There was a blur of activity. Bags and passengers were unloaded and another confrontation between Burt and Zoë was narrowly averted. An ancient Chevy pickup moseyed its way up the tarmac to be greeted by the joyous exclamations of the children as they jumped into the back.

"Greta, do you want to ride in the cab?" Dinora's voice brought Greta back to the moment.

Greta looked at the woman driving. She looked to be about a hundred years old and mean to the marrow. A worn baseball cap covered a mop of gray hair. Dirty overalls hung on her bare-bones frame. She wore old cowboy boots and a weathered flannel shirt.

"Is that Tia?" Greta asked nervously.

"Who? Her?" Dinora began laughing. "No. Definitely not." Greta was encouraged by her tone. "That's Edith. She's…."

"You girls gonna stand there wastin' daylight and testin' my patience or you gonna get in the truck?" Edith's voice sounded like rocks in a blender.

"I'll ride in the back with you," said Greta quietly.

"Don't worry," Dinora said sympathetically. Edith had started driving just as the last leg was pulled over the edge, causing Dinora to tumble down into the truck bed. "She's all bark and no bite." Dinora rubbed her knee, wincing. "Okay, well mostly bark."

The truck meandered along the coastline as they wound their way up the island. Greta looked around and saw steep cliffs looming above her. At the foot of the cliffs she glimpsed dense forest where even the sun didn't seem to brighten. They had made it just in time. The sun was just beginning to set over the western horizon, casting a pink glow across the water. It looked so calm, and for a moment, Greta doubted what she had learned in her science classes, about the dangers that lurked below the waves. As if the ocean itself was responding to her skepticism, her eyes were drawn to a fury of white foam erupting as waves crashed down on jagged rocks.

Her face must have shown some sign of her concern.

Seymour leaned towards her and shouted over the booming muffler, "Don't worry. We swim on the western side of the island. It's much calmer. Are you a good swimmer?" Greta thought of the pool at the YMCA where she had gone a few times with her mother. She had never even been to the deep end. She didn't know how to answer his question.

"It's okay. The rest of us are *very* strong swimmers. We'll teach you."

His voice sounded reassuring but there was something in his choice of words, or maybe it was the way he accentuated the "very" that concerned her. She remembered what Dinora had told her about the crash landing the previous summer. She had assumed that meant crashing on the ground. Now a picture came into her mind of crashing into the ocean and having to keep afloat until help came. That image was a lot more.... Greta searched for the word and found it instantly. Unsettling.

"Greta, if you look off to your right, you'll be able to see Tia's as we round this bend up here." Mario had been listening to her conversation with Seymour. Greta wondered if he was trying to distract her. Whether he was or not, it worked.

She looked, and there, set against a sheer rock face, was the largest, most beautiful house Greta had ever seen. It took her breath away. She wasn't sure if it was actually a dusky mauve color or if that was just the sunset coloring it. It was like a small castle right out of a storybook with three stories and a tower at either end. Greta also counted three chimneys, at least two balconies and windows everywhere. It looked like you could spend a year exploring it and discover something new each day.

"It was built in 1822 by Tia's grandfather, Captain Lowe," Mario informed her.

"He was our great, great grandfather." Seymour smiled easily as he indicated his cousin on the other end of the truck.

Greta looked at Zoë, who appeared a different person entirely from the girl she'd met a few hours earlier. This girl looked as if she didn't have a care in the world. She looked content and something else — something that shone from within her. The road turned again and the house was out of sight. A silence came over the children. This wasn't out of the ordinary for Greta, since she hardly spoke anyway, but her companions had never been this quiet. She looked around at them. They all shared the look she'd noticed in Zoë. Dinora seemed excited but somehow in a calm way, as if her heart knew there would soon be no more waiting. Then her eyes brightened and Greta turned.

There was the house, looking even grander than it had from the road below. Greta could also see an enormous garden off to one side of the house, a large barn and what looked like an orchard farther out. She discovered the house was not right against the cliff face as she had first thought. Instead it was surrounded by fields which dipped on one side into a bluff overlooking the ocean, still sparkling in the setting sun. On the other side, the fields met a thick forest, which surrounded the base of the cliffs; these in turn towered above them all. At this moment they looked as if they were made of bronze.

"Well, well!" A warm voice boomed as the truck sidled up the gravel driveway. "Looks like you just made it. Just made it."

Greta turned her gaze from the cliffs to meet the twinkling eyes of a very large woman.

"Dinora, I told you before sunset and I see you barely made it. Barely made it."

"Tia!" Dinora climbed quickly out of the truck and ran into the woman's outstretched arms. "I tried, Tia," she said rapidly. "I kept telling them we needed to hurry but no one listened to me, and I told them what you said but still —"

"There, there," Tia giggled, her round shoulders bouncing up and down. "It's alright now. Alright now. You're safe and sound. Safe and sound."

Greta couldn't help but smile at this odd, sweet lady.

Seymour and Zoë had also gotten out and made their way over to her where Tia grasped Zoë in a huge hug, pulled her shoulders back, touched her face, patted her hair and murmured something Greta couldn't hear. She repeated the gestures three more times and then turned to do the same with Seymour. Mario helped Greta out of the truck and they waited their turns.

"Mariotzo! Mariotzo!" Tia cried, her eyes brimming with tears. Greta swallowed to keep from laughing at the silly pet name for such a serious boy. Lastly, it was her turn.

"And you must be Greta," Tia said as Greta braced herself to be pulled to the bosom of this grandiose woman. But Tia didn't hug her. Instead she reached out and took Greta's hands in hers. Greta was relieved and disappointed at the same time.

"I am so glad you came. So glad, so glad."

Greta wondered if Tia's habit of echoing her own words had anything to do with living so close to the cliffs.

"Now, did Dinora meet your plane alright?" Out of the corner of her eye, Greta saw Dinora's posture tighten.

"Yes, ma'am," she said matter-of-factly as she tried to contain the grin that was fighting to spread across her face. Dinora relaxed.

"Well good, good. See, Edith? I told you the girl could do it. You said she was too scatterbrained." Tia pointed to Dinora's head. "There isn't a scatter in this child's brain. Not a scatter!"

Edith made a "hmph" sound and gave Dinora a narrow-eyed look before heading off behind the house.

"Now, we're not going to do any good standing out here are we? No, sir. No good at all. Not at all." Tia clucked as she corralled the children into the house through a side door.

They entered a massive kitchen with a high-raftered ceiling and stone-tiled floor. There was an empty fireplace at one end with a large tabby cat sleeping on the armchair in front of it. Nearby was a round oak table with eight or nine chairs and in the center of the room stood a long counter top with pots, pans and various drying herbs hanging from the beam directly above it. On the counter, Greta saw four different projects in the works. Pie crust in the middle of being rolled out, next to two pies which were already finished and waiting to be put in the oven. Potatoes, onions and carrots were lying on a cutting board or chopped up in a bowl. Loaves of bread were rising in baking tins of various shapes and at the end Greta could see a large roasted chicken about to be basted. The kitchen smelled wonderful.

"Get! Get!" Tia said, sweetly but sharply. Apparently, Tia felt her guests had been sufficiently greeted and that any more pleasantries would be coddling. She was all business now. "You know what to do. Don't stand here dawdling. Get going and let me finish. Dinner will be at seven sharp. You hear me? Sharp," Tia said, already moving towards the sink where she washed her hands vigorously and dried them on her apron. Almost as an afterthought, she added, "Zoë, honey, show Greta where the girls' room is and see she gets settled. And don't forget, I said seven sharp. Se-ven sharp!" She made her way over to the chicken where she picked up her basting brush.

"Sure, Tia. This way, Greta," Zoë motioned.

Seymour and Mario headed off in another direction and Greta saw them start up a staircase she hadn't noticed.

"We're on the other end of the house," Zoë explained. "The boys get to be above the kitchen but we're above the music room and that is infinitely better."

"I'm going to go ahead," Dinora said eagerly. "I want to get a shower in before dinner." She sprinted through the doorway and never slowed as she turned back to shout, "I'll meet you up there, Greta!"

"I swear that girl can't do anything unless she can do it fast," said Zoë.

Greta laughed. It was a perfect description of Dinora. Zoë led her through a series of rooms including a large dining room with a table already beautifully set, an even larger living room stuffed with furniture and finally a room where Greta would have loved to linger a little.

"The music room," Zoë explained, although no explanations were necessary. The fact that there were easily twenty different musical instruments in the room gave it away. There was a grand piano next to a window and other smaller instruments lining the shelves along the wall. There were also some overstuffed chairs and a bunch of pillows piled in a corner. It looked like a perfect spot for an impromptu concert or jam session.

"Tia loves music. She was an opera singer in Germany before she retired. Now she plays the organ at church. Do you play anything?" Zoë asked without slowing down.

"No."

"Well, that won't last long around here. C'mon."

Greta was tempted to have a closer look at, and perhaps try, the instruments, only half of which she recognized from her music class at school, but Zoë was climbing a set of stairs in the hall outside the room and Greta didn't want to get left behind.

The girls' bedroom was a long rectangular room with four beds on one side and a sitting area on the other where a sofa and three armchairs circled a thick rug. Behind the sitting area was a door and Greta could hear the faint sounds of a shower and Dinora's singing.

"Go ahead and pick the bed you like," Zoë said, going to the far end to close the window. A fresh ocean breeze had been coming in but now it was definitely chilly. "The ones on this end are nice. Their windows look over the gardens and more moonlight comes through. If you like it darker, choose one of these. The boys get the view of the water but we get the sun in the morning."

Greta looked out each of the windows and took Zoë's suggestion of one of the two beds close to the garden windows. She noticed Dinora's bag open on the bed closest to the door and was glad she wouldn't be starting the summer by fighting over beds with her new roommates.

"Dinora will probably take awhile but I'm quick, so if you are too we should both have a chance to bathe before dinner," Zoë said, unpacking her few things and putting them in the small bureau next to her bed. The bureau had a lamp on top of it. Greta looked around and saw the rest of the beds were outfitted in the same way along with a thick down duvet and two feather pillows. The furniture, bedding, curtains and wallpaper were so perfectly unmatched that it all just seemed to fit. The room was like a giant, busy and beautiful garden.

"Will we have time before seven?" Greta asked, looking around for a clock and not finding one.

Zoë chuckled. "Tia has been saying 'dinner at seven sharp' for a million years and not once has it happened," Zoë said. "I'm not even sure she *has* a clock. She never knows what time it is and even if she did, it wouldn't matter. In Tia's house, 'seven sharp' is whenever dinner is ready." Zoë saw Greta's confused face and added, "You get used to it after a couple of days."

Zoë had finished unpacking and made her way over to another door off of the sitting area. "Come check out the closet," she beckoned. Greta followed and watched as Zoë opened the door and flicked on the light switch. The "closet" was bigger than Greta's bedroom at home. It was lined on both sides with three mismatched bureaus underneath a long row of clothes on hangers. At the very end were shelves filled with boxes and baskets marked *big warm gloves, medium church hats, skinny belts* and so on. The clothes on hangers were similarly organized. Greta saw rain slickers of various sizes on one end and frilly dresses in just as many sizes on another. Between these were overalls, vests, jackets, smocks, blouses, sweaters and who knew what else. Each was in about every size a girl from eleven to eighteen might be.

Zoë opened one drawer marked *old jeans* and rummaged through until she pulled out a well-worn pair which she held up to her waist as she extended her leg. "Yup," she said decidedly, "they'll last another summer." She looked up at Greta, "Feel free to look around and choose whatever you like. Just make sure you always have a sweater or pullover or something. It can get cold quickly on The Island."

Zoë had grabbed a light green, long sleeved shirt with faded white lettering and a thick, rusty orange turtleneck sweater. She continued as Greta opened a drawer herself. "Dinora likes to wear dresses with jeans and a sweater. I'm a jeans and tee shirt gal myself. The boys too — except Mario likes his without rips and Seymour likes his broken in. Whatever you want is okay — just be comfortable." Zoë must have heard the shower stop. She grabbed her clothes and headed towards the door. "I'll be quick. I promise."

Greta wore a uniform at school and hated it. Not because it looked bad, which it probably did, but because it was so uncomfortable. She was beginning to like the idea of wearing whatever she wanted the whole summer. She chose a pair of jeans almost as worn as Zoë's figuring if Zoë liked them, she might also. Then she chose a long sleeve shirt with purple and pink stripes. She was trying to decide between a red sweater and a brown velour hooded jacket when Dinora came in.

"Definitely the sweater. Tia never turns on the heat and it gets cold in the evenings."

Dinora was drying her hair with a towel and had already changed into her standard outfit. She wore a yellow flowered dress over jeans with a matching yellow cardigan. Greta thought it was a little peculiar but somehow suited her.

"Did you see those pies?" Dinora asked. "Did Zoë tell you Tia was a famous pastry chef in Paris before she retired? I hope one of them is raspberry. I love raspberry. I love blueberry too…and strawberry. Well, of course apple, I mean that's just a given…." Dinora kept listing pies as she made her way back to her bed to grab her brush.

Greta went to sit down on the sofa while she waited for the shower but changed her mind when she noticed bookshelves lining the back wall. Her gravitation towards them was an automatic response. Greta, an avid reader, had brought seven new books with her and four she wanted to re-read. Her mother had assured her Tia would have plenty but it definitely put her heart at ease to see upwards of three hundred books in such close proximity. As she perused them, Greta was delighted to find Tia hadn't just included books which might be appropriate for the "girls' room". Before her were amassed an eclectic assortment spanning nearly every discipline and genre.

The Island

She was just starting the second chapter of *The Sea Maiden: a Captain's Tribute* by Ignatius Sewall, when Zoë emerged from the steamy bathroom and told Greta to be quick about it. Fifteen minutes later, the girls were clean, dressed and curled up contentedly in their sitting area. Greta was reading, Zoë was plaiting Dinora's hair and Dinora was talking. Zoë had just finished the second braid when a buzz sounded from the corner. Zoë hopped up. She went to a small white box by the door and pushed a blinking green button. A boy's voice came out and said something in a language Greta didn't recognize. Zoë responded and the two went back and forth for a minute. Greta assumed they were speaking Chinese (Zoë had flown in from Shanghai) and deduced the voice must belong to Seymour. It was a strange notion: this big, blond, white boy, speaking Chinese. And yet, Greta thought, certainly no stranger than anything else she had witnessed today.

Zoë removed her finger from the intercom and smiled at the other two girls. "It's seven," she said.

4

❧ The Dinner ❦

The dinner table was crowded with serving platters, steaming bowls of food, a soup tureen, baskets of bread and a myriad of smaller dishes heaped with their own delicious offerings. Greta wouldn't have known the color of the tablecloth if it hadn't extended past the edge of the table and halfway to the floor. Even the plates and bowls were practically on top of each other.

The rest of the children were seated and it looked as if the boys too had showered and changed into more comfortable clothes. Greta sat down in the seat closest to her, between Dinora and Seymour. Edith came in grumbling and sat down. There were two places left and only Tia was still up, bustling around making sure she had everything. Greta wondered who the other guest would be.

Then Tia sat down and picked up the hand of Edith to her left and Mario to her right. When all were holding hands, Tia bowed her head. Nearly a minute passed before she said simply, "Let us be the change we seek."

After the odd blessing there was a flurry of activity as dishes were passed, food was served, requests were made and overlapping conversations began. The dinner table was much noisier than the one to which Greta was accustomed. It sounded like an entire restaurant had been shoved into one room. She could only pick up a part of one conversation before another drew her attention. Seymour had asked Mario about his current project, and now Mario resembled his sister as he talked animatedly about chemicals and compounds, all between bites of mashed potatoes. Edith seemed to be going through a long list of things that needed to be fixed, supplies to be ordered and decisions to be made. Tia didn't appear to be at all concerned or even paying attention. She was too busy making sure everyone had enough to eat.

"Dinora, the pumpkin soup you like is over here; pass me your bowl before it gets too cold. That's right. Pass it, pass it. And Seymour, darling, have you tried the stuffed squash? I want your opinion. I couldn't decide whether to use walnuts or pecans. Here, take one of each and let me know. Now Mario, Mario! There you are, don't fill up on all those potatoes — nothing exciting there. I made this mushroom pastry just for you. Greta, pass that blue dish in front of you over to Mario and are you getting to try everything? I can't even see your plate. Hold it up, darling. Hold it up. There, well that's not very much but I see you have some of everything. Good girl — oh, except for the bread. Now that bread is right out of the oven. Right out. Zoë, cut off a small piece for Greta and make sure there's plenty of butter on it. Now, Edith, eat up before it's all gone. What? The barn door? Oh, darling, I don't know, I don't know. Did you get some quiche? It truly is divine...."

A large piece of freshly baked bread appeared underneath Greta's nose. She thanked Zoë and took a bite. It was delicious. Everything was.

"Rufus. Here, Rufus," Dinora whispered, and Greta felt the large cat move underneath the table to where Dinora's hand was hanging down. In it was a small piece of chicken.

Once Edith recognized she wasn't going to get any answers from Tia, she dedicated herself to her dinner. Within ten minutes she was done. Pushing back her chair, she mumbled something about getting back to work.

"Tia, is the sailboat fixed?" Zoë asked. The other children stopped their conversation and waited expectantly for the answer.

Tia held up her finger as she chewed the food in her mouth. She swallowed and took a sip of water before answering, "Yes, darling, and this time try to be a little more careful. Just a little more careful."

"Excellent! Let's go out tomorrow. We could leave first thing after breakfast and spend the whole day out."

"Just be back by seven. Se-ven sharp," Tia said, getting up from the table. Rufus emerged at the same time.

"Well, for goodness' sake, Rufus. For goodness' sake." She chuckled as the cat followed her back into the kitchen.

The children were already immersed in plans for the following day. Mario wanted to sail out to a smaller island and go hiking. Dinora wanted to ride horses. Seymour was happy to do anything that involved swimming and Zoë wanted to spend the day on the ocean.

"What about you, Greta?" Mario asked her. "It'll be your first day on The Island. What would you like to do tomorrow?"

Greta didn't know what to say. "They all sound fine to me," she said meekly.

None of the four pressed her. Instead they continued the discussion as they got up and began clearing the table. As they put food away and washed dishes, they argued, bargained, pleaded and debated over how to spend tomorrow. By the time the kitchen was clean, they had reached a compromise. Zoë had given up sailing for half of the next day so they could spend a full day sailing later on in the week. Now the plan was to ride horses, swim and relax on the beach.

Greta had never ridden a horse and was already afraid to swim in the ocean. She was beginning to regret not taking her companions up on their offer to let her choose tomorrow's activity. She tried to picture their reaction if she had suggested staying inside and reading all day. She wasn't sure if the image in her head was accurate, but it was certainly amusing. *Still*, she thought to herself, *even if I drown or get trampled by a horse, already this day has been worth getting out of going to Poor Camp.* Greta tried not to worry about it as she followed everyone into the living room.

Mario and Seymour got out a chess board and set it up in one corner.

Dinora left and came back with Tia and a basket full of yarn. "She's teaching me how to knit," Dinora explained as Tia returned to the kitchen.

"For the third summer in a row," Zoë said wryly. She was sitting at a large table with a map so weathered it looked like it might have belonged to Captain Lowe himself. Greta thought the girl looked as if she were planning quite a voyage for later that week.

This time, Greta had no difficulty deciding what to do. She went back to the bedroom and retrieved *The Sea Maiden: a Captain's Tribute*. She settled in an armchair underneath a standing lamp and read. Within moments, each of the children was absorbed in their own activity. Perhaps an hour had passed when Greta got up to stretch her legs.

"Greta?" Tia called her from the kitchen. Greta entered and saw Tia sitting at a table surrounded by books. She assumed they were cookbooks, although none of them were in English. Tia looked up from the notes she was taking. "Sit down, darling. Do you want a cup of tea?" Tia motioned to a small tea pot next to her. Steam was curling lazily out of the spout and it smelled like oranges and honey.

"No, thank you."

"What about a cookie? Would you like a cookie?" Greta's mother had taught her it was impolite to refuse but Greta suspected a summer with Tia would include frequent offers of food and she'd have to refuse often if she were going to survive.

"Thank you, but no."

Tia looked at her with a quizzical expression. The idea of declining an offer of food seemed to perplex her.

"Suit yourself, suit yourself. Oh, now I remember." She looked up again and pointed to a black box on the wall next to the refrigerator. "Why don't you call your mother and let her know you got here alright. We only have one phone line coming to The Island, so you might have to try a couple of times to reach the operator."

Greta walked towards the box and found it was one of those old-fashioned phones — the kind she'd seen in movies. There was a small stool nearby and she pulled it over and stood on it to reach the mouthpiece.

She picked up the receiver and a scratchy voice came over the line. "How may I direct your call?"

Greta gave the phone number.

"What city, please?"

"Trenton…New Jersey," Greta replied.

"One moment please while I try the line."

Greta heard some clicks and buzzes followed by a distant ringing.

"Oh, and Greta?" Tia called softly from the table.

"Hmm?"

"Be sure if you want to talk about anything too personal, you don't use the phone. Not everyone respects the privacy needed with a line shared by an entire community."

Greta nodded.

"Hello?" Her mother's voice sounded a world away.

Greta started to answer but stopped when she heard the operator say, "Call from Deer Isle, Maine. I'm patching it through. Caller, you may begin speaking."

"Hello?" Greta began, tentatively.

"Greta? Is that you, baby?"

"Hi, Mama. I wanted to let you know I got here okay."

"Huh? What's that you said? I can't hear you. Speak up!" Mrs. Washington seemed to be screaming herself.

"I said, I got here okay!" Greta yelled as loudly as she dared.

"Wonderful! How is everything? Are you having fun? Are you getting enough to eat?" Mrs. Washington laughed at this last question.

"Very funny, Mama! Yes, everything is fine. Tomorrow I'm going to ride a horse."

"Oh, baby, I'm so happy for you. I miss you already but I'm so happy for you."

"I miss you too." And as soon as she said it, she realized it was true.

"Huh?"

"I said, I miss you too!" Greta didn't look in the direction of Tia and Dinora who were cutting into pies at the other end of the kitchen.

"Hey, write me a letter. That way you won't have to yell."

"Okay, I'll do it right now."

"Tomorrow is soon enough. And Greta?"

"Yeah?"

"I love you, baby." Greta wasn't sure if the catch in her mother's voice was static from the phone line or something else.

"I love you too, Mama."

"Okay, goodnight honey, sweet dreams."

"Goodnight." Greta hung up the phone and waited a few more minutes before joining the others.

Dinora had gotten her wish. There was a raspberry and a blueberry pie set out on the buffet in the dining room. Next to them were some plates, saucers and tea cups. It all looked delicious and Greta wished she hadn't eaten so much dinner. She made up her mind to leave room for dessert tomorrow.

Greta followed the sounds of voices and laughter to the music room where Tia was at the piano. Dinora and Seymour were standing next to her searching through piles of sheet music.

"How about this one?" Seymour asked.

"No, it's too high. Let's do the one with that nice harmony."

"It's in the red book over there," Zoë shouted. She was standing on a chair and reaching for two small drums attached to each other.

"Greta, take these will you?" she asked. "And Mario, you're taller. Will you grab the one on top?" Zoë stepped down and Mario replaced her, retrieving a larger drum from the top shelf and passing it down to Zoë. "Thanks. Are you going to play?" she asked him.

"I think I'll be the audience tonight. I want to finish this book on Madam Curie."

"You lead a fascinating life, Mario," she quipped. "Oh, well. Suit yourself. What about you, Greta? Would you like to try something?"

Greta very much wanted to but she had never played an instrument and everyone else seemed to know what to do.

Zoë sensed her hesitancy and suggested, "Why don't you take the harp?" She pointed to a large gilded harp standing near the piano. "I'll show you a way to kind of cheat. It's easy but it'll sound very cool." Zoë showed her which three strings to pluck and in what order. "Just follow the chords of the song. Start with G and keeping plucking to the beat. I'll nod when it's time to change chords so keep an eye on me," Zoë instructed.

After a few false starts, they fell into a nice rhythm. Later, Greta took a turn on the djembe and then the cello. The rest of the evening passed too quickly, and before they knew it, the children were yawning and Tia was hustling them off to bed.

"There will be plenty of nights for this foolishness. Off to bed with you. Off to bed."

Greta managed to stay awake long enough to brush her teeth and put on pajamas. She crawled into her bed and was drifting off to sleep when she heard a beautiful song coming from beneath the floorboards. This must be what Zoë meant when she said it was better to sleep above the music room than the kitchen.

"Brahms," Zoë muttered from across the room.

"Waltz?" Dinora asked.

"Mmm hmm." Zoë yawned. "In A flat. That's too easy, Tia."

"What is she doing?" Greta asked in Dinora's direction.

"It's this thing — a game, I guess. Tia plays pieces and we guess what they are. Usually there's some sort of code or hidden message. I can only get the easy ones — but Zoë, she's been doing this forever. Tia rarely stumps her."

Tia began a new song, much more fast-paced than the one before.

"Oh! I know this one. It's from *Peer Gynt!*" Dinora sat up in bed.

"Composer?" Zoë tested.

"Greg?"

"Greig," Zoë corrected. "Title?"

"The dance, the dance by…uh…. Oh, Anita!"

"Anitra. You're getting much better, Dinora."

Greta couldn't see her expression but she pictured a complacent smile as Dinora lay back on her pillow.

"Was there a clue in that one?" Greta asked.

"Maybe."

"Like that we'll learn to dance or go to a dance?"

"Sometimes it's like that. Sometimes it's just a song." Another piece had begun. It was slower and a little sad. "This is ours." Zoë's voice was barely audible. "Gershwin." She began to sing along softly, "*Summertime…and the livin' is easy.*"

As Tia played the soothing melody, Greta found it impossible to keep her eyes open. Just before she fell asleep, a strange thought occurred to her. She remembered the extra place setting at dinner and wondered who hadn't come. Before she could think of any possible explanations, she was fast asleep.

Greta awoke and rubbed her eyes. She started to get out of bed, already wondering what her first day on The Island would be like. Something was out of place. She looked around. Dinora and Zoë were both still sleeping. She looked out the window and saw it was still dark. *Well, something must have woken me*, Greta thought sensibly. She wondered what it was as she walked to the window overlooking the garden. The window also looked over the long driveway stretching from Tia's house to the main road. And at that precise moment, the night was clear enough to reveal the dark outline of an approaching car. It was the gravel, Greta realized, or the sound of the wheels on the gravel, that had woken her. It was the middle of the night. She shook her head and rubbed her eyes, trying to shift her brain from sleep mode into whatever mode could figure out what was going on. It must have worked because she noticed two things immediately afterward. First, that she couldn't hear a motor and second, that the headlights were off. In fact, if she hadn't heard the car approaching, she might not have even seen it at first glance.

The car slowed and stopped at the side of the house, directly beneath Greta's window. She heard a door open and saw the top of Tia's head emerge from the house. Three figures got out of the car and, after a few low murmurs, Tia stepped aside and they entered the house. She paused a moment and then glanced around in all directions, almost as if she were trying to determine if anyone was watching.

Tia may have looked up and seen Greta watching but Greta had pulled her head away from the window and turned with her back to the wall. Her heart was beating quickly and her mind was racing. She kept telling herself it was ridiculous to react like this. Tia had obviously been expecting the strangers. Maybe they were detained somewhere and were running very, very late. There was probably a reasonable explanation for the car arriving so furtively. Despite her efforts, Greta was not able to convince herself these events were normal in any way. Her gut said something was going on — something very much out of the ordinary.

Greta wasn't sure how much time had passed when she heard the door open again. She risked a look and could make out only two figures returning to the car. Together they pushed the car around and headed back down the driveway. Greta watched it until it met the road. The engine started, headlights shone and in a matter of seconds the night had returned to normal.

Greta's head was clogged with questions and only one of them was answered. The last dinner guest had arrived.

5

❧ The Visitor ❦

Sunlight was pouring into the bedroom when Greta next woke. Immediately she was in a good mood with no memory of the previous night's strange events. This time she went to the window to let in the crisp morning air. She looked below and saw that Tia, Zoë and the boys were near the garden and moving in slow synchronicity. Greta watched their peaceful, intricate gestures and felt a calm come over her. Tia was such a big woman. Greta was surprised she could move so delicately.

Dinora joined her at the window. "Isn't she..." Dinora yawned before finishing, "...beautiful? She was a professional dancer before she retired."

Greta reached for her jeans. She found a green swimsuit in the closet and put it on, not knowing if there would be a place to change at the beach. The YMCA had lockers and Greta heard people talk about changing rooms at beaches. Still, little so far had been as she had thought, and Greta decided to err on the side of caution. She put on the jeans and a tee shirt that fit perfectly. The sweater looked too burdensome so she grabbed a light jacket instead and ran down the stairs.

Dinora was at the buffet, where Tia had laid out another magnificent meal. Greta took a plate and linen napkin and chose two pancakes topped with fresh strawberries and real whipped cream. She joined Dinora and they ate together in happy silence. The screen door in the kitchen banged shut and Zoë and the boys tumbled in. They were all out of breath.

Mario poured himself a cup of coffee and sank into a chair. "Zoë, you must have passed your prime. I almost beat you today." Mario took a sip of his drink.

"Oh, and I'm sure that had nothing to do with your giant helper here." Zoë shoved Seymour before they adorned their plates with breakfast.

"Hey, don't blame me if you can't keep your concentra —" Seymour stopped in mid-sentence and stared at the doorway.

The rest also turned.

That must be him, Greta thought, memories of last night rushing back. She had expected an adult but before her stood a young man. Despite the conservative suit he was wearing, he looked to be only fifteen or sixteen at most. He was a boy. Greta was confused. Dinora had said it would just be the five of them. Why wouldn't Tia have mentioned anything?

Tia came out of the kitchen and put her hands on the boy's shoulders. "Peter, good morning. Good morning," she said in a chipper voice as if nothing strange was going on at all. "Everyone, this is Peter. He'll be with us for a while. Peter, these are Seymour, Zoë, Mario, Dinora and Greta."

Peter nodded his head slightly forward. "A pleasure to make your acquaintance." His voice was deeply resonant and he spoke with what Greta thought might be a British accent. In fact, if she didn't see this black boy in front of her and just had his voice to go on, she'd assume he was white — a businessman or a butler for a rich family. Greta had thought Mario was formal. This boy was positively distinguished. He made Mario look like a.... Greta couldn't find the right word. She settled for "goofball".

"Hello," everyone mumbled in unison, looking nonplussed.

Greta liked the idea that here was one thing where she knew more about what was going on than her companions, even if it wasn't much. "It's nice to meet you," she added.

"Peter, there's breakfast on the buffet and plenty of it. Plenty of it. You just help yourself. Would you like some coffee? Or tea perhaps?" Tia twittered nervously.

"Tea, yes. Thank you."

"Seymour, pour Peter some tea, will you? Thank you, darling." Tia had guided Peter to the buffet where he took the cup and saucer offered by Seymour. Again Greta saw a slight nod of his head before he rounded the table and sat down, leaving an empty seat on either side of him.

"Peter, the children were planning an outing today. Sailing was it?" No one answered her. Everyone was preoccupied with trying not to stare at Peter. Save Greta, none were succeeding. "Seymour?" There was a slight edge in Tia's voice.

"Hmm?" her nephew was startled back to attention.

"Is it sailing today?" she repeated.

"Uh...no. We're...uh...horses. I mean, we're taking the horses.... We're going swimming on the west side of The Island." He looked at Peter. "You're...uh...welcome to join us. That is, I mean...." Seymour took a visible breath. "We'd be happy to have you." Greta had no trouble finding the word to describe Seymour. He was flustered.

"Thank you, but no," Peter said evenly.

"Are you sure, Peter? It'll be a lovely time. A lovely time," Tia encouraged.

"No. Thank you, Miss Witherspoon." Greta had no idea that was even Tia's surname. No one had ever used it. *Everyone* called her Tia. Who was this boy?

"Well, whether you're coming or not, we need to get going." Zoë apparently was the first one to get her wits together. "It's at least a two-hour heavy ride to the shore and it must be almost nine. We need to be out of here in a half an hour if we're going to have enough time at the beach. No sense in showers — we're just going to get dirty again." Zoë shoved half a muffin into her mouth before continuing. "Seymour and Greta, you're in charge of the food. Saddlebags are on the counter." She swallowed. "Dinora, you and Mario get the horses ready. Greta, do you ride?"

Greta fumbled her response. "No. I mean, I never have so I guess…"

"Better get four ready. Greta can ride with one of us. I'll get towels and other basic provisions. If anyone wants anything special, you better get your butt in gear and go get it. Greta, come with me first and we'll get you some better shoes. You do *not* want to ride a horse in sandals." Zoë half-jogged out of the room and instantly the rest of them were up, clearing dishes and rushing off to their assignments. No one seemed to have noticed that Peter had already left the table.

After she had been outfitted with heavy socks and boots, Greta tried to think of anything and everything she might need for a day at the beach. Finally, she chose two books and figured she'd just have to live and learn.

Seymour had packed most of the food when Greta joined him in the kitchen. "Perfect timing," he complemented. "I can't decide: oranges or plums?"

"Plums might bruise," Greta suggested.

"Good point. Oranges it is." He put the plums back in the large fruit bowl.

"But oranges could get sticky," Greta added as an afterthought.

"That's not helping, Greta."

She felt a smile creep across her face. It was the first time one of them had teased her.

"How about strawberries and we can put them in a container?" said Greta.

"Sounds good! They're over there. After that, get the canteens on the hook by the sink and fill them up. We don't want to be without water."

Greta performed her tasks eagerly and when Zoë stormed in, they were all ready. "Looks good," Zoë ruled, after quickly surveying their work. "If the horses are ready, we can go."

Mario and Dinora had chosen and saddled three horses. Now Dinora seemed to be pleading with a young boy for something.

"Who's that?" Greta asked Seymour, handing him a saddlebag.

"Oh, that's Daniel. He stays here and helps Tia out. Hey, Daniel!" Seymour shouted with a friendly wave.

"Seymour!" Daniel came towards them and hugged Seymour unabashedly. He held out his hand to her. "And you must be Greta. It's nice to meet you."

"Thanks, you too."

"Did the trip go okay? I was sorry to miss dinner last night. I wanted to see everyone but Mr. Whitcomb's cow was delivering and he said I could help. It was amazing! Anyway, I see you decided to forgo the dip in Penobscot Bay this time." Daniel chuckled.

"Yeah, we felt like once was enough," Seymour said.

"Seymour," Dinora called, "please tell Daniel to let me take Diablito."

"You can have Sophocles or nothing," Daniel shouted back.

"But Daniel, I don't *care* if he's temperamental. I *love* temperamental. Sometimes *I'm* temperamental. Please, Daniel. Please?"

"If you get hurt…" He seemed genuinely concerned.

"I won't. I promise I won't. I'll be extra careful. Plus, he needs the exercise and you said yourself you wouldn't have time today. Please, Danny."

"Fine," Daniel grumbled. "Take him, but you better be —"

"Absolutely!" Dinora beamed with delight and gave him an impulsive hug.

Daniel blushed.

Tia emerged from the house just as they finished getting the reins on Diablito. "Now dinner is at seven sharp. Se-ven sharp. And I'd prefer you don't stink to high heaven of horses so you should plan to be back here by six. You hear me? By six."

"Yes, Tia," they promised.

"Greta, with whom are you riding?" Tia asked and Greta looked around to find everyone had already mounted a horse.

"Ride with me, Greta!" Dinora shouted. "It'll be great fun — very exciting."

Greta knew there was no way she was getting on that horse. Zoë must have sensed her reluctance and quickly offered hers. Greta readily accepted and Zoë dismounted to help her up.

When they were all ready, Tia asked, "Greta, darling, what would you like for dinner tonight?"

"Uh, I don't know. Anything is fine." Dinner was the furthest thing from Greta's mind. All she could think of was not falling off.

"Alright then. Dinora, what would you like?"

Dinora started to answer when Diablito took off through the open field, leaving them with a reverberating, "Enchilaaaaaadaaaaas!"

"We'd better catch up!" Zoë shouted and signaled their horse to follow. Their summer vacation had officially begun.

6

❧ The Beach ❧

Upon reflection, it was an utterly perfect day. The first hour on a horse, galloping across the island, was a complete blur for Greta. She had been entirely focused on not falling off the chestnut mare. Finally, her brain sent the message to her nerves that if she was going to be thrown to her death, it would have happened by now. Soon after that, her heart slowed down and Greta was able to make room for the incredible burst of joy which flooded through her. Riding a horse at full gallop was like nothing she had ever experienced.

It was noon when the children reached a steep cliff overlooking The Island's western shore, which Greta admitted looked significantly calmer. Perhaps she wouldn't die today after all. While the rest took a break, Seymour and Dinora scouted along the cliff to see if there was a way down to the beach. Both returned quickly with bad news.

"There has to be a way down," Mario insisted. "Are you sure you went far enough?"

Seymour and Dinora explained that the cliff went on for many kilometers with no signs of meeting the beach.

"We could go back a ways and try it north of here, or south?" Seymour suggested.

"Yeah, but who knows how long it will take and it would leave us with even less time actually on the beach," said Mario.

"What's Zoë doing?" Dinora pointed to where Zoë was walking along the cliff's edge, looking around. Then, before anyone had a chance to realize what she was doing, she jumped off.

"Zoë!" Seymour shouted, running towards her. The others were right behind him.

"I'm fine. I'm fine," came Zoë's muffled voice.

"Where are you?" Seymour yelled again.

"It sounds like she's underneath us," said Dinora. All the children looked down but there was only ground covered in tall shafts of heather and sea grass.

"I'm right below you!" Zoë started laughing.

"Zoë, it's not funny!" Mario shouted at the ground. "I think you're about to give Seymour a heart attack."

"Okay, okay. I'm coming."

Seconds later they heard a scuffling and Zoë peeked over the cliff's edge. She looked up at them and grinned. "This is so cool! You have to see this."

Seymour looked like a worried parent ready to scold a misbehaving child. Then, his curiosity got the better of him. The rest of the children followed, kneeling down on the edge.

"It was so weird," Zoë explained. "I was walking along the cliff, looking for a way to get down. I thought maybe there might be a path, or a place where it wasn't as steep. But I didn't see anything." She was building up to the good part. "So there I was, staring at this little ledge here." She indicated the outcrop less than a meter wide, on which she was standing. "And I thought if we got down here, we could scale it."

It sounded from Zoë's tone that she had ruled out this possibility. Greta was relieved and suspected she wasn't the only one. "Then I found it! It was right in front of me the whole time. Do you see it?" Zoë acted like she was pointing out something new but it looked the same to Greta.

Then Mario yelled. "I do! I see it! Zoë, that's incredible. Have you been in? Does it lead anywhere? Let me down." Mario started to jump but Dinora held him back.

"Oh, wow! I see it too!" Seymour shouted. "It's so obvious once you know it's there but I had no idea at first."

"See what?" Dinora demanded petulantly. She sounded angry, like they were playing a joke on the little kid.

"Dinora," Seymour said calmly, "look straight down and tell me what you see."

"I see a *tiny* ledge sticking out of a *big* cliff," she said impatiently.

Seymour didn't take the bait. "Okay...now right above the ledge, what do you see?"

"A bunch of weeds and grass and stuff, why?" She seemed to be losing her patience.

"And in which direction is the grass moving?"

"Away from the cliff, but how is that supposed to.... Oh!"

Dinora and Greta got it at the same time. Greta had been answering Seymour's questions to herself. She was thinking there was something strange but she couldn't place it. Then suddenly, it dawned on her. There was a breeze coming up from the ocean onto land. It was blowing the grass by her feet, softly towards her, inland. But the grass next to the outcrop was blowing out to the ocean.

"A cave!" exclaimed Dinora.

"In fact, more than a cave," Mario corrected. "It has to be a tunnel."

"It's acting like a chimney — drawing air through—" Zoë added. "And a pretty wide chimney at that if the breeze is this strong."

Mario climbed down. No one seemed to be as brave as Zoë when it came to jumping off a hundred-meter cliff. He disappeared into the tunnel and emerged a minute later to report. "It looks wide enough, and since it can't go up, it can only go back, sideways or down. Whichever way, it's open at the other end." He was looking at them to see if anyone was going to make the suggestion.

Zoë did. "Let's go! If it reaches the beach, great. If it doesn't, we get to go caving and have our lunch inside the island itself. Either way will be fun!"

"We have no guarantee the exit will be any lower down." Mario said. "But, it seems to me we have just as much of a chance getting to a beach this way as we do if we go back and search along the cliff. I'm in."

Seymour looked at Greta and Dinora. "What do you think?" It was clear he wanted to go.

"Sure, why not?" Dinora shrugged casually.

This left Greta as the only remaining member of the party to weigh in. Her first instinct was to run screaming back to the house. Go into a cave they had no reason to believe was safe? Were they crazy? This could have disastrous results. Mario was the oldest. He should be looking out for them. He should be the responsible one who says "it's not safe" or "it's too risky". *It definitely shouldn't be me. I'm eleven!*

Greta looked around at their expectant faces. Even though she was just getting to know them, she knew already that they weren't going to pressure her. They would go on without her but they wouldn't force her to come. A picture came to her mind of how the rest of the summer might play out: adventure after adventure where the four of them asked if she wanted to join in and she continually declining the invitation. *The invitation to break my neck — that's the kind of offer this was.* Greta sighed. She had to admit, it was also the offer to have fun. She decided it was now or never.

She put on her best game face and said, with more confidence than she felt, "Let's do it!"

The rest of them cheered and Zoë shifted immediately into organization mode. "Mario, why don't you go ahead in and see how far it goes. Actually, wait a second. Dinora, there's a torch in June-Balloon's satchel, will you get it?" Dinora ran back to the horses and Zoë looked down at Mario who was about to climb into the opening. "It may not be dangerous at all, but we shouldn't tempt fate."

Mario nodded and waited for the torch. When it arrived, he gave them all a hearty salute and vanished into the cliff face.

Zoë leaned down after him. "Try not to get too far ahead, in case something happens," she cautioned. "Seymour, help me up." Zoë stretched out her arm and her cousin clasped it. "Thanks," she said, brushing off sand and dust from her hands and knees. "Now what?"

"Let's find a place to tether the horses, get our stuff and join Mario before he gets to have all the fun on his own," Seymour suggested. Dinora pointed out a good spot where the animals could have shade or sun, depending on their preference, and plenty of grass. With alacrity, Seymour and Zoë removed saddles, as Dinora showed Greta how to take out their bits.

"Don't miss me too much, my sweet Diablito!" she called as they returned to the cliff's edge, each carrying a heavy bag over their shoulder. Zoë jumped down to the ledge. Even this time, when Greta knew it was going to happen, it made her stomach leap into her throat. Together, Zoë and Seymour helped the younger girls down. Soon, they were inside with no trace that five children had been above ground only moments before.

Greta noticed that while she had to bend down to get through the entrance, the tunnel quickly opened up and even Seymour was able to stand. Dinora immediately called ahead to Mario and her voice boomed along the chamber in a barrage of echoes.

"Careful!" Zoë warned.

"Sorry," Dinora apologized.

Mario's voice called softly, his message rolling back to them in a confused jumble.

"I'm not exactly sure what he said," Seymour whispered, "but I liked his tone."

They made their way down the steep incline of the rock corridor. Soon, the light from the opening was all but gone and Zoë had to take out the second torch. The yellow beam threw distorted shadows on the wall and did little to improve the gloom. It was difficult to tell where they were going, where they'd been, or how long they had been walking. Eons of wind had smoothed the rock which had both advantages and disadvantages. Greta didn't worry about tripping on something — at least not rock. On the other hand, there wasn't anything to grasp in case she fell. An image of a waterslide made entirely of granite came to her mind and she shuddered. It wasn't her only thought though, as she slowly followed Zoë. Greta's teacher had taught them about the pyramids of Egypt this year. He had vividly described the narrow stone passageways within those ancient tombs. Greta was beginning to get a very good sense of what it would be like to be in one of them.

"Dinora?" she asked softly.

"Yes?" came the hushed voice behind her.

"Just making sure."

Dinora placed her hand on Greta's shoulder. The warmth of the hand and the reminder that she wasn't alone made Greta feel a little better.

A loud cry came from deep below them and a shiver of terror and delight sped through Greta's veins. The children quickened their pace. About ten minutes later, they all saw the source of Mario's jubilation.

It was as if a lagoon had been magically created just for them. It was perfect in every detail. The cliff ceiling surged up and over, creating an amphitheater. Half of the sandy floor was bathed in the warmth of a sun nearing its apex. At the rim of the cave, an assortment of boulders slipped into clear blue water.

"I wonder why we couldn't see it from above," Seymour asked of no one in particular.

"Because we're still in the island. Look there." Mario indicated where two arms of the cliff circled around, creating a small enclave of water. And except for the sun, which angled its way through, the pool was inaccessible. It was a little piece of heaven and banished all trepidation from Greta's mind.

"I got to see it first," Mario said. "Why don't the rest of you try the water and I'll get lunch ready. Will you pass me those bags, Seymour?"

"Here. Thanks, Mario." Seymour didn't waste any time. He tore off his shirt, shoes and jeans, revealing bright-red swimming trunks. He dashed down the rock steps and across the sand. He found a flat rock and dove smoothly into the water. Nearly a minute later, his head popped up at the far end of the lagoon. "There are fish!" he cried. "We should have brought our poles!"

"Next time!" Mario shouted back, laughing.

Dinora and Zoë joined Seymour moments later. Greta had experienced enough excitement for the time being. She decided to help Mario instead. Maybe later she would be able to muster enough courage to try swimming.

"Something I can do?" she offered.

"Thanks, Greta." Mario passed her a satchel. "There should be some sort of tablecloth in here. Let's set up over there where the rock juts out into the sun."

Now that she took this second glance, the large flat rock actually resembled a table. She opened the bag and found a slightly torn piece of cloth decorated with faded pink roses. Together, she and Mario laid out the food Seymour had packed. There was plenty — cold chicken and freshly baked bread from the night before, tomatoes and cucumbers from the garden, a thermos of real lemonade, a huge container of strawberries and a smaller container of cream. When all was set out, Mario announced that lunch was served. Greta was ravenous.

"The swimming is great!" Dinora said breathlessly, drying herself off with her tee shirt and laying it out in the sun.

The children spent the rest of the afternoon in absolute bliss. They swam in crystal-clear water and napped as they dried on sun-drenched rocks, only to wake and dive back in. They ate, talked and laughed. At times they were just still, silently admiring their incredible find. Greta took out her book and found a spot which suited her perfectly. She could alternate between the sun and the shade with a short scoot and her legs could dangle in the cool water. She had a handful of berries on a napkin and a canteen filled with the spring water they had found trickling out of a fissure in the cavern. Nothing could have made the day more pleasant. Seymour even found a thin tree limb and created a crude spear with which to catch fish.

"You need a net!" Zoë yelled.

"I'm fine!" he yelled back, but still he didn't catch anything.

The day stretched on, endlessly. Finally, Greta had to admit it was probably time to head home. She yawned and turned over, letting her eyelids close for just a minute more. When she opened them again, the sun had sunk even farther into the sky. "We're late!" she shouted.

The rest of the children looked at the sky to contradict her, only to realize they too had let their private paradise distract them from the time. "Seven sharp" might occur at any time for Tia but none of the children wanted to be galloping across the island at dusk. This thought seemed to reach all of them at once. Each of them rushed to shove things in satchels and put socks and boots over wet, sandy feet. Without slowing down, they hurried through the dark tunnel and climbed back onto the grassy bluff. Even the horses seemed anxious as the children hastily saddled them.

They sped over the fields as quickly as safety would allow and Greta thought of where she was and how she had spent yesterday and today. She had traveled alone on a plane. She had seen the ocean and ridden a horse for the first time. She had faced her fears and experienced an adventure. She had helped discover the most perfect place in the entire world, and she had made friends with the most interesting people she'd ever met. So much had happened to her in just two days and this was only the beginning. A pair of thoughts settled in her mind simultaneously. She was not the same girl she had been two days earlier, and she wondered what she'd be like by the end of the summer.

7

☙ The Garden ❧

An exhausted sleep only served to rejuvenate the children's enthusiasm. At breakfast the following morning they were still talking excitedly about their adventures. Tia had not been pleased at the state in which they returned. They'd been coated in salt, dust and sweat (both human and equine). They had been on time, however, so she let them off easily, with only a few thinly veiled comments on their odor.

Even Greta couldn't help herself. "Tia, I was so scared," she blurted out, for the fifth time. "I thought for sure I was going to die but I just thought…. I can't think of the right word. It was so much fun!"

The rest of the children laughed at Greta's exuberance and agreed heartily with her sentiment.

"Greta, I think that has to be the most we've heard out of you yet," Seymour said.

Mario had found a piece of paper and was making a list of supplies they should be sure to take with them today.

"Definitely another torch," Zoë started.

"Make it two — that tunnel is creepy," Dinora insisted.

"And fishing poles," Seymour added excitedly.

"And how are we supposed to carry fishing poles on horses?" Zoë asked.

Mario looked up and tilted his head in his signature pondering pose. "Well, if we tie them together and don't go through the woods — oh, good morning." Mario clumsily greeted Peter, who had entered the room, clothed less officially this morning with a simple blue blazer over his white shirt and khaki pants.

Zoë noted he still wore a tie and possessed the same air of superiority. "Nice tie," she commented coldly. "*Ow!*" She glared at Seymour who seemed to have kicked her underneath the table.

"Thank you," he responded without any emotion at all. Peter still hadn't made it to a single meal on time. The night before he'd come to dinner at the very end, taken a tiny bit of food, eaten half of it and gone back upstairs. He hadn't even helped clean up with the rest of them. In fact, he had made it pretty clear: he didn't want to spend any more time with them than he absolutely had to. Still, even Peter couldn't quell the tide of cheerful energy at the breakfast table.

"Peter, you should've come," Seymour said sincerely. "It was incredible fun."

Dinora and Greta too offered their encouragement.

Mario suggested, "Why don't you come today? Do you ride?" Peter glanced at Tia.

"Oh, I'm sorry, darlings. You probably won't have enough time to go back today. I need your help in the garden. Market is tomorrow and there is a lot of work to be done. Those weeds are practically strangling my Cavendish strawberries."

No one made any outward sound but the disappointment at the table was palpable. None of them was much in the mood for eating after their hope of another visit to the beach had been eliminated — at least for today. In silence, the children picked at their food until Tia left the room.

After the breakfast dishes were done, the children went back upstairs to change into clothes better suited for heavy labor in the garden instead of an afternoon lounging at the beach.

Daniel was waiting for them outside and explained what needed to be done.

"It's not like we haven't done this tons of times already, Daniel," Zoë reminded him.

"Greta hasn't," Mario reasoned. "Perhaps she'd like to know." Greta listened attentively as Daniel finished his instructions. After getting gloves, tools and large baskets they began their various assignments.

They worked in tense silence until Dinora blurted, "I don't know how you stand him."

Placing a ripe tomato in his basket, Daniel asked, "Who?"

"Peter," came simultaneous responses.

"Oh, the new kid?"

"If you can call him a 'kid'," Zoë muttered under her breath.

"So how do you do it?" Dinora asked again.

"Whom?" Seymour asked.

"Stop playing, you know what I mean." Dinora wiped some sweat from her forehead but the dirt on her glove just made her face muddy.

"No, I mean whom are you asking?"

"You!" Dinora barked. "Well, you and Mario, anyway."

"Why us?" Mario and Seymour asked.

"Because you have to stay in the same room with him. We only have to see him at meals — and barely then."

"He's not staying with us," Mario informed them.

"He's not?" Zoë turned to face them. "Why wouldn't he stay with you? The boys always stay together in the boys' room. That's why it's called the *boys'* room."

"I thought that was strange too," Daniel said. "But Tia was adamant. She wanted your rooms ready as well as the guest bedroom next to hers."

"Why didn't you tell us this before?" Seymour asked.

"I don't know," Daniel shrugged. "I figured you would know what was going on. Plus, this is practically the first time we've even had a chance to talk. Beginning of summer is always the busiest."

"Why would she do that?" Mario asked.

"We're missing the point altogether," Dinora argued. "What is he even doing here? Tia told us there would be five. It just doesn't make sense."

"You're right," Seymour agreed.

"She told us about you, Greta," Mario added. "Why wouldn't she tell us about Peter at the same time?"

"I'd like to get back to why he's not out here busting his butt like the rest of us," Zoë complained. "I don't care who he is or who he thinks he is or why he came or why Tia didn't tell us. I just want to know one thing —"

"Why he's not out here busting his butt like the rest of us," chorused the others.

Greta giggled.

Zoë cast a look at them indicating she didn't think it was at all funny, and then said, "Well, I *do*."

Greta wondered if she should share with the others what she knew about Peter's strange arrival. Perhaps if the conversation had continued in this same vein, she might have. But after a few minutes of grumbling about Peter and why he thought he was so special, they hunkered down and re-focused on their work. By the end of the first hour, they had fallen into a steady, if backbreaking, pattern of work.

Of course Seymour loved it, but he was clearly the only one. By the time they accumulated enough food to sell at tomorrow's market, they were in miserable spirits. And to top it all off, Zoë had gotten sunburned on her back and shoulders which affected all of them. Zoë was the immediate recipient but since she updated the rest of them so frequently on her pain and discomfort, they were also burdened.

"At least we can go back tomorrow," Greta reminded the others. No one had said anything in a while and the tension was growing. She had thought it might ameliorate things if they remembered how recently they had all gotten along and had fun. "You should come too, Daniel. Do you think you could make it?"

"I'd love to, Greta, but I've got Market tomorrow. The day after I'm free though. Edith won't need my help on Thursday."

"Shoot!" Mario threw a weed into his basket, stood up and stretched.

"What?" Daniel asked, a worried look on his face.

"Market." Mario looked at the rest of them.

Everyone groaned, except for Daniel who nodded his understanding and Greta who just stood there looking puzzled. "What about the market?" she asked hesitantly.

"If Tia needed us today, she'll need us tomorrow," Mario told her. "It'll be still another day before we can get back."

Greta felt the day's second wave of disappointment wash over her.

"Well, at least Daniel can come with us. That's good," Seymour offered, trying to lift their spirits.

But no one was cheered. Instead, the news seemed only to make the children more tired, hot and frustrated.

"And why is it again that Peter isn't out here?" Zoë yelled at her friends, her temper rising.

"Probably doesn't want to get his precious suit dirty," Dinora growled.

Greta again felt an urge to say something about what she had seen but couldn't think of how to start. It was probably nothing anyway.

"Look, we're almost done. Let's not make things worse, okay? Let's just get through and then we can get out of here," Mario said.

"Oh, I'm terribly *sorry*, Mario," Zoë said snidely. "I didn't understand my pettiness was making it hard for you to concentrate. I had forgotten picking lettuce was such an extremely *complicated* job!"

"Don't make fun of my brother!" Dinora shouted, standing up to face Zoë.

"Dinora, it's okay. Calm down." Seymour put his hand on her shoulder.

"Oh, and of course you'd take her side. Come on, Greta. Let's pick from the edge," she scowled at Zoë, "where it's a little quieter!"

Greta didn't know what to say. She was an only child and had never experienced this before. She hadn't even acted this way with her friends. She didn't want to say "no" because then Dinora might be mad at her. She also didn't want to give everyone else the impression she agreed with Dinora. For a moment, Greta thought she was going to cry as she stood there, hot, frustrated and tired, not knowing what to do.

"Fine!" Dinora shouted, tears quickly filling her eyes. "I guess if no one wants to pick with me, then fine. I'll pick on my own! I'll do everything on my own! I'll spend the whole stupid summer alone!"

"Oh, stop acting like such a baby," Zoë chastised.

"Dinora…" Daniel began, but didn't seem to know how to finish. His voice was calm, but not calming.

Dinora just gaped at Zoë and began gesticulating wildly. Greta was afraid the girl might inadvertently hurt someone. Then, Dinora looked up at the house suddenly and grimaced. The rest of them followed her gaze. Peter was at a window looking down on them.

"What do you think you're looking at?" Dinora shouted at him, hands on her hips.

"Dinora!" Mario hissed at her, followed by something in Spanish Greta couldn't understand but which didn't sound very nice.

"Oh, I get it. Even my own brother doesn't like me now!" she yelled back and bolted out of the garden, sobbing.

"Dinora, wait!" Daniel called after her.

"Great. Now Mr. High and Mighty gets to see us put on our little show," Zoë grumbled, standing up and brushing the dirt from her clothes and hands. Greta looked up at the window again but Peter had gone. She thought she had noticed something in his expression. She wasn't sure what, but it didn't seem to be malicious. Sure, he hadn't been friendly or seemed interested in them but maybe he was just being shy? *Maybe Tia has a reasonable explanation for keeping him away from the rest of us.*

"I'll be right back." Mario's shoulders sagged as he walked after his little sister.

"I don't know about you three," Seymour said, rising and throwing an onion into the designated basket, "but I think we've done about as much work as we're able. Why don't we pack up some lunch and go down to the pond?"

"Sounds great. I'm dying to get in the water," Daniel said. He was the only one whose mood hadn't been hampered by the hard work and bickering. For a second, Greta had almost forgotten he was there. He had kept working so quietly.

"The pond?" Greta asked.

"It's down behind the house a bit, maybe ten minutes from here, through the woods." Daniel replied.

"What do you say, *Zo*?" Seymour asked kindly.

"Don't patronize me…*See*."

Seymour was about to say something but seemed to think better of it. Mario came out a few minutes later and saw them cleaning up the gardening supplies. He helped them load the baskets of produce into the truck bed and cover it with a tarpaulin.

"How's Dinora?" Seymour asked him.

"I don't know," Mario answered. "I couldn't find her. Tia packed us a lunch though. It's on the counter. Anyone up for the pond?"

Zoë sighed dramatically and held up her hands in mock surrender. When she spoke, much of the bitterness had left her voice. "I give up."

Mario looked to the others for an explanation.

"Yes, Mario," Zoë sounded more like herself. "The pond sounds great. I'll just grab my suit."

"I too," Greta added.

They changed into swimsuits and sundresses. As they finished, some very loud sniffling came from underneath Dinora's bed. Greta looked to see how Zoë was going to respond. She hoped it wouldn't result in more melodrama and posturing. Greta wanted lunch and a swim. But apparently Zoë was quick to anger and quick to let go.

"Dinora?" she said contritely.

"*¿Si?*" came the muffled reply.

"Listen, I'm sorry. You're not a baby. If anyone is a baby, I am. I was grumpy and hungry and my sunburn was hurting. I shouldn't have lashed out at you. I'm sorry."

"I don't like people yelling at me," Dinora said, crawling out from underneath her bed.

"Of course you don't," Zoë said, going over to her. "I'm very sorry, Dinora. Next time, I'll try harder not to lose my temper."

"Okay."

"We're going down to the pond, all of us. You want to come?" Zoë asked. "Tia packed a lunch."

"She did?" Dinora perked up. "Do we know what's in it? Has anyone checked? Maybe she made those special sandwiches. I love those sandwiches. Oh, I am so hungry, but I'm dirty too. I wanted to take a shower but.... Oh, we're going to the pond. That'll work. Mostly, I just want to cool off. It was so hot out there and dusty and.... Oh, you're already dressed. Will you wait for me? I'll just be a second. I'll change quickly, I promise. Will you?" She looked at Greta and Zoë with a hopeful expression.

Zoë smiled. "Sure," she said.

8

❧ The Market ❦

They left before the sun rose. Mario drove with Greta, Dinora and Seymour in the cab. Zoë and Daniel squeezed in between baskets of fresh fruits and vegetables in the back. It was a twenty-minute drive into town and they had just started setting up their stall when the sun peeked over the eastern islands in a blaze of orange and violet.

After the children had unpacked the food, Daniel and Dinora offered to take the first shift, leaving the others with a few hours to fill.

"Do you want to go down to the beach?" Seymour asked the remaining four.

"Or we could check out the rest of the market," Mario suggested.

"Does the town have a library?" Greta asked hopefully.

"Yeah, but whatever we do, let's get the shopping done first," Zoë reminded them. "Tia is very picky about her food and the best stuff is always the first to go."

They grabbed canvas bags and split up to cover the substantial grocery list.

Greta looked at the things she and Zoë needed to find and began reading them off one by one. "Honey, preferably wildflower, large jar; Serrano peppers, 200 grams; Casper eggplants, six medium; Gruyère cheese from Marcia's stand, 300 grams; bacon, one kilo —"

"Let's order the meat first and have the butcher set it aside for us. Then we can pick it up before we head back. Tia would not be too happy about bringing meat that had been left to sit in a hot truck all day," Zoë said, leading Greta through the town square to a small shop on the opposite end.

As they were leaving the butcher, Zoë noticed a group of boys watching them from the wharf. When they began to approach, she guided Greta into the closest store. "Let's check this place out, okay?" she said tightly.

"Oh…sure." Greta wondered what might possibly interest Zoë in this small tourist shop. It was filled with knickknacks, tee shirts, postcards and other items which didn't exactly coincide with Zoë's persona. They wandered around the store for a few minutes.

"Can I help you girls?" said a thin lady standing behind a cash register.

"No, thank you," Zoë said. "We're just looking."

"Well maybe if you tell me what it is, I can help you find it," she said snidely.

"Like I said, we're just looking."

Just then the bells over the door jingled and in came the four boys. Zoë had a bad feeling about this.

"C'mon, Greta," she said, trying to sound as casual as possible, "let's go back to the stall and see if they need help."

It looked to Zoë that Greta hadn't become suspicious of the boys, although she did seem confused by Zoë's behavior.

"Hi there."

Zoë's gut lurched. She turned. It was the largest of the boys, maybe fifteen or sixteen, with close-spaced eyes and a crew cut.

"Let's go." Zoë grabbed Greta and tried to slip past the boy.

"What? You're not even going to say 'hello'? That's not very friendly, is it guys?" he asked the other boys, who all shook their heads in uniform accordance.

Zoë had managed to get herself and Greta past the first boy but now the other three were blocking her way. The first one turned to seal the other end of the aisle. They were trapped.

"I thought a pretty girl like you would have better manners. Isn't that what you *Orientals* are supposed to be — real polite and all?" Greta felt Zoë's hand tense on her shoulder at the word "Oriental" and she started to get nervous. This was not right. Why wasn't the saleslady doing anything? Was she still there? She had to be able to hear what was going on. Greta tried to peer between the three boys to see the counter but they were too big. Quickly, Zoë shoved hard against them, trying to protect Greta as much as she could. They were through in a second and out the door in another.

Each girl breathed more easily as they put some distance between them and the store. Zoë risked a quick glance back but the boys weren't following them. They walked in heavy silence, both immersed in their own thoughts.

"I hate that about the States," Zoë finally said. "China has plenty of problems but at least I don't have to deal with *this*."

"Does it happen a lot here?" Greta asked.

Zoë seemed confused for a moment, then said, "Oh, you mean on The Island? I don't know. What's a lot? I guess it happens every once in a while. It's just so stupid!"

"I know," Greta echoed her sentiment. "I hate the way it makes me dwell on whatever they say."

Zoë nodded. "He says hateful things and stops thinking about it, but it'll be days before I do."

"And you never forget it," Greta said. Most of her neighborhood was black, her school and church too. Still there had been plenty of times she had been other places and people had said unkind things to her or her mother — for no reason, just to hurt them.

They returned to silence until they reached the stall, where Mario and Seymour had also arrived.

"Why so glum?" Seymour asked them.

Greta looked at Zoë, wondering if she would say anything about the boys in the store.

"Oh, nothing," Zoë said. "Do you want to take a break?" she asked Dinora and Daniel. "We can handle the stall."

"Sure — oh hello, Officer," Daniel said, standing up.

Greta and Zoë turned to see a policeman. He was so wiry that his uniform looked as if it was still on its hanger.

"Hello there, son," he acknowledged Daniel in a nasal tone. "How's business?" He didn't seem to really want an answer to his question.

"Fine. May we help you with something?"

"Well, I think that's for the little girl here to say." He looked down at Greta. "Is there something you'd like to tell me, honey?"

Greta loved it when her mother called her "honey". It made her feel warm and safe and loved. She even liked it when it came from her teachers or from Tia. She definitely did not like it coming from this man who didn't even know her name. In fact, the way he was patronizing her and Daniel, she decided she didn't like him at all. She said nothing.

"I'm not sure we understand, sir," said Mario, stepping up next to Greta.

"I'm waiting." The officer kept staring at Greta.

"Sir, if you'll just tell us what you think —"

"What I *think* is that this young lady took something from that shop back there and," he paused, "how should I put this…forgot to pay for it?"

"What?" Greta asked indignantly.

"You heard me, honey. Now just come with me back to the shop and we'll take care of this. I'm sure Mrs.

Edson won't press charges, but maybe you could do something for her — sweep up the shop, maybe — show you've learned your lesson."

"I didn't take anything." She pulled herself up to her full height, which wasn't very much.

"Little girl, just give back what you took and we'll try to forget all this unpleasantness."

Greta thought if the man didn't believe her the first time, he wouldn't believe her the second or third. In fact, probably the more she tried to convince him, the more guilty she would seem in his eyes.

The police officer quickly moved from irritation to anger. "Young lady —"

"Sir," Mario approached him. "She said she didn't take anything."

Zoë looked beyond the policeman to see the boys who had harassed them a few minutes earlier. They were laughing over the prank they had pulled at Greta's expense. Sweet Greta, who wouldn't hurt anyone. A fury began to build within her. Zoë scowled at them and looked back at the police officer. She couldn't do anything with *him* around.

"Look," Zoë said, stepping directly in front of the officer. "She didn't take anything. I was with her the whole time so it's *whoever's* word against ours. Are you going to make a federal case out of it? Huh? Are you going to arrest us?"

"Now you listen here, missy —"

"I believe what my friend meant was that unless you are going to officially charge us, we would appreciate you letting us go about our business," Mario said politely. Greta saw his fist clenching at his side.

The police officer must have realized this was not going to be a simple case of intimidation and confession. He decided they weren't worth the bother and left, but not without saying to Greta, "Probably best if you don't go into Mrs. Edson's shop anymore."

"I agree," Greta replied coolly.

The rest of the day passed uneventfully. The festive spirit of the morning hadn't lasted long, but at least things were quiet until mid-afternoon when the market closed.

The six children were loading up the truck when a voice called out, "What's wrong, Daniel?"

The children turned. Greta and Zoë recognized the boys from the store.

"Are those the guys?" Seymour asked in a hushed voice. After the incident with the police accusation, Zoë had shared the story.

"Yeah," she said, still staring at the leader.

"What are you talking about, Jake?" Daniel asked.

"I'm talking about what's wrong with you. Don't you like hanging out with your own kind?"

"Shut up, Jake. Leave us alone."

Jake said something to his friends and they laughed. He continued taunting Daniel, slowly coming closer. "What's wrong with white people? Huh? You got a problem with whites?" He pushed Daniel hard to the ground.

"Hey!" The children crowded to defend Daniel. Dinora helped him up and guided him closer to the truck while the others faced Jake and his three friends.

Jake smiled. "Just 'cuz you're poor and stupid —"

"And ugly," another boy added.

"And ugly," Jake continued, "doesn't mean you have to stoop to going around with a bunch of uppity —"

"Alright, that's enough." Seymour stepped up to Jake, towering over him, "why don't you just stop right there, turn around and leave us alone? Okay?"

"No, it's not 'okay'." Jake's derisive sneer flashed into shock as Zoë flew at him in a rage. Next thing everyone knew, she had punched him and he had punched her back. She fell, clutching her face. Immediately Seymour grabbed Jake and pinned his arms to his side.

"Hold him there, Seymour, and I'll get the police," Mario instructed.

"No!" Zoë shouted as she rose.

An eerie calm had come over her. She lowered her hand and Greta winced at the bruise forming over her left eye.

"I didn't want to have to use my *karate* on you boys but if you don't leave us alone, I won't have a choice."

She made her way towards Jake's friends, talking slowly, almost hypnotically. "Oh, and you might find it interesting to note that my grandfather is Lau Ye, the famous Japanese Sensei. He's been training me since I was four. But don't worry, I haven't killed anyone..." she paused, "...*yet.*"

"I thought she was Chinese?" Greta whispered to Mario.

"She is," he replied. "I think she's counting on them not knowing the difference, which sadly is probably the case."

Zoë began to make movements, which Greta thought looked a lot like her exercises the other morning, only much faster. She had also added peculiar yowling noises.

Greta tried to help by making her own expression look as scared as possible. "No, Zoë!" she yelled. "Don't do it. They're not worth it. You could end up in jail. Zoë, please!"

Perhaps it was the combination of their performances that worked. The boys looked briefly at each other before turning to run down the street.

"Cowards!" Jake yelled after them. "A girl can't hurt you! Get back here!"

"They don't seem to be coming back, Jake," Seymour said, releasing the boy. "And it's probably best if you join them."

Jake looked as if he was about to talk back but without his friends watching, he'd lost his bravado. He didn't run away but he walked quickly.

"Who was that boy?" Dinora asked as they got ready to leave.

"Jacob Sewall, school bully," Daniel said quietly. He didn't offer more information and Dinora could tell he didn't want to talk about it. She wondered if he was embarrassed that he had been pushed down. She almost reminded him Jake was practically twice his size but decided that probably wouldn't make him feel any better, at least not now. She climbed into the back of the truck with Zoë and Greta. It just seemed right to let the boys be alone for a bit.

The truck started and began its crawl up the hill and back to Tia's. As they got closer, each of them relaxed a little more.

"How did you think of it?" Greta asked.

"You mean the whole karate thing?" Zoë clarified.

Greta nodded.

"I don't know really. When I fell it just became clear to me. He wanted a fight and he was going to keep going until he got one. Except it wasn't as if he was brave or anything. He was showing off for his friends." Zoë shrugged. "So I thought if I could get rid of the others, he'd have to leave us alone."

"But why karate?"

"Oh, that?" Zoë smiled, grimacing at the pain. "They just seemed like the types who think they know everything about an entire race of people, just from watching movies. I thought I'd use their stereotypes against them."

Greta half-smiled. "Well, at least they're good for something," she said sardonically.

When the children arrived home, no one suggested going out. Instead they gathered in the large library on the second floor where they engaged in effortless and mindless occupations.

"Well, there's one good thing," Dinora said dispassionately. She was standing in front of the floor-to-ceiling windows, which overlooked the ocean.

"What's that?" Zoë asked, shifting the ice pack from her eye to her cheekbone so she could see Dinora.

"Tomorrow we can go back to our beach."

Even this thought only slightly cheered the children. They'd had two hard days. Recuperating in their sunny cove was just what each of them needed.

9

❧ The Attic ❧

When the children woke, there were only gray skies and a chilly drizzle to greet them. Tia was surprised the children were not more disappointed. In truth they probably would have been, if not for the incident at the market. The night before, Zoë had not come to dinner, saying she wasn't feeling well. She was desperately hoping her black eye would fade before she ran out of ways to hide her face from Tia. But Tia herself seemed preoccupied and didn't bat an eye when Zoë emerged the following morning, wearing a black velvet Sunday hat complete with veil.

The children spent the morning in a variety of activities. Daniel worked in the barn, mucking out stalls, and Dinora had offered to help him. Surrounded by the scent of rain and horses, the two were quite happy in each other's company. Daniel was probably one of the few people on the planet who could listen endlessly as Dinora rambled on about horses. And of course, Dinora loved having such an attentive listener. Occasionally she even had a question for Daniel. Mostly, the physical labor had a cathartic effect upon both of them. Lifting, hauling and sweating are wonderful remedies for pent up frustration and anger. When they joined the others in the large dining room for lunch, both Daniel and Dinora were rosy-cheeked and famished.

Seymour was in the greenhouse. He had built a hydroponic garden the previous summer and decided to put it back together and see if he could achieve any more success in cross-pollinating dahlias and chrysanthemums. To be in the warm, humid air, with only the sound of rain falling heavily on the glass roof, had healing results for him.

He had been going over the events of the previous day in his mind. *Why are people cruel?* He figured it probably stemmed from someone hurting *them*. Maybe it was the fear of being hurt — lashing out before you are attacked. He felt guilty that he had not done a better job of defending his friends, especially Zoë. As he fit pieces together and hooked up hoses, he kept imagining different scenarios. His favorite was one where he would punch Jacob Sewall over and over until his face was bloody and swollen.

The shiver of satisfaction he felt in his body scared him. He thought of himself as a peaceful person. Perhaps it came from being so big. When you are always looming over other kids your age, people can get intimidated. Many kids would assume he was the bully because of his size, but often it would be the smallest kid in the class out to prove he wasn't afraid.

Seymour had never truly felt fear — at least not of being physically hurt. Being separated from Zoë, after they had practically been raised as brother and sister, had been the most painful thing he had experienced. *Why am I bringing up bad memories?* He took a deep breath and tried harder not to focus on what he could have done — or should have done.

By the end of the morning, his garden was set up and running. He had also come to terms with the fact that he wouldn't have done anything differently even if he could have lived it over. He was sorry Zoë had been hurt but knew if he had struck back, things would be worse. For one thing, he wasn't absolutely sure he would have been able to stop. Setting aside these thoughts and his tools, he joined Dinora and Daniel who were leaving the barn.

Mario had also returned to a project from the previous year. Six years earlier, when he had first been invited to The Island, he hadn't wanted to come. His father had been teaching him the ways and laws of chemistry and they were just getting to the part where he was going to let him start conducting experiments. Mr. Enriquez had finally convinced Mario to go by sending him with a wide array of chemicals and scientific equipment. Mario had set up his lab in a corner of the basement where the sun wouldn't affect his work. He spent the rest of June and nearly all of July in the dark recesses of the cellar, testing and re-testing his theories.

Since then, his lab had always been a place he could go to clear his mind. Chemistry calmed him. There was a reason for everything — if you could find it. This was something he could control. The only variables were ones which *he* introduced when *he* chose. It was nothing like life and definitely nothing like human beings. They were unpredictable and noisy and emotional. It flustered him. He marveled at Seymour's ability to grasp a situation and not get swept up with it. Mario just wanted to run and hide in his lab. He had been here all morning and felt like he could easily spend the day here.

When he heard the call for lunch, Mario felt himself tense. If he joined them, they'd be laughing and talking or still be angry and hurt, or full of some other set of emotions he hadn't even considered. He decided he just needed to be alone. He needed more respite from the fray. He continued his work, despite the rumbling in his stomach.

A little later, he heard soft footsteps on the cellar stairs. He looked up and saw Greta descend with a tray of tiny sandwiches and pot of tea. She set it down on a nearby table, smiled at him and went back upstairs without saying a word. Mario liked Greta. She was the only person who could have come down here without saying something and without being offended if he didn't say anything. It was as if they had an understanding.

He poured himself a cup of tea and picked up a sandwich. Tasting it made him appreciate Tia and her culinary talents. Now that he thought about it, Tia probably chose Greta to bring him some food. Tia understood what he needed and didn't judge him for not joining the others. She rewarded him for taking care of himself.

And if Tia noticed Zoë too was missing from the table, she made no mention of it to the others.

Zoë had spent her morning skulking around the house in fear Tia would discover her, or rather, that Tia would discover the evidence on her face that she had been fighting. Tia had very strong opinions about violence. Two summers earlier she had even threatened to send Zoë home if she found her fighting again.

As Tia worked in the kitchen or her downstairs study, Zoë made a point of remaining on the upper levels. And when Tia started up the stairs towards the girls' room, Zoë flew down the hallway, up to the third floor and clear over to the other side of the house. "Phew!" She sighed and sank down to the floor.

"Hello?" The voice startled her and she let out a tiny shriek. "Miss Witherspoon? Is that you?"

It was Peter.

Zoë stood up and backed down the hall. It was no use.

Peter came out of his room and she was caught. "Oh, hello. I thought it was Miss Witherspoon. Are you lost?"

"Oh no…. Not lost. I was just, I…. Oh, please don't tell. Please. I know you don't like us and I don't blame you. We've been just horrid to you, but I don't want to go back, and if she sees me, she's sure to do it. I just know she will."

Peter looked confused. "I am not exactly sure what it is you don't want me to tell, so in that you seem to be safe."

Zoë breathed a sigh of relief.

"Unless of course, it is the shiner."

"The what?"

"On your eye — the shiner. Someone hit you."

"Oh, shoot!" Zoë stamped her foot.

"Surely Miss Witherspoon would not blame you. You are the victim and she seems a very kind woman."

"Well, it's not exactly —" Zoë paused for a moment and recognized a way out of her predicament. "Yes, you're right. I am the victim," she lied. "But Tia's very strict and…. You won't tell will you?"

Peter smiled. "Let us just say I will not volunteer the information. But if my hostess asks me, I will not lie to her. Is that a good enough promise?"

"It'll have to be," Zoë muttered to herself. "Say!" An indignant look came upon her face. "Why don't you like us?"

"Why would you think that? As I recall, *you* were the ones yelling up at *me* the other day."

"That was Dinora, not all of us. Besides, you were spying on us," she accused.

"Perhaps," Peter said calmly.

"What do you mean? Are you saying you weren't spying? It looked an awful lot like —" Zoë stopped to listen.

"What is it?"

"Shhh," she silenced Peter.

Slow, heavy footsteps were coming up the stairs. Zoë looked around. Across from Peter's room was the stairway leading to the attic. She had no way of knowing if Tia would turn left or right when she reached the landing but either was more likely than going to the attic. Hardly anyone went up there.

Zoë slowly opened the door and motioned for Peter to come with her, in the hopes of preventing an impromptu conversation with Tia. The two slipped quietly upstairs into the stuffy warmth of the attic.

The air was stale and Zoë imagined it might be the same air that had been there since the great house was built — well over a hundred years earlier. It looked as if the attic's contents had been here just as long. Huge black trunks bound with leather straps filled much of the large room. There were also hat boxes, wooden crates and shelves filled with faded books, tins and bottles.

"Over here," Zoë whispered, creeping towards a small round window. The clouds had cleared and the sun had lit up the sky. Zoë pulled a couple of crates over and sat down.

"This place looks like a historian's dream," Peter said.

"Huh?" Zoë looked around. "Yeah, I guess. Anyway, why have you been snubbing us? Why didn't you come with us when we went to the beach? And for that matter, why didn't you help in the garden? I mean, really! Why should *you* get out of the work?"

At first Peter didn't say anything, just gazed out the dusty window. Finally he said, "I do not mean to be rude...." he hesitated, trying to remember her name.

"Zoë," she offered.

"I do not mean to be rude, Zoë, and I wish I could answer your questions. I am afraid I cannot, at least not most of them. I can say I meant no offense when I declined your offer and I hold no disregard for any of you. You all seem rather nice. I am sure if the situation were different, we might have a pleasant time together."

"What do you mean? What situation? What are you talking about?"

Peter sighed. "I am sorry. I have told you as much as I —"

"You haven't told me *anything*," she interrupted.

"Please, just know my...behavior has nothing to do with you or your friends." He was still looking out the window. "I will stay in my room, at least as much as I can. It is for the best, honestly."

"Look, I don't know what's so important —"

"Get down!" Peter shouted, pushing Zoë off her crate and onto the floor.

"What are you doing?" she yelled back. Peter was also on the floor, breathing heavily, a look of sheer terror painted on his face. He didn't answer her. Instead, he pushed the crate aside and moved so his back was leaning against the wall, his face right next to the window.

"Zoë?"

"Yeah?"

"I need you to do something but I cannot tell you why." He swallowed. "Will you?"

"What is it?"

"Come over here, to the other side of the window. Do not go in front of it." He was talking to her but still looking out the window's edge.

She moved as he directed.

"Good, thank you. Now, carefully turn and look out and tell me if you see anything."

Zoë did as he asked. She saw the garden below them, and the woods. She scanned them and didn't see anything out of the ordinary. She moved her eyes up, into the rock face of the cliff. Still nothing.

"Wait a second…. That's weird," she mused to herself.

"What?" Peter insisted. "What do you see?"

"Well, it's like a flashing, like a bright light, which isn't so strange in itself. The sun catches on shiny things all the time, bits of glass or rock, but…." she trailed off.

"But what?"

"Well, if it was that, it seems like the light would be smaller and there wouldn't be flashing, just a steady stream of light. There might be wind, but enough to move a rock? Even a small one? It doesn't make sense."

"So what is it?"

"Well, the flashing means it's moving, but since it is coming from the same place it means it is moving just a little. It isn't going anywhere. And…."

"And what?"

"Well, it has to be big, maybe the size of a fist or something. I don't know. Mario is the scientist. We could ask him."

"Can you think of anything *natural* that would do this?"

"Natural? I don't know. I guess if an eagle or some other bird was making their nest and they grabbed a piece of tinfoil or something, that might do it, except...."

"*Except what?*"

"Well, eagles build their nests higher up; this is coming from lower down, in that clump of trees. And also, if it was tinfoil it would stop flashing as the bird secured it. I don't know, Peter? What do *you* think it is?"

Peter hesitated, then looked away from the window for the first time. He was trying to decide whether or not he should tell her. He wanted to but was afraid of what would happen if he did. "I think..." His voice was shaky. "I think it may be a lens."

"You mean like from a camera?"

Peter nodded.

10

❧ The Footprints ❧

"Will you at least tell us where we're going?" Seymour hauled himself up the cliff.

"Just a little bit more," Zoë urged. "When we reach that clump of trees, we'll stop there."

"I still can't believe you actually talked with Sir Peter," panted Dinora, accepting Seymour's help.

"If it was anyone but you saying he wasn't so bad, I would never have believed it," said Mario.

Zoë stopped to let the rest catch up. "I know. I was so surprised he didn't turn me in to Tia," Zoë said. She continued to herself, "Although I did lie to him...."

"You did *what*?" Seymour shouted up at her.

"I'll tell you in a minute — besides it was only a little lie."

"There's no such thing," Mario admonished.

"Will you all just hurry? I'm dying to tell you but I want to check something first."

The rest joined her one by one. Daniel was still back at the house finishing a job with Edith. As a result, the children had a few hours to spare before going sailing for the afternoon. They would have returned to their cove but it was too far away — by the time they got there, they would have to come back. Zoë had courteously reminded the others, with her jaw clenched, of their promise earlier in the week to sail with her. This tipped the scales and they agreed to go — except of course Peter, who had again declined Zoë's invitation. She thought this was just as well since it would give her the chance to tell the others of his strange behavior the previous day. The children reached the rim of trees as Zoë disappeared among their branches. When they joined her she had found a clearing and was moving dead leaves around with her feet.

"What exactly are you looking for?" asked Mario.

Zoë was absorbed in her job and didn't answer.

"We might as well help," said Dinora. "Even if we don't know what she's hoping to find, we certainly have brains ourselves. Chances are, if we find anything strange, it could very well be the thing we want to find. After all, when you think about it —"

"Let's try looking quietly, eh?" suggested Seymour. "Might help us to concentrate."

Dinora shrugged her shoulders, apparently feeling as if her searching skills wouldn't be impeded in the least by conversation. Nevertheless, she was silent as they worked.

"This is strange," observed Mario, after they'd been exploring the clearing for fifteen minutes or so.

"What?" asked the rest in unison.

"Well, look here," he said, pointing to two footprints embedded in the ground.

"So someone's been up here — that's not exactly out of the ordinary. Tourists hike up these mountains, hunters too," Seymour said.

"Yes, but it's not hunting season is it? Not for months yet and if they belonged to a hiker, they'd be pointing in the opposite direction. A hiker would face the mountain."

"And they'd be spaced differently," noticed Greta.

"What do you mean?" asked Dinora.

"If you were hiking, it's pretty much the same as walking. You put one foot in front of the other. These are side by side."

"And wide apart too!" contributed an enthusiastic Seymour, moving behind the prints. "I'd say maybe a shoulder's width apart. And see how they're deeper in the back? I think he wasn't standing. He was squatting — and for some time too."

"He?"

"Most likely. Look, these shoes are larger than mine. Definitely a man. And if I'm almost 180 centimeters, this guy has to be at least that."

"But why would someone spend that long just staring. There's not even a view from here," said Dinora. "You can barely see through the trees and if you do, you can't even see the ocean."

"All you can see is the house," whispered Greta.

"Exactly!" Zoë shouted, startling the rest.

"Okay Zo, 'fess up. What do you think is going on?" Seymour demanded.

Zoë paused dramatically, and then blurted, "I think someone's spying on Peter." She then proceeded to tell them about the odd occurrences of the previous afternoon.

"But that could have been anything or anytime for that matter," Mario said sensibly.

"Not anytime," countered Dinora.

"Huh?"

"The rain. These footprints had to have been made while it was raining or soon after. If they were made before, the rain would have washed them away, or at least blurred them. It was a heavy summer shower and these are clear and defined. Plus," Dinora looked around at the intent faces and smiled, "the sun came out and it got hot in the afternoon remember? So hot we decided to go for a quick dip in the pond after all. See how dry the ground is now? I'd say they were made before night."

"Dinora!" exclaimed Mario, sweeping his sister up in fierce embrace. "Ingenious! What beautiful logic! Such deductive reasoning!" Dinora glowed with her brother's praise.

"So, we know it was yesterday, and even if the flashing you saw wasn't a lens, we still know the guy was focused on the house — and for quite some time," Seymour summed up the situation with a slightly furrowed brow.

Zoë looked frustrated. "We just don't know *why*. Peter wouldn't tell me anything. He looked pretty upset at even sharing his suspicion at all. And he clammed up right after."

"Why would someone want to spy on Peter?" asked Mario.

This is it, thought Greta. *It's time*. She took a deep breath. "I might know."

Everyone looked surprised. Slowly Greta told them of Peter's arrival under cover of night.

"That's enough proof for me!" Zoë exclaimed.

"We still don't know why," Mario reminded her.

"No, but we know someone is watching him. I bet that's why he doesn't accept our invitations. Have any of us seen him even leave the house?" said Zoë. No one had. She continued, "And Tia must know. Why else would she let a perfectly capable child get out of work?" They had to agree on that point as well.

"We also know why *not*," said Mario. "Think about it. If he had done something bad —"

"Like killing someone," Dinora interrupted conspiratorially.

"Dinora!" all but Greta exclaimed.

Dinora shrugged. "You never know. I once heard about this girl who —"

"We know he didn't do anything bad," Mario reclaimed the conversation, earning a glare and a grunt from his sister. "If he had, Tia would never be hiding him, which she clearly is. Also, if he had broken the law, it would be the police who would be trying to find him."

"And they'd just come to the front door and ask if we were *harboring a fugitive*," Dinora said before turning to Greta and adding, "That's how they talk. I've seen it on television."

"Then it must be a bad guy who's trying to find Peter," said Seymour.

"Or already found him. Our watcher has left. Maybe he got what he needed," reasoned Mario.

"He could have given up," Greta said, trying to sound more optimistic than she felt.

"We're still missing pieces, though. Like why would he even think to look here for Peter? What connection do Peter and Tia have? It's not like they're close. If they were, he'd call her Tia."

"Do you think we should tell her?" asked Greta. The children looked at each other.

"It could be nothing," said Seymour.

"It's not. We know that." Zoë's tone was emphatic.

"Then we have to tell her," Greta said softly. "Peter's in danger."

When they arrived at the house, however, they found Tia had gone into town. Telling Peter what they had found only seemed to make him more nervous and more reluctant to share why someone would be spying on him.

The children weren't able to concentrate on much of anything as they anxiously waited Tia's return. Sailing was definitely out of the question. Finally, late that afternoon, Tia came home, only to hurry them out of the kitchen so she could prepare dinner for the guests who would be arriving any minute.

Reverend and Mrs. Eaton stayed late into the evening and none of the children had a chance to relay what they had found. The children were so distracted with their recent discoveries that they did not pay much attention to the adults' conversation until Mrs. Eaton squealed in delight.

"Oh, that would be simply divine, Miss Witherspoon," her shrill voice warbled. "You're sure the children won't mind?" she asked, as if they weren't all right there in the room with her.

Tia smiled sweetly. "They'd love to do it. Wouldn't you, darlings?"

None of them had the heart or courage to confess they hadn't been listening. Tia tolerated many things but never bad manners. Instead, each of them nodded their head with vigorous enthusiasm.

"This is just great!" Zoë complained when the children were cleaning the kitchen. "Now we have two mysteries to solve."

"What's the second?" asked Dinora, drying the porcelain teapot.

"Whatever it is we volunteered to do."

It wasn't until after Reverend and Mrs. Eaton had left that the children got their chance to tell Tia about the footprints. She had assured them it was probably nothing but her behavior indicated the contrary. For one thing, she didn't join them in the music room as usual.

"Did you see the way she rushed to her study?" Seymour asked.

The rest of them, Daniel included, had also chosen to pass on music for the night. Instead they brought tea and pastries and gathered in the boys' room. Greta had just assumed the girls' room was better. As she looked around, she couldn't imagine why. The boys' room was huge, nearly twice the size as theirs — almost as big as her whole apartment at home. There was a loft too, with a view of the ocean, where they were ensconced in two sofas and an assortment of armchairs. Zoë sat on the floor, leaning against Dinora, who was intricately plaiting her hair. It was a symbiotic relationship, helping Dinora to concentrate and Zoë to relax.

Seymour continued. "First, she picked up the phone but didn't make a call. It almost looked as if she were about to contact someone and then thought better of it."

"She probably didn't want the whole town to know," Dinora said.

"I wonder what she has in her study then," said Greta. She was stretched out on one of the sofas, her book resting unopened on her chest.

"I have no idea. This is my seventh summer and I've never been inside it," said Mario.

Daniel took a sip of the tea. "I've lived here for almost two years and have never seen it unlocked."

Together the children pondered their collection of mysteries but as no new insights surfaced, the conversation found its way back to their secret cove on the other end of the island. They shared with Daniel the story of how they found it, including a drawn out and slightly exaggerated version of Zoë's leap off the cliff.

Daniel's enthusiasm was energizing. "It sounds incredible. I can't wait to see it."

"You don't have to wait," Dinora said excitedly. "We can go tomorrow."

"I can't. Edith's haying tomorrow and I said I'd help." The others groaned but Daniel seemed resigned to the task.

Greta heard a click and the faint sound of voices. None of the others seemed to notice. "Dinora, will you help me take the dishes back?" she asked.

Dinora looked up from where she was just finishing Zoë's braid. "Sure," she said, proceeding to return plates, cups and saucers to the silver tray. Greta grabbed the teapot and napkins.

They took the back stairs which led to the kitchen. Greta turned on the landing and heard the voices more clearly. There were three: Edith, she'd recognize that gravelly voice anywhere; Tia; and a third person — a man.

"— but not ready yet. That's my concern, Tia. It's safer here, for all of them," the man said.

"David, you have to do something," Tia pleaded.

"I'll try, but I can't promise. You know how it is out there."

Greta heard a chair scrape against the floor as someone stood up from the table. "Edith, I could use your help," the man said.

"Only if Dot feels —" Edith began.

"Of course, Edith. If David says it's safe —"

"He didn't say *safe*, Dot. He said *safer*." Edith said sternly.

"Darling, I'll be fine."

A few seconds of silence passed before Edith consented, "I'll get my gear."

"Make sure you bring your —" the man began.

"Greta? Darling, is that you?" Tia called out and the man abruptly stopped what he was about to say.

Greta stepped forward. "I'm sorry, Tia. I didn't mean to listen. I just didn't want to interrupt —"

"Greta?" asked the man.

Greta descended the stairs. The man was staring at her. She could tell he was trying to turn away, like he didn't want to be rude or make her uncomfortable. He had the kindest eyes she'd ever seen — and the saddest. So much so it was almost contagious. *That's the word*, she thought. *It's like I feel sadder just looking at him.*

"When did she…." he asked Tia gruffly.

"Just this week." Tia paused to make sure she had his attention. "David, she doesn't know."

"No, no, of course not. I…I just wasn't expecting…." He took a deep breath and shifted his focus. "Edith, I'll meet you outside."

"Give me two minutes," Edith said, walking out the door. The man turned to follow.

"David?" Tia stopped him.

"Yes?"

"When will you be back for the pickled peppers?"

"Saturday night. I'll pick them up at the bazaar if I don't make it back sooner."

He risked one last look at Greta, who was staring openly at him. "Goodbye, Greta. I…" He looked at Tia who had a serious and disapproving expression on her face. "…well, goodbye."

Greta was speechless.

11

❧ The Library ❦

It seemed ages since the children had been to their cove. Greta hoped nothing had changed. She was worried someone else — maybe some other kids — had found it and ruined it somehow. Looking at her friends, she figured she probably wasn't the only one concerned. Everyone was enjoying the ride but there was definitely a feeling of anxious anticipation in the group, as if they had been away so long they were beginning to doubt if their perfect day had actually happened or if their hideaway even existed.

"Look!" Zoë shouted. It was the cliff. They urged the horses towards the rocky edge. Everyone seemed to hold their breath.

Dinora was the first to see it and she squealed in delight. "It's here, it's here!" she yelled back, Diablito prancing along the edge. "It's all still here."

The children rushed to tether the horses and move supplies through the tunnel. The passage wasn't nearly as terrifying this time, in part because it was familiar but mostly because they had brought enough torches for everyone.

"Oh!" Greta gasped. She had forgotten just how beautiful it was. The sea sparkled even bluer, the sun more golden. Even the sand seemed softer. Fearing it might not be true had magnified its splendor.

When they returned, dinner was waiting for them on the table, along with a note from Tia.

Darlings,

My apologies — a little busy with a project at the moment. Enjoy dinner and get to bed early. Please work in garden tomorrow. Also, if I have not returned by Monday, there are some errands I need you to run. The list is on the kitchen counter.

All my love, Tia

Perhaps other children would have relished this opportunity to be left unsupervised and to their own devices. These children did not. Instead they worried about Peter. He now refused to come out of his room at all, and only spoke to them to say "thank you" when food was left at his door. They tried to maintain a cheerful mood but as dinner progressed, their conversation again found its way to the man spying on the house, the stranger from the kitchen and Tia's mysterious departure.

"I hate this," said Seymour on the second evening, when Tia still hadn't returned. They had spent the day in the garden and were now relaxing in the music room with cups of hot tea and sore muscles. "I feel like we're sitting ducks."

"That's the thing though," said Daniel. "If we were in danger, Tia never would have left us."

"Then why is Peter afraid to come out of his room?" Dinora asked.

"That I don't know," he replied.

"It is possible," offered Greta, "Tia thought we'd be in *more* danger if she didn't leave us."

"That's a comforting thought," remarked a sullen Zoë.

"I just wish there was something we could do," Dinora grumbled, reaching for a raspberry tart.

"But we don't even have all the pieces of the puzzle," Seymour complained as he paced the floor.

"Yeah," said Zoë, "it's like one of those thousand-piece puzzles and we have about four pieces. We don't even have enough to guess what the puzzle is supposed to resemble."

"Let's think about this logically," suggested Mario. "Let's review what we do know."

Zoë's frustration was palpable. "We've done this already. We know a bad guy is after Peter. We now know Tia is scared and I think we can rule out that she thinks we are safe here since that is pretty much the whole reason she left — that we aren't safe here — that someone has found him."

"But are we sure of that?" asked Greta.

Daniel poured himself another cup of tea and silently offered the pot to the others. "Well, he hasn't left the house, so it *is* possible he hasn't been found and the bad guy just *thinks* he could be here."

"Thanks," Dinora said offhandedly as Daniel refilled her cup. "I do wish Peter would just tell us what is going on."

"It's futile," said Zoë. "I've been trying for two days straight. He won't say a word."

"This is getting us nowhere," said Mario. "We might as well get some sleep. Don't forget, we need to run Tia's errands tomorrow."

"Wonderful," groaned Zoë. "Just when my eye has healed."

"This time let's try to get through the day without any fist fights, shall we?" Seymour encouraged.

"He was the one who started it."

"Yeah? And who threw the first punch?"

"You two can stay and argue," Mario stood up. "I'm going to bed. I'll see you in the morning."

The rest followed suit.

"Zoë?" Dinora asked softly, a few minutes after the lights were out.

"Yeah?" came a groggy voice.

"Do you think he's watching us now?"

There was a long moment of silence before Zoë answered truthfully, "I don't know, Dinora. I hope not."

Greta was so scared she wondered how she would ever fall asleep. The sound of the surf, a branch tapping against the window, the creak of birch trees, all made her skin crawl. Her mind was inundated with thoughts of someone out there: watching and waiting. Planning.

At the breakfast table the next morning, the other children too looked as if their nights had been plagued with the same restlessness.

"Right when I want my brain to be working its best," said Mario over coffee, "it feels like it doesn't work at all."

Fortunately, Jake and his cronies were nowhere to be seen, and everything went smoothly. Again, they divided the list in half and the girls set out for the Lobster Co-op, Historical Society Museum and jeweler.

It was a beautiful day and a tour bus had deposited its passengers on Main Street. Elderly ladies in sunhats wandered about looking in shop windows and discussing how *very* lovely all the lovely things were.

After placing an order of nine lobsters for the following Monday, they delivered an old book to the office of the museum's curator.

"Fascinating," said the intern, clearly titillated. He reached for a pair of tweezers and began turning pages. "Simply fascinating."

As they left the office, Dinora whispered to Greta, "I bet that's why Edith calls them the *hysterical* society."

The girls continued walking down Main Street until it met Sunset.

"Here it is." Zoë stood before a small shop. The windows of the second story boasted bright yellow curtains and Greta assumed it was the proprietors' home. A wooden shingle hung next to the door. It read: *Pruitt & Son, Jewelers.* They walked in to the empty store. "Hello," Zoë called.

"Coming," a voice responded. A television clicked off and a middle-aged woman emerged, wiping crumbs from her dress. She looked at them and smiled broadly. "Hello, girls. Back again for the summer?"

"Yes, ma'am." Zoë and Dinora said together.

"Wonderful. There's nothing like being a kid in the summer — no worries, no pressure, not a care in the world. Am I right or am I right?"

"You're right, Mrs. Pruitt," Zoë replied. Greta wondered what her friend *really* wanted to say.

"Mrs. Pruitt, we have something for you." Dinora held out an envelope. "Tia asked us to give you this."

"Well, let's have a look-see." The woman opened the envelope and read the note inside. "I didn't even realize he'd gotten this old. Well, I suppose time marches on." She looked up at Dinora. "You tell your brother to stop in and see me sometime next week. I should have it ready by then. To think of how many of these we've made over the years. It makes me feel so old." Mrs. Pruitt stared wistfully out the window. "Well, no matter. Is there anything else girls?"

"No, ma'am. That's it." Zoe said, and the three departed the store.

"I wonder what that was all about?" said Dinora. "Do you think Mrs. Pruitt is suffering from dementia? I heard about this woman once who…" Dinora continued hypothesizing as they went to meet the others at the post office.

The boys were already there, sitting on the wide, shallow steps.

"The mail hasn't arrived yet," Seymour held up his hand to shade his eyes. "Walt said it should be here by noon."

"What's this?" Zoë asked, reaching for a small package lying next to him.

"Something for Tia, I assume. It must have come on Saturday."

"What pretty stamps." Dinora took the package from Zoë, admiring the postage. "I'm so glad they didn't ruin them with all that ink. Look Greta, I think that one's a gardenia. I love gardenias."

"We have an hour to kill," Mario said. "It doesn't make sense to drive back to the house."

"Rum Raisin!" Dinora exclaimed.

"Huh?" Daniel asked.

"Let me translate," offered Mario. "My sister is proposing we pass the time by purchasing and eating ice cream cones. She herself will order Rum Raisin. Why, you ask? She's working her way through all the flavors in *alphabetical order.*"

The others looked at Dinora.

"I'm on 'R'," she confirmed.

"I don't know," Seymour feigned disapproval. "Dessert before lunch? I'm not sure Tia would approve."

"Hah! Are you kidding me? Tia *invented* dessert." Zoë shoved him. Greta noticed Zoë always hit Seymour in the same spot. *I wonder if he has a permanent bruise.*

"If you don't mind, I'd rather just go the library," Greta told the others.

"Instead of ice cream?" Dinora asked incredulously. "They have sprinkles."

Greta laughed, "Yes — instead of ice cream."

"I'll go with you," Seymour offered.

"I don't mind going alone, really."

"You sure?"

"It's two blocks away. You can all see it from here. Plus, there's a librarian inside." Seymour looked as if he wasn't sure if this was a "yes" or "no" so Greta added, "I'll be fine. Thank you."

"Okay," Seymour said hesitantly. "We'll be at the truck if you need us."

Greta nodded and began walking quickly to the tall white building next to the Town Grange. She pushed open the large front door and inhaled the familiar and comforting scent. She knew it was just the smell of people and old books, but to her, libraries were perfumed with knowledge. She had finished *The Sea Maiden: a Captain's Tribute* and was looking for another story involving adventures on the high seas. The librarian was happy to help.

"If you liked that one, you *must* see these over here. They are all stories about seafaring. But these right here," she pointed to the top shelf, "are all by sailors who eventually settled on The Island. Most of their descendants still live here to this day."

Greta thanked her, chose one of the smaller volumes and found a comfortable chair in a tucked-away corner. Soon all of her worries had been ousted. Now she was immersed in the regaling of storms, pirates and mutiny.

She wasn't sure how long she'd been reading when a cloying voice distracted her from the book.

"Ah yes, excuse me, ma'am. I was hoping you could help me find something."

"Certainly, sir. For what book are you looking?"

"Well, it is not exactly a book. I'm a...a journalist from *The Boston Globe*, up for the day on a story about old New England families."

"We have a lot of information on —"

"Actually," the man interrupted, "I'm particularly curios about the...uh, Witherspoon family."

"Witherspoon?"

"Yes, I believe there is even still a descendant living on The Island today, a Miss Dorothea Witherspoon?"

"Yes, she does — and the Witherspoons did play quite a prominent role in The Island's history."

"I see. Well, I'm more interested in sort of a 'then and now' comparison. For example, I understand she has a number of children."

"Yes, in the summer she has, for certain."

"She has a camp?" he asked.

"Oh, no — just nieces and nephews, friends of the family. From all over the world they come — quite a kick, really."

"Yes, a kick indeed. And where did you say they come from?"

"Now let me think. Well, I believe China...and Mexico and of course the U.S."

"Fascinating."

"Yes, isn't it?"

"You said China and Mexico but not any other countries? No African countries, per se?"

"African?" the librarian paused. "No, not of which I know. But one of the girls is here. Perhaps she could tell you."

"One's here?" The man's voice heightened with interest.

Greta's inner alarm blared — this man was not to be trusted. Looking around, she noticed the back door had been propped open to let in some air. Quietly, Greta set down her book and crept out of the library.

She ran as quickly as she could back to the post office. When she saw the others, she pushed herself even harder. Her lungs felt like they were filled with cement.

"What the blazes —" Seymour began, but something in Greta's expression made him stop.

Zoë rushed towards her. "Are you okay? What happened?"

"Get — in the truck — now," she panted. "We — need to go — now!"

If they had been adults, no doubt they would have questioned her. Probably even other kids would have asked why or argued with her. After all, she was an eleven-year-old ordering them around. But that was the thing about this group. Somehow, Greta knew they would trust her and when she saw them following her instructions without any hesitation, she knew her trust had been well placed.

By the time they reached home, Greta had told them everything. As soon as they arrived, the group marched up the stairs to Peter's room. When he opened the door it was to view six very serious faces.

This time it was Mario who spoke. "We need to talk."

12

❧ The Truth ❦

It was after dinner that evening when Peter finally confessed. He'd argued with them the entire afternoon, trying every strategy from being evasive to telling them it was for their own good that they didn't know. But the children were persistent.

After they cleared the dishes and put out tea, Peter finally told his story. "Well, there are two stories, really. I suppose I shall tell the easiest one first. Then you can decide if you want to hear the other," he said softly. "I do not know who they are, honestly. The men…following me…I do not even know…."

"Maybe you should just start at the beginning," Mario suggested.

Peter was silent, then nodded and began again. "I was studying at Northfield Academy."

"That's the private school, right?" asked Daniel, "The one in Massachusetts?"

"Yes, it is. I was just finishing my sophomore year. Before that I was at another boarding school, in London. I was there for six years."

The Truth

"Do your parents travel a lot?" Dinora asked. "Is that why they put you in boarding schools?"

At the mention of his parents, Peter's lips tightened. He didn't answer her question. Instead, he took a deep breath and continued his story. "I have been in boarding schools, or had tutors, for as long as I can remember. I barely even knew my parents. Maybe I would go home once a year for a couple of days. Even in the summer I would work with private tutors or take extra classes. It is not that they did not love me —" he assured them, a little too strongly. "They had a great many responsibilities. It is done now, so...." He left the sentence unfinished.

"Then about two weeks ago, I was walking back from class when I noticed this man. I remember, at the time, thinking it was peculiar — on campus one does not see many adults. Even parents are not very common unless it is Parents' Weekend or the beginning of school. It was also strange because the man was somehow familiar to me, even though he seemed out of place. But I could not think of where I had seen him. Regardless, I was focused on exams and I just put it out of my mind.

"Later that night I was studying in my room and there was a knock at the door. I answered it and there were two men in suits and they looked..." he paused for a moment, "...*official*. Like they were from the government or something. And they called me by my full name, which not many people know. I was disarmed by that. I figured they must be legitimate. They said they had something very important to tell me and asked to come in. They entered and as soon as I closed the door, one of them grabbed me and the other held a wet cloth over my mouth, soaked in something which made me dizzy — probably chloroform."

"What's *chloroform*?" Dinora asked.

"$CHCl_3$, also known as trichloromethane. It's a colorless, sweet-tasting liquid, usually derived from acetone, acetaldehyde, or ethyl alcohol — used formerly as an anesthetic," explained Mario offhandedly.

"It knocks you out," clarified Zoë.

"Oh," said Dinora.

"And it did. Next thing I knew I was in the trunk of a car with my hands and feet tied."

"Oh, dear!" said Dinora.

"Then what happened?" asked Seymour.

"I do not know how long I was in there but eventually the car stopped and I heard voices, then new voices — I am not sure how many. Then scuffling and then..." Peter looked around before continuing, "...gunshots."

Dinora gasped.

"I thought the men who had taken me were dead and the ones who shot them did not know I was there. Eventually they opened the trunk and untied me. They too called me by my full name. One of the men told me to get in their car — that we needed to hurry — that they were taking me to a safe place."

Maybe this was David, wondered Greta. *Who is he?*

"But you didn't know if they were good guys because they saved you from the bad guys or if they were just more bad guys who took you for some other reason," said Daniel.

"Well," said Seymour, "what else could he do?"

"I must have still been in shock. I did not even consider running. I let them lead me to the car and we drove off. Maybe it was an hour later when it occurred to me to ask what was happening. That is when they told me." Peter's voice descended into a whisper.

"Told you what?" asked Zoë.

"About my parents. They were dead. They had been killed that morning, back home."

"Oh, Peter!" cried Dinora. "I'm so sorry."

"It is odd. I know I should feel awful, but I do not. Then I feel *bad* that I do not. After all, they were my parents — even if I did not really know them."

"Do you know why they were killed? Did the men say?" Seymour asked.

"They did not have to. I already knew. Lesotho is not a powerful country but it is located in a powerful place. Our whole history is filled with one occupation after another, as different nations vie for control of my land. Then the occupiers put the military in the hands of their staunchest supporter. They always leave the monarchy intact. They think it makes the people calmer if they can see their king is still in power even if the General is making all of the *important* decisions. And they are right."

"It sounds too simple," Seymour said.

"It *works* because it's simple," Mario explained.

"Is that why your parents were killed?" Daniel asked.

"They were getting too powerful, fighting to be more independent, saying Lesotho should not be run by outsiders. They were garnering much support, even from many of the soldiers."

"But why would that endanger their lives?" asked Zoë. "They're just two people. How could they be such a threat?"

Then Greta said softly, "He was the king wasn't he, your father?"

Peter looked up at her and slowly nodded.

"Then that makes you…" began Dinora.

"A prince," finished Seymour.

"A prince who is not safe in his own country," Peter added flatly.

"Or in this country either, apparently," mumbled Zoë.

"We don't know that yet," insisted Dinora.

"But I don't understand something," said Greta.

"What is that?" Peter asked.

"I don't mean to be…" she paused, "…insensitive, but if they wanted to get you out of the way just like your…parents, why didn't they simply…well…"

"Kill me when they had the chance?" he asked.

"Basically…yes."

"It must not have been their purpose. I was not exactly under armed guard when I was at school. If someone wanted to hurt me, or…kill me, they could have done it easily, at any time."

"In a way, that's good news," offered Mario.

"How do you figure that?" Zoë arched an eyebrow.

"Well, it means even if Peter is in danger of being taken again, he isn't in danger of being killed," answered Mario.

"Or us either, for that matter," said Daniel. "What good would that do? That's probably why Tia felt comfortable enough to leave us here alone."

"I'm not sure. If the whole aim is to keep Peter safe, he hardly seems safe here in the house, unguarded."

"You think there is a guard, *don't* you?" said Seymour.

Dinora looked around the room.

"Not here in the *house*, Dinora," scoffed Zoë.

"But somewhere," Seymour said.

The children were quiet as they thought about this.

"Why Tia?" asked Dinora after a while.

"I do not know. I did not meet Miss Witherspoon until the night I arrived."

"Did the men say why they were bringing you here?" asked Seymour.

"They just said they were bringing me here — to be safe — while they found a permanent place for me."

"You mean you won't go home?" asked Dinora.

"No," Peter replied softly. "I probably will not be able to go home for a very long time."

"But you're the prince," said Dinora.

"Actually, you're the king," corrected Mario.

This thought seemed to startle Peter. "It was hard enough to grow up carrying the responsibility of being a prince. I do not even want to think about the burden of being king. Although at this point it hardly matters."

"Well, that is at least one problem we can solve," declared Dinora. "If you only want to be a prince, then that is what you'll be."

Peter smiled at her sweetness. "Thank you," he said.

The Truth

There was a rustle outside and all of the children froze. Zoë was closest to the door. She picked up a guitar from a nearby stand and held it like a baseball bat. A door opened and footsteps sounded.

"Darlings?" came Tia's voice "It is I."

The children heaved a collective sigh of relief.

"Good Lord, Zoë. That is no way to hold an instrument. For heaven's sake, it is not a golf club! I certainly hope this is no indication of how you've been treating my house while I've been away."

The children flooded to her, covering her with hugs and kisses. All except for Peter, who stood back politely. Before Tia had a chance to catch her breath, Greta blurted about the strange man from the library who was looking for Peter.

"Hmm. I suspected as much," said Tia. "Peter, I'm afraid you won't be able to stay with us much longer. I've made arrangements with a friend of mine. He'll be here Thursday night."

"But Tia, if a man comes here looking for Peter —"

"He won't find him," interrupted Tia, her eyes sparkling mischievously. "At dawn you children must be off and out of sight. Now, if we could only think of a place where you could be safe and not completely bored."

"Our cove!" they shouted.

"Perfect. Now I suggest you try to get some rest before you leave."

"But we have to pack and get ready. There's so much we'll need: tents and clothes —" blurted Zoë.

"And food for the horses," added Dinora.

"Leave that to me and Daniel. Didn't I ever tell you I was a highly regarded excursionist before I retired? Your job is to sleep. Now off you go."

The children went.

"Oh, Peter," called Tia. Peter turned towards her and Greta overheard her whisper as she drew him close. "Might be best to sleep in the boys' room tonight, just to be on the safe side."

13

∞ The Tunnel ∞

It seemed to Greta she had just fallen asleep when Tia woke her and told her it was time to leave. She looked out the window. The sky held not even a hint of dawn.

"Try to be quiet. Don't turn on any lights. Zoë?"

"Yes, Tia?"

"Go wake the boys. Tell them they just need to get dressed. I've taken care of everything else. And girls…" all three of them turned in her direction, "…*hurry.*"

Zoë splashed some cold water on her face and pulled on her boots. She had slept in her clothes and was the first to leave. The other two were not far behind.

The children gathered soundlessly in the dark kitchen. Each of them was wide awake, despite their lack of sleep.

"Now, listen carefully," said Tia. "This is Tuesday. I want you back by Thursday — no sooner. Do you understand?"

They nodded.

"Tia?" Dinora fidgeted nervously with her jacket zipper.

"Yes, darling?"

The Tunnel

"Is someone watching the house?"

Tia sat down at the kitchen table and drew the children to her. It would have been completely dark if not for a faint trail of moonlight seeping through overcast skies. Greta could make out the silhouette of this woman she had come to love so easily. Tia's shoulders sagged. She looked tired — tired and scared.

"Probably, Dinora. I'm not certain, but most likely. Don't worry. If there was cause for worry, I'd tell you — be sure of that. Whoever they are, I believe they still aren't convinced Peter is even here. They'll watch the house just like they are probably watching twenty houses. Think about that. You could probably even stay here and be safe. I just don't want to take the chance. They won't look elsewhere on The Island — they've no reason. Go to your cove. Have fun. Try to relax and enjoy yourself. Be back on Thursday."

Even in her groggy state, Greta noticed Tia was speaking strangely. She didn't sound like herself. Then it occurred to Greta — it was the first time Tia was speaking without repeating every other word. For some reason, this seemingly insignificant detail worried her more than anything else. Tia might be telling the truth but she wasn't telling them everything.

"If they are watching the house," Mario began pragmatically, "won't they see us leaving?" Greta thought he didn't look as frightened as the rest of them. Of course with Mario, one never really knew for sure *what* he was feeling.

"Taken care of," assured Tia, rising from her chair. "Follow me, my darlings. Follow me."

Greta felt some small comfort in the return of Tia's patter as she and the others descended the basement stairs. When Greta had last been there, she had only noticed Mario's simple laboratory. She couldn't see much more now, with the faint light sifting through the windows, but she could sense the room was much larger. Tia led them down a long hallway. Even with the light completely gone, she didn't risk using a torch and Greta was grateful for every precaution. They stopped and she could hear the sound of keys jingling, the rusty click of a lock and the creaking of an opening door. A short gust of cold, damp air greeted them, followed by an earthy smell — like dirt after a spring rain.

"Zoë, darling. You go first, but slowly. The slats are about a hand's width apart." Tia stepped aside to make way for her charge. "Mario and Seymour, you next."

The boys quietly entered the passageway.

"Girls, step inside but wait for me," instructed Tia. Greta and Dinora did as they were told. Tia came after, pulling the door closed and locking it. They were in complete darkness.

A second later, the passageway was flooded with light and Greta shrieked. Instantly she covered her mouth with her hand and looked contritely at Tia.

"It's alright, dear. It's alright. I should have warned you."

A parade of light bulbs ran the length of the passage — or at least seemed to. Greta couldn't see the end of it.

"Tia, what is this place?" Zoë asked excitedly.

"Sorry, darling," Tia whispered back. "We still shouldn't talk. The tunnel acts like an amplifier. I'll give you a history lesson later. Go ahead and set a fast pace for us. We haven't much time. Just make sure you stay on the slats."

Greta looked below, curious about what she'd touch if she did misstep. It was nothing. Not "nothing" like nothing-to-worry-about. Just...*nothing*. A shiver went up her spine just as Tia clutched her hand tightly and started walking quickly after the others.

They had walked for nearly an hour when Greta looked up for the first time and noticed the same door they had entered. *Have we been walking in a circle? No, of course not*, she thought as she shook her head to get it working right. She was so tired. She couldn't remember the last time she'd slept free from worry. This did not bode well for the rest of the night. Zoë was brave and Seymour was strong. Mario was astute and Dinora had moxie. Greta knew she had been useful to the group before. She knew she was "book smart" but that didn't do much good. What *had* been helpful was the fact that she was observant. She noticed things. This was a valuable skill which would aid them, help keep them safe. But if she couldn't recognize a new door that simply looked like one she had used an hour before, then who knew what else she'd miss. Silently, she reprimanded herself for slacking off and vowed to stay alert. She needed to keep her wits about her.

Tia stepped forward and turned out the lights. Once again they were plunged into utter darkness. The only difference was this time Greta knew what was beneath her. Tia unlocked the door. Greta expected a blast of cool night air to meet them. Instead she heard a latch and another creak. Tia ushered them into a tiny room. *It's a cottage,* Greta thought, *and barely that. This is a shack.* She held the familiar feeling of finding the right word. It gave her hope that her senses were returning.

Zoë stepped out the front door, looked ahead and could just barely distinguish the outline of five horses and a young boy.

"Daniel?" she whispered.

"Zoë?" the familiar voice responded. "Are you all here? Are you alright?"

"We're fine. Where are we?"

"About two kilometers southwest of the house. How was the tunnel? I'd heard about it but never really believed it was true."

"You'll see for yourself soon enough, Daniel," Tia said. "Right now we need to get these children off."

In fewer than five minutes, they were on their horses — Greta again with Zoë — and saying goodbye to Tia.

"No need, no need," she chuckled softly. "This is just a little harmless adventure — good for the circulation. I'll see you on Thursday, around seven. Now get!" This time

Dinora was ready as Diablito sped off. The rest were seconds behind her.

Except Mario.

"Tia, will you be alright? Are you in any danger because of this?" he asked gravely.

"Of course, darling. We all are — every day — from all sorts of things," she matched his tenor.

"You know what I mean."

"And *you* know what *I* mean," she said firmly.

"I just —"

"I know, I know. It'll be fine, Mario. It has to be," she paused. "It's the right thing to do."

Mario looked at her a moment longer, smiled resignedly and turned to face the slowly lightening fields. He signaled his horse and headed west.

Tia and Daniel watched him even after he could no longer be seen through the haze of the island dawn.

"Come, Daniel," Tia said distractedly, "our work has only just begun."

Approximately two kilometers northeast a man was squatting next to a CB radio. "This is Red Dog. Over."

"Yeah, Red Dog. This is Eagle." A bored voice crackled through the static. "Do you have confirmation? Over."

"No confirmation yet, sir, but I do have some abnormal activity. Over."

"Go ahead, Red Dog. Over."

"Sir, there's still no sign of the item in question, but the farmhand left an hour ago with horses. Over."

"And where are the children now? Over."

"They're still inside — far as I can tell — but they might be planning to rendezvous with the horses and escape. Over."

"We've got a guy at the ferry and one at the airport. If they try to leave, we'll know about it. Are you tracking the horses? Over."

"Yes, sir. Put a device inside a saddle. I only had a chance to do one — but from what I've seen — those kids stay together. Over."

"Any movement? Over."

"Just a few minutes ago they started moving in a southwesterly direction. Over."

"Is that toward the coast? Over."

The man rolled his eyes and muttered to himself, "We're on an island, aren't we? Everything's toward the coast."

"Red Dog? Over."

"Affirmative, sir — toward the coast. What do you want me to do? Over."

"Could the kids be on the horses? Over."

"I suppose it's possible, sir. But I've been watching the house all day. No one's left except the farmhand. Over." There was a pause. "Eagle?"

"Hold on, Red Dog — waiting for further instructions. Over."

A few minutes passed and the man fidgeted with a cigarette he wasn't allowed to light. *Who cares*, he thought. *I'm surrounded by trees in the middle of nowhere. Still, better to wait until after the call. That man could hear a thought in your head.*

"Red Dog? Over."

The man jerked to attention. "Red Dog here. Over."

"Boss says stay put and check in at noon — unless something happens. Over."

"Got it, sir. Over and out." He hung up the receiver, lit his cigarette and hunkered down to watch the house.

14

❧ The Tide ❦

It took over an hour to unload the horses, transfer the supplies over the ledge and make their way down to the cove. The idea of relaxing had seemed impossible the night before when Tia suggested it. Now, looking around at their haven, each of them knew it would be hard *not* to do just that. Even Peter seemed like a different person. Of course, much of that had to do with the fact that he was wearing old jeans and a Red Sox tee shirt.

"There's enough food here to last us a week," said Dinora, lugging another satchel to where Peter had created temporary shelves and a little kitchen area.

"I guess Miss Witherspoon wanted to make sure we had enough to eat," he replied in his clipped British accent.

He and Dinora looked up as they heard Seymour emerging from the tunnel, followed by Zoë. Simultaneously, they dumped their final load of provisions next to Mario and Greta, who were preparing some food. They hadn't eaten since dinner the previous night. Even then, they were too distressed to do more than pick at the delicious meal Tia had made.

"Were the horses secured?" Mario asked.

Seymour had taken awhile to tie up the horses, unsure of himself. After the fifth try he had finally done it. "They're set. Watered and everything. I put their saddles back on after I rubbed them down, just in case."

"Food's ready," announced Greta with a self-conscious flourish.

They all turned to see her posing next to her creation with a proud expression on her dust-covered face. Along with Tia's bread and a wheel of cheddar cheese from the dairy, Greta had laid out half a salami; small, tart plums from the overgrown orchard behind the house; and a container of creamy milk, still cold from being packed in ice. "I figured we should drink this first, since it won't last for very long."

"Sounds wonderful," Peter exclaimed. "I am positively famished."

The others quickly joined him, except for Seymour, who went to wash up from the horses. "Peter, did Tia pack a bucket?" he called.

"Yes. I put it underneath the big basket."

Seymour retrieved it, and along with a few other items he found in the supplies, was able to fashion a crude water-catchment system. "It'll take forever," he explained later, between mouthfuls of food, "but if we keep it going, we can use it for bathing, washing dishes, everything."

He looked at his friends, who hardly spoke as they cut off slabs of cheese and salami, took bites of plums, poured milk and passed the bread back and forth. Although they didn't seem particularly interested at the moment, he knew they'd be very appreciative when they wanted to bathe.

The children devoured their breakfast quickly. Afterward, they could barely keep their eyes open.

"I say we finish unpacking and set up later," suggested Zoë.

No one argued. They took blankets and found warm spots on the sand. Within minutes they had fallen fast asleep.

Perhaps three or four hours had passed when Greta woke. Her whole body ached from the lack of sleep, the worry and the long ride that morning. She yawned, stretched and made her way over to the water Seymour had stored. He too was there, changing pails. Now he had added something new to his contraption, which diverted extra water off to a handmade pool of sorts.

She washed her face and took a long drink. "Seymour, it's ingenious. Thank you."

"My pleasure. How are you feeling?"

"Stiff."

"Best idea is probably a swim. It'll help you work your muscles out. If you want I can look in the first aid kit for some medicine."

"No. I'll be fine." She looked at him and tilted her head to the side. "Seymour?"

"Mmm?" He was still maneuvering pieces to perfect his design.

"It feels weird."

"What does?"

"I don't know. It's so beautiful — so serene and sunny. Then I think of last night — of being in danger. It seems like a whole different world."

"You're right. It is strange. Me, I'm just going to think of it as a holiday. Why worry about something over which we have no control? Tia told us to spend a couple of nights here." He shrugged. "We might as well have fun."

Greta wrestled with his logic. "I'll try."

"Good girl. Now help me take this pail over to the fire pit."

The Tide

Greta hadn't noticed the pit until Seymour mentioned it. Now she saw he had built it in such a way that a pail could rest on top and they could boil water.

"What's this for?" she asked.

"Last time we were here I noticed a lot of clams. I thought they'd make a nice dinner." He indicated a basket in the shade which held a handful of sand and shells. He set the pail next to the unlit fire so it'd be ready.

When the others woke, they worked together to erect their tents.

"Make sure you don't set them up too close to the beach," Mario cautioned, "for when the tide comes in."

"I wonder how far it reaches," Zoë said as she fed poles through the loops of the girls' tent.

"Look on the rocks. You should see water marks," Mario told her as he laid down a tarpaulin and spread out the larger tent for the boys.

"Here, let me help you," offered Peter.

For the next hour the children worked without much talking, as they established their cozy, temporary home.

Afterward, everyone went swimming — except for Peter and Seymour who were determined to gather every clam and mussel to be found; and Greta who was still trying to muster up the courage to even wade in the water. The children sat down to eat a few hours later. They didn't bother to set out proper place settings, preferring instead to eat casually from the communal pail of perfectly steamed shellfish. They basked in the setting sun, the warmth of the fire, sated appetites and good company. It had been a long day and even with their morning nap, each of the children was worn out.

"Zoë, you might want to bring in your tent a little bit. The tide is beginning to come in," said Mario.

Zoë groaned. She was lying on her back next to the fire with eyes closed. She looked like she never wanted to move again. "I tried to find the watermarks, Mario, and I couldn't see any."

"Well, I'd definitely move your tent. Look, it's only four meters away right now and the tide's still coming in."

"I'll get it," offered Dinora.

"I'm coming." Zoë dragged her body up and went over to help. Together they pulled out the stakes and moved it much closer to the mouth of the cave.

Ten minutes later, the tide had already surpassed where their tent had been and was beginning to encroach on the boys'.

"I thought for sure it wouldn't reach this far." Mario sounded nervous. He, Peter and Seymour moved their tent next to the girls'. The children became increasingly uneasy, as moments later the waves began lapping softly less than a meter away from the tents. "This just doesn't make sense." Mario struggled to rationalize what was happening.

"Maybe we should just bring the tents inside the cave, to be safe," Peter said.

"Mario?" Greta called softly.

He was helping Peter pull the tarpaulin and didn't respond.

"Mario?" she repeated.

"Yes?"

"I think you should see this." Mario released the tent and walked towards her. "Look," she said, pointing at the top of the cliff. "Are *those* watermarks?" Terror was creeping through her.

Mario's jaw dropped as he stared at the cliff in disbelief. "You guys...." his voice began to tremor. Everyone stopped what they were doing and looked at him. "We have less than an hour before this whole cave fills with water."

No one said anything.

"We need to get out of here...." He tried to keep his voice calm, but failed. "*Now!*"

There was a flurry of activity as the children scrambled to pack their belongings and climb back up the tunnel. Food was thrown haphazardly into any bag available. Tents and sleeping bags were bundled together. Soon Seymour ordered them into an assembly line. Mario scouted ahead to find a place where they would be safe and Seymour gave the rest of them their assignments. Greta and Dinora rushed to form one end of the line while Seymour and Zoë continued packing as rapidly as they were able. Peter grabbed bag after bag and raced half way between Seymour and Dinora, over and over.

"Just pack the important stuff first!" Zoë yelled at Seymour as she took a turn running supplies up to where Peter would meet her. "We may have to just let some of it go!"

Seymour looked up. The ocean had already reached the mouth of the cave. "Zoë!" he bellowed. "Get everyone back down here. We need to at least get it into the tunnel."

Zoë relayed the message but with all of the echoes it served only to confuse the rest of them. Finally, all of the children came back to the cave, which at this point was filled with over half a meter of water.

"There's a strong undertow," Seymour warned as he forced his way through the ocean which grabbed at his calves and ankles. "The rest of you should stay out of here."

"Seymour, there isn't time." Zoë looked as if she were about to cry. "Just leave the rest!"

"We can't!" Mario moved past her and jumped into the water. The receding wave snatched him instantly and dragged him under.

"Mario!" Dinora screamed.

They all stared at the water, transfixed in terror. Then they saw him. The waves brought him up only to thrash him down again. His body was flung against the jutting rock they had used as their table. This time his hand reached out and clutched the edge. Even with the dusk and the distance the children could see the gash in Mario's forehead.

"Mario!" Tears were pouring down Dinora's cheeks. Greta was afraid the girl might go into hysterics.

Mario waited strategically for the undertow to pass him. He wiped blood away from his eye before edging his way back along the cavern side. As he reached the supplies he shouted, "Seymour, go long!" Seymour turned just in time to catch a satchel Greta knew to hold their extra batteries and a torch.

"Start taking this stuff out of here or we won't be able to get through," Zoë instructed coolly as she too jumped into the water. Her timing was better, giving her a few seconds to get her bearings before the water came at her.

"Zoë, don't! Get back in there!" Seymour shouted at her.

"Don't tell me what to do!" she shouted back. "We don't have time for this. Throw me something!"

Seymour only hesitated a moment before tossing the small cooking stove in her direction. She caught it easily and passed it to Peter who set it next to a whimpering Dinora.

"Greta?" asked Peter, keeping his composure.

"Yes?" She was paralyzed with fear and desperate for instructions.

"You and Dinora have to take this stuff up past the water level, way past, at least until the little cave. Do you understand, Greta?" He was referring to a place near the top of the tunnel which flattened and widened out to create a small cave in and of itself. Originally, when they were first exploring, they thought this was the end and the rest of the tunnel was only wide enough for the wind. Then they discovered another smaller tunnel coming out of the floor in a corner. "Greta?"

The combination of Peter's tone and having something to do both soothed and energized her. "Got it," she said.

"Good."

"Dinora!" she said sharply to her friend. "You can cry later. Right now, take this tent and this torch and go up to the little cave. I'm right behind you."

Dinora slowly picked up the jumbled tent, accepted the torch Greta pressed into her palm and began the assent.

"Faster, Dinora! You can do this." Greta spoke with an authority she didn't know she possessed.

Dinora didn't stop weeping but she did begin to move more quickly. Together the two girls transferred the provisions until there was nothing left to clog the opening of the cave. Greta was dumping the last load when she heard muddled sounds. Something was wrong, but because of the layered echoes, it was hard to discern exactly what. Then it stopped.

She heard Mario's distant voice, "— too late — let the rest go —" followed by silence.

A moment later she heard another voice. This time, it was from above.

15

❧ The Trek ❦

Six children huddled together against the cold stone of the cave. Some were still damp from swimming. Two were wearing jeans soaked nearly to the waist. One was drenched completely. Most of them had scrapes and bruises from where they had fallen or grazed the rock surrounding them. One was still crying. All of them were scared.

Although they hadn't heard the voices for over an hour, they didn't dare go outside to see whether or not it was safe. They had decided together, in hushed and urgent discussion, it was better to stay put and leave when it was light. The bluff was flat and they would be able to see if anyone was around.

"Unless they're in the woods." Zoë was shivering more than the others. Her teeth chattered as she spoke. "It's so dense — we wouldn't be able to see four meters in."

"Here." Seymour passed her his sleeping bag. "This one isn't as damp."

Greta was sure Zoë would refuse. She seemed too proud to admit her thin frame was taking this the hardest.

But she accepted the gift gratefully and handed hers back to her cousin.

"Thanks." Zoë curled up even tighter and Greta scooted closer to her.

She thought she couldn't possibly admire Zoë any more than she already had. The girl was just three years older but nothing seemed to scare her. Greta could still see her jumping back into the water, her mind and will set. Come to think of it, the behavior of her friends during tonight's terrifying escapade had heightened her respect for each of them. Despite the fact that she had seen her brother nearly bashed unconscious against the deadly rocks, Dinora had still managed to draw on some reserve fortitude. *She may be crying,* Greta thought, *but she did what we needed her to do. We wouldn't be here right now if it weren't for her. Sure, we are cold and tired and scared. But we're alive, and for the moment at least, safe.* Each of them had given all of themselves. Together they had survived an ordeal where survival wasn't a guarantee — not by a long shot. She was proud of them, proud of herself.

Mario could not have felt more differently. *How could I be so stupid?* Desperately, he tried to think of the clues he'd missed. He blamed himself. *I'm the oldest,* he chastised. *I should have been more alert, more careful.* He tried not to let his mind admit his real feelings but he was drawn there nonetheless. He was angry with himself, certainly. He was disappointed in how careless he'd been. Mostly though, he was scared — terrified actually. *I could have gotten them killed.*

It was with this thought in his mind that he drifted off to sleep.

When Mario next opened his eyes, the cave was still pitch-black. He listened intently and was able to distinguish five separate patterns of slumbered breathing. As depleted as he was, he still wasn't able to do more than rest his eyes. This was due in part to his incredible discomfort — wet jeans and beaten body against ice cold rock. Mostly, however, it was his conscience which kept him awake. He knew they were probably safe, and logic dictated he would be of more use to the group tomorrow if he were rested. Still, he stayed awake, guarding the people he'd endangered, the people who were dearest in the world to him.

When he judged it to be close to sunrise, Mario rose — still soaked and sore but now stiff as well. He took the torch and crept into the tunnel. A few minutes later he saw the soft light of dawn peeking through the entrance. He turned off his light and trod slowly out into the open. The sky and sea couldn't have been more peaceful. It was a mockery of the night before and struck a bitter chord in Mario's heart. He turned and hoisted himself up just enough to peer over the edge. Nothing. It was as tranquil as the view behind him. Whoever had been there the night before, they were gone. Now there wasn't a soul in sight. Not even their horses.

"For the millionth time, I know I tied them correctly." Seymour's voice was hoarse from screaming in the salt air of the night before. His was not the only one. They were all still wet and many had begun sneezing. Mario's wounds, now that there was enough light to see, were even worse than he had let on. Zoë had a fever. They might have been a formidable team any day of the week, but now they were a dismal bunch, bedraggled and in need of more than a little tender, loving care.

Dinora decided she was just the girl to put things right and so took matters into her own hands. "Look, whether he did or not is irrelevant." She addressed her friends before whispering to Seymour, "I'm sure you did. I have the utmost faith in you."

He smiled wanly at her and she beamed back.

"Okay now.... These are the times that try men's souls.... The stuff of which dreams are made and stories are told. We can get through this! We've gotten through a lot worse when you think about it, but I won't go into that. I don't want to distress you. Basically, what we have here is a situation, do you hear me? A situation." Even Zoë looked up. Dinora continued. "And what do we have to do with a situation? We have to take care of it, find a way out, pull ourselves up by our bootstraps and put the pedal to the metal. So, here is what we are going to do. We're going to prioritize. Triage — that's what it's called, right? Mario, right?"

"Uh yeah, I guess," he muttered.

"Well, then you guess right, because it is. Well? What's most important? We need to be safe and we need to be together. Well we have the latter, at least for the moment. So what if we are sore and tired and wet. So what if we almost saw our brother...." she faltered. "Never mind, these are all secondary concerns. First, if we are going to keep safe, we need to get out of sight. I don't know who was here last night or who took our horses. I do know we can get warm and fed anytime. This is our only opportunity to get out of the open. So here's what we're going to do. Anyone know first aid?" They were all silent. "Okay, okay. Don't worry. You all look like a bunch of nervous-nellies-jams-and-jellies. I know first aid, pretty much. I just didn't want to keep all of the fun stuff for myself."

Peter smiled. He liked this spunky side of Dinora.

"Let's see...well, uh...." For a moment there it looked to Greta like Dinora might have lost her train of thought, or worse, her momentum. "Seymour, you're probably the best with the woods and stuff like that, right?"

"I guess."

"There's a whole lot of guessing going on here, boys. A whole lot of guessing." It was like a miniature Tia standing there before them. "I'm hoping that'll change pretty quickly into a whole lot of yes ma'am-ing. Seymour?"

"Uh...yes, ma'am?" He almost started to giggle.

"That's more like it, and it's not funny. I need you to go ahead and find an adequate place for us to stop for a while. It needs to be secluded but still close enough to a clearing where we can dry our stuff. It will be hot today. It has to be," she said, looking up at the sky, as if she were even ready to give Mother Nature orders if it came to that. "Do you understand the kind of place we need, Sergeant?"

"Uh, Dinora, I'm not a —" he began, but when he saw her expression darken he quickly changed his tune. "I mean yes, sir! I mean ma'am."

"That's better, sailor. Now, would you like to begin this mission in clothes that aren't sopping wet, maybe?"

"Yeah, but —"

"I'll do the 'buts' around here and there are no 'buts' about it. Did you or did you not haul out any bags which have dry clothes in them."

"I'm an idiot!" he shouted, all of a sudden realizing they had been sitting next to bags the whole night which held clean, dry clothes.

"No worries, mate." Dinora was on a roll. "Don't blame yourself. You were in a state of shock. So this is what you're going to do, my friend. Go back to the little cave. Get dressed — leave your wet clothes there. Grab a bag or backpack, whatever, dump it out and fill it with some food, a canteen, a torch, a knife — you know what we need. Take a sleeping bag too and bring me the first aid kit. You have ten minutes. Go!"

Seymour darted off, encouraged both by Dinora's goofy speech and the idea of dry clothes. He had just finished changing when Peter and Greta entered.

"And what are your missions?" he asked, his playful personality finding its way home.

"We are in charge of sifting through this," Peter motioned to the piles before them, "and making five bags of bare essentials."

"It seems such a shame to leave most of it behind," Greta lamented as she dumped a bag out.

"It won't seem like that when it's been your fifth hour of hiking with it on your back." He grabbed his bag and the first aid kit. "Okay, I'm off. I've got Zoë's sleeping bag and one of the tents too, just so you know." He quickly made his way to where he'd tied the horses. He was so sure he'd done it right.

"Here's the kit," he handed it to Dinora. "Zo, will you be alright?"

"I'm fine, Seymour. I just need some rest." She took the medicine Dinora handed her along with the half-filled canteen.

"I'll find a good place, I promise," he told her.

"It doesn't have to be perfect, Seymour," Dinora reminded him. "We just need somewhere to rest. Did you get some food?"

"Yes, I have some. When everyone's ready, start making your way northeast, up the mountain. I'm thinking we should be able to find a spot above the tree line, maybe an hour's walk at the most but we need to be moving east. We're due back tomorrow night."

"Done. Now get," said Dinora as she focused her energies on her brother's wounds. He winced as she none-too-delicately dabbed his scrapes with alcohol. "Don't be a baby," she chided warmly.

He smiled at her and then at Seymour. "My sister," he said proudly.

"She did well, Mario. We'll see you in a bit." He ran ahead into the woods.

Thirty minutes later, Mario was bandaged enough to meet any den mother's standards, and the children had amassed the most crucial supplies. Zoë's bag was the lightest and Peter carried the second tent. Dinora set the pace, and using her compass, directed them into the woods.

"Well, my friends, this is it," she announced. "This is what separates the men from the boys."

They had been hiking for less than an hour when Seymour rejoined them. Immediately, he took Zoë's bag. She was grateful, knowing she would not have been able to last much longer. Her fever still hadn't broken and now her eyesight was blurry. In addition, none of them had taken into account the drawbacks of hiking through the woods. While the group had started out with somewhat restored spirits, it wasn't long before the burst of optimism had dissipated. They were left with the drudgery of hauling gear while trying not to get eaten alive by the mosquitoes and black flies swarming around them. To make matters worse, when Greta focused on the bugs, she'd miss the roots below her, which seemed to peek out of the forest floor and trip her the moment she wasn't looking.

"It's just ahead," called Seymour, after they'd hiked another kilometer. Within minutes, they emerged onto a vast ledge, cresting the mountain. Greta set down her backpack, grateful the insects hadn't followed them.

Seymour had spread out two damp sleeping bags on the lichen-covered rocks and the others arranged theirs in a similar fashion. Once completed, they collapsed in physical and emotional exhaustion. All but Dinora, who first went to check on Zoë. Once she was assured all of her charges were comparatively well and safe, Dinora too, let herself succumb to sleep.

The children dozed into the early afternoon, accompanied only by the ocean breeze drying them, the summer sun warming them and a few creatures that passed by to inspect the visitors: a bald eagle which nested five meters above them; a small red fox; and an assortment of crickets, beetles and doodlebugs.

Seymour woke first and went immediately to his cousin. Although he was only a month older, he had always thought of himself as her protector — a fact which annoyed Zoë to no end. He felt her cool forehead with relief. Her eyes fluttered open.

"Seymour?" She raised her hand to shield her eyes from the sun.

"How're you feeling?"

"Better, I think. How long did I sleep?"

"Over three hours. We all did. The rest are still sleeping."

"Hey, you know what I was dreaming?"

"What?"

"Our fort — you remember — when we were little?" She looked at him expectantly.

He thought about it. "You mean the one in Guangzhou?"

"No, stupid. The one here — on The Island. Remember when we ran away? I forget why. Our moms wouldn't let us do something. What was it? I don't remember…. Oh wait, I do now," she giggled. "We wanted to shave Rufus and they wouldn't let us and we thought that —"

"That they never let us do anything fun and we decided to run away. Now I remember."

"Do you remember what we took?" she said, laughing easily.

"Oh, right — you took all of your stuffed animals," Seymour said.

"And you must have taken close to twenty books."

They smiled at the memory. Then they were silent as they recalled what happened not long afterwards.

"That wasn't why, was it?" Zoë asked the cousin she'd grown up with as a brother. She already knew the answer.

"No. It wasn't," he said.

They sat in silence on the ledges overlooking woods and ocean.

It was some time before Zoë spoke again. "Anyway, that's what I dreamt — about the fort."

A thought occurred to Seymour. He stood and looked around. "Do you feel well enough to walk? It's flat from here, mostly anyway. I thought we'd just stay along the ridge and then find a place to camp tonight."

"I think so, if we go slowly."

16

❧ The End ❧

"Do you even know where we're going?" Zoë asked her cousin.

"Just wait. I think we're almost there — if it even exists. I'm still half-convinced I've imagined it."

The two of them had been walking for over an hour but the terrain wasn't too rigorous and they had taken it slowly.

"You're trying to find the *fort*, aren't you?" Zoë said.

"It wasn't a fort. Don't you remember anything?"

"I remember a fort."

"You called everything a fort. You'd crawl under the dining room table and call it a fort."

"You know why, Seymour?"

"Why's that?"

"Because it was a fort," she teased.

"There it is," Seymour pointed excitedly. "At least, I think it was there."

"That's a cave."

"It *was* a cave."

"I thought it was a fort."

"You really want to have that argument again?"

They walked closer and she saw, whether or not it had been their childhood refuge, it was certainly the place to spend the night. While not nearly as lavish as their cove, it was dry and big enough for all six of them.

Seymour set down the backpack he had brought. "Wow, it's so much smaller than I remembered." His eyes scanned the cramped space. It was like opening a time capsule. There was a crevasse at the top which served as a skylight illuminating the projects of two young children, crumbled now by time, other inhabitants and the elements. "Zo?"

She turned and he could see she was holding an old book in her hands. She smiled as she held back tears. "*The Story of Doctor Doolittle: Being the History of His Peculiar Life at Home and Astonishing Adventures in Foreign Parts Never Before Printed*," she read, starting to choke up. "Tia used to read this to us, remember? It was our favorite."

"I remember."

Zoë sat down on the ground and let the book slip from her hands. Shifting to Mandarin, she said, "I'm so tired, Seymour."

"I know," said Seymour, discarding his English as effortlessly as she. "You stay here and rest. I'll get the others. It won't take long. We'll be able to move more quickly. Two hours tops."

She stared at him, her eyes unfocused.

"That's not what you meant, was it?" he asked.

Zoë shook her head.

"Look Zo, we can't do this to ourselves, especially not now. We need to get through this, get Peter to safety and then we have the whole summer left." He had knelt down beside her and taken her hands in his. They were cold and he worried he had pushed her too hard. He took the sleeping bag, dried and warm now from the sun, and placed it over her. "Are you going to be okay?"

"I'll be fine," Zoë said flatly.

The End

Seymour knew better than to try to reason with her when her mood darkened like this. "Alright, I'm going to get the others," he said, rising.

Zoë just stared at the ground, dejected. Seymour turned, left their childhood sanctuary and started to make his way back to the others. Anxious about leaving Zoë, he broke into a run. Exerting himself helped mollify those heartrending memories he knew were still plaguing his cousin. Zoë and he were so different. It had always been easier for him to shake off the past, to forgive those who had hurt them. Zoë couldn't. She carried everything with her still. This inability to let go and move on troubled him. If she was this embittered and sad at fourteen, what would she be like in ten years? Life was never free from pain. How would she ever be happy if she couldn't cope with disappointment?

"Great directions!"

Seymour jumped. Lost in his worries, he hadn't noticed his friends twenty meters in front of him.

"What?" he shouted back.

"I said 'great directions'," Peter repeated, running to meet him and smiling broadly. "I always liked the simplicity of the basic arrow."

For a moment Seymour was confused. Then he remembered he'd laid out a brief message with rocks and twigs on the ledge.

"Sorry about that. I wanted to let you sleep."

"Don't worry," Mario said. "We figured you'd take the easy path if you had Zoë with you. Where is she?"

"She's at the camp. It's not much of one but it should be fine for tonight. Dinora, do you think I should go back to the little cave and try to get some more of our things? I could easily make the round trip before dark."

Dinora considered this. "I don't know. There are definitely things we could use but we'd risk being seen, and then followed."

"I could go with you, Seymour," Peter offered. "That way we could at least make the risk worthwhile."

"I could too," Mario said half-heartedly.

"Who are you kidding?" Dinora reprimanded. "Alright, the two of you go. Try to get as much food as you can, otherwise we'll be eating bugs and berries. If you can bring the stove too and some dishes and —"

"Dinora, there are only two of them," Mario reminded her.

"Right, you're right. But if you see or hear anyone, don't risk it. We've come too far already and we're so close." She rifled through her bag. "Take the torch and the canteen and be back by dark or..." she looked intently at them, "...or I'll cry."

Seymour hugged her and assured her they'd be careful. He and Peter wasted no time as they ran westward back to their provisions.

"I don't like being separated like this," Dinora said to Greta and Mario as they watched their friends go. "We're so much stronger when we're together."

Not long afterwards they found the cave and a much improved Zoë. Her fever had crept back slightly so she took two more aspirin before showing off her efforts. She'd swept out the cave, which upon further inspection hadn't been as untouched as she'd originally thought. Then she'd used the Swiss Army knife to cut back the grass from the skylight so her fort seemed almost homey.

Together the rest of them set up camp. Greta and Dinora gathered firewood while Zoë unpacked. Mario rested on the hillock, which formed their roof. In her search for wood, Greta came upon a small stream where they could fill their canteens.

Just before dusk Peter and Seymour joined them, looking for all intents and purposes like Father Christmas and his favorite elf. Seymour was relieved to see Zoë's gloom had passed and there seemed to be some color returning to Mario's face. Dinora prepared a soup over the fire and handed out the only bread which hadn't been stolen by the tide. There were also a few plums but they agreed to save them for breakfast.

The End

"I think we're closer than we thought," Mario said, adding another log to the fire.

It was a cloudless night and the children brought their sleeping bags out into the open. This inspired Greta to dub their temporary home *Star Rock*.

"Remember, we only have to get to the little hunting cottage. We can spend tomorrow morning resting up and head back after noon." He looked at his friends, who were well-fed, warm, dry and drowsy.

They murmured their agreement and drifted off to sleep under a blanket of stars.

Late in the morning, the children piled their supplies underneath the tarpaulin and covered it with rocks. They had all agreed, after recuperating at Tia's, they would love to return to Star Rock for a longer stay.

"Wait, we forgot something," Mario called as he started lifting off the recently situated rocks.

"What in the world are you doing?" said Dinora, her arms akimbo.

Mario found a box, opened it and passed four items to each of them: a pocketknife, a torch, a canteen and a box of matches.

"Mario, we're just walking a few hours, what could happen?" Zoë said, as he handed her the things.

"We'll not be unprepared again — not on my watch." He replaced the rocks and headed off down the ridge, refusing to discuss the matter any further.

Hiking down the mountain was less strenuous and Seymour set a leisurely pace. This time, because she was rested and in better spirits, Greta was able to handle the roots with more aplomb. Perhaps it was the lack of tripping or a good night's sleep that made the forest seem like an entirely different place. Greta had been in plenty of parks but this was nothing like that. The first thing she noticed was how delicious everything smelled. It felt as if she were inhaling the sweet, dark scent of life itself, burgeoning around her. Then there was the silence. Even with the footsteps and occasional voices of her traveling companions, there was a quiet so heavy and dense it dwarfed everything. Beyond the quiet she noticed the murmurings of an entire universe. *It is breathtaking*, she thought.

Then she saw a deer — *no, a fawn*, Greta corrected herself, noticing the white spots on his back. He had been chewing leaves but froze when he noticed her. She stopped as well. The others were far enough ahead that for a moment the world just seemed to pause altogether, as if creating a little time-pocket solely for her and this creature. She had seen a deer at the zoo but this was completely different. Somehow it didn't even look like the same animal. And he was so close — less than three meters away. The fawn's ears turned towards her. She couldn't help but giggle at the wide-eyed expression on his face with the leaves sticking out of his mouth. Her laugh jarred against the stillness and the spell was broken. The fawn bounded off and the world resumed its turning. She sighed wistfully before running to catch up with her friends.

Soon after, the children heard a familiar voice call out to them, "Hello?"

"Daniel!" they exclaimed, running excitedly to meet him.

"I'm so relieved to see you. When the horses came back that first night I thought something horrible…. Well, never mind. Tia told me not to worry, that you'd gotten yourself out of stickier pickles than this — her words, not mine," he added in response to some raised eyebrows. "Anyway, we should hurry. The man is already here, waiting for Peter."

The children's mood changed instantly. It was over. Peter would be safe. This is what they all wanted. Still, it meant the end of their time together. Just when they were beginning to get to know — and like — this unusual boy, he had to leave. For Peter, it meant having to face a world full of worries and new problems. For all, it meant the end of their adventure. Scary at times, uncomfortable to be sure; but now that it was coming to a close, they could all see it as a glorious adventure. And now it was over.

According to Daniel, Tia was anxious to get Peter to safety, so the two boys walked ahead of the rest. The rush was over and the surge of excitement gone. Lost in their own thoughts, the children took their time as they wandered down the long passageway.

Not Greta. As soon as she heard Daniel mention "the man" all she could think of was David, the mysterious man she'd met in Tia's kitchen, with his kind, sad eyes. There was something about him. The way he acted so strangely when he saw her, the way Tia cut him off when he tried to talk to her. She wanted to see him again.

Peter and Daniel were able to move more quickly than she, plus Greta was desperately afraid of falling through slats. When she reached the basement, the boys were already in the kitchen. She heard voices, including a familiar one not belonging to Tia, Daniel or Peter. It was a man's voice but it wasn't David's.

Something was wrong. She crept up the stairs and peered around the corner. She knew if Tia saw her, she wouldn't be allowed to stay.

The man standing next to Tia spoke. "I don't want to waste any more time. David's at the airport holding the plane."

"Certainly, thank him for us and tell him —" Tia began.

"I'm sorry, Miss Witherspoon. We really must go. Your Highness?"

"Yes," said Peter. "I'm ready."

Greta sat back on the steps. She knew that voice from somewhere. Somewhere not good.

17

❧ The Piano ❦

None of the children slept more soundly than Zoë. Her fever still lingered and she was worn out. The excitement, intrigue and danger had taken their toll, not to mention the effect of memories long set aside. Each of these combined to push her deeper and deeper into the comforting recesses of dreamless sleep. This is why she missed the first clue.

It was Greta who woke at the sound of the piano. It seemed odd Tia would be playing this late and this loudly. "Zoë?" she whispered. Not a sound. Greta went over to her bed and shook her.

Zoë mumbled something in Chinese.

"Zoë, I think it's important." Greta whispered again. For some reason she was afraid to make any noise.

"*Bi Zui!*" Zoe grunted.

Greta could only assume what this meant. She began to panic. What was she supposed to do? The more awake she became the more she realized Tia would not be bothering them, especially after this whole ordeal, unless something was wrong. Maybe the ordeal wasn't over.

The Piano

This made her think again of the man's voice and how it had seemed both familiar and unsettling.

She remembered.

"The library." The words came on her exhaled breath and the memory rushed back. Peter had gone with the wrong man.

"Zoë, please," Greta pleaded, shaking her friend more vigorously.

"What's going on?" It was Dinora. She sat up in her bed and yawned loudly. "Is Tia playing the piano?"

"Yes. I think something's wrong. Help me wake her." Together the girls tried to bring Zoë to consciousness.

"It's the medicine," Dinora explained. "It's made her too sleepy."

"Please, Zoë," Greta began to cry, "please —"

"*Fatal Hour*," Zoë interrupted.

"What?" Dinora and Greta asked simultaneously.

"The piece she's playing." She still seemed more asleep than awake.

"It's what?" the girls asked urgently.

"*Fatal Hour* — by Purcell."

As if sensing she'd gained the clue, Tia transitioned into a new piece.

Zoë got it instantly. Her eyes shot open as the adrenaline won out over the medication. "Schubert's *Marche Militaire*. Oh no, oh no. We've got to get out of here. Something's happened."

Quickly the girls threw on clothes suitable for a nocturnal escape. Just as they were leaving, Tia began a new song.

"Wait," Zoe whispered, listening for the clue.

"It's *Danny Boy*," Dinora tried to contain her pride. "Does she want us to tell Daniel?"

"No," Zoe said decisively. "She wants us to take him with us. This must really be bad."

The girls climbed carefully up the stairs, thankful Tia's playing had continued. It masked the creaking steps of the old house. They followed the unlit hallway to the other end of the old manor. Zoë stopped before a closed door and listened. Silence.

"This is Daniel's room," she whispered. "You two wake him up, tell him what's happening. Then come quickly and quietly to the boys' room."

Greta and Dinora did as she said. Daniel woke more easily, and in minutes, they joined the others. They had just started down the back stairs when they heard a voice in the kitchen.

"— sign of him yet. Not to worry, sir. The boy will come here. It's the only place he knows.... Yes, sir.... Yes, sir."

The children hovered in silence, afraid to move.

"Sir, she's harmless — an old lady. She made us tea if you can believe that.... No, sir. Mike's with her now. She's playing the piano — says it calms her. Sweet, if you think about it.... Yes, sir. I understand, sir. We'll make sure she doesn't leave the house. Sir, that wasn't my fault. The boy.... Yes, sir. You're right, sir.... Yes, I understand, sir." The man stopped to take a sip of his tea and a bite of something, probably one of Tia's pastries.

"No, the other kids didn't come back. She says they're in the village with friends. Said she wanted them out of the way in case anything happened. I suppose she could be lying — hard to say. Still, it's not like they're a threat. I figure we stay here tonight — wait for the boy — then back to the original plan. It was a stroke of luck we intercepted her message. All I had to do was show up and have the boy handed to me."

The man had finished the pastry and was now rummaging around Tia's kitchen looking for something else to eat.

"Yes, sir. I understand we then lost him. Still.... Yes, sir. Got it. I'll check in when he gets here. It may take him awhile — he's a boarding school prince. He hardly knows the first thing about surviving on his own. He'll be here soon enough.... Yes, sir. I know. I won't underestimate him again. Yes, sir. I understand, sir." The man hung up, grabbed another éclair and left the kitchen.

The children looked at each other. They didn't dare talk, but without talking how could they decide what to do? No one was taking charge and time was of the essence. They each seemed paralyzed.

It was Daniel who poked Dinora and motioned for her to bring the others back upstairs to the boys' room. In panicked whispers they planned their next move.

"The guy could be coming back at any second."

"The door makes too much noise."

"What if all of us don't get out?"

"What happened to Peter?"

"Who was that guy?"

"What's happened to Tia?"

"Should we try to rescue her?"

"She wanted us to get out — and fast," finished Daniel. "We daren't leave through the kitchen. It's too dangerous. We can't take the risk. The best way is out the window — here," he pointed to the one facing the orchard. "The tree is probably too far for the smaller of us but we could climb the trellis down." The wisteria-smothered trellis scaled the side of the house, nearly reaching the second story.

"If we lower you down, can you grab hold of something?" Seymour asked him.

"I'll try. I can't think of any other way. It's too far to jump."

Seymour held Daniel by the wrists as his feet worked their way through the vines to find the wood underneath.

"It's old," he whispered. "It'll probably take me, Greta and Zoë. I'm not sure about the rest."

Daniel found his footing and was now feeling for something to grip. He settled on the gutter. Silently, he made his way down. Just as he was nearing the bottom, one of the laths broke beneath his weight.

"Zoë, you go next. That way you and Daniel can catch —" Seymour began, glancing at Dinora, who was also beginning to realize the predicament: Seymour and Mario were too heavy for the trellis but they were both tall enough to jump to the tree. She was too short *and* too heavy.

As this settled in Dinora's mind, Zoë was being hung out the window, tracing Daniel's path. Greta followed. She was light enough but not nearly as experienced as the rest of the group. She slipped half way down but Daniel caught her easily.

"What do you think?" Seymour asked Mario.

"I don't know. If it couldn't hold Daniel's weight…."

"She'll never make the tree. I'm not entirely sure *we* will," Seymour said. They turned to look at Dinora. She was gone. A moment later they saw her below, waving impishly up at them. They also saw Zoë start to berate Dinora for her foolishness but without being able to make any noise, her scolding was rendered useless, and somewhat comical.

"No time like the present," Seymour said, as he crawled onto the window's edge and leapt onto the tree branch. He made it with a solid *thump* and quickly descended the large maple. Next, Mario jumped, although not as gracefully.

Once they were down, Daniel led them around the back of the house. As they neared the barn, Mario whispered, "Daniel, we can't take the horses. It'll make too much noise."

"I know. We're using the barn to block us, just in case anyone looks out."

"Of course — sorry."

The five followed Daniel, who knew these woods far better. Within minutes of entering the forest, the nearly full moon was of little use. Still, Daniel managed to lead them along a faint path, gradually climbing the mountain. As her eyes adjusted, Greta was surprised at how much she was able to see. The trees, which at first had been indistinguishable, now separated into distinct shades of black. The foggy outlines of her companions too became more pronounced — almost as if lit from within.

When Daniel judged they were at a safe enough distance, he stopped. "Is everyone okay?" It was the first time someone spoke and the sound clashed with the subtle murmurings of other forest conversations. One by one, they checked in.

"It's not just you though, is it, Dinora?" Zoë picked up right where she had left off. "You put all of us in danger. If they saw you they would have known the rest of us wouldn't be far off."

"I didn't think of that," Dinora said contritely, "sorry."

"You're sorry? You don't even get it —"

"Forget about it," Seymour said. "It turned out fine. Plus," he spoke in Zoë's direction, "I'm not sure what else she could have done."

"Hmph," Zoë grunted.

"Settled? Great," Mario announced. "Now let's try to figure out the rest of this." Methodically, Mario proceeded to review the facts. "What do we know for certain?"

"Tia is being held captive," said Dinora.

"Although she doesn't seem to be in any immediate danger," Seymour said. "The question is, what will happen when Peter doesn't show up? We need to get her out of there." Seymour's voice betrayed his anxiety.

"Either her or them," Daniel added.

"I think there are only two bad guys at the house." Mario said. "If there were more, then it seems like the kitchen guy would have mentioned it."

"We also know they somehow intercepted Tia's message," said Zoë.

"Which means the good guys still think Peter is here — and safe," said Daniel.

After much discussion, Seymour summed up the little they knew, "So basically, we don't know where Peter is or if he's okay. We do know he's not with the bad guys, but

Tia is. What we don't know is how to get in touch with the good guys so we can get Peter to them, assuming he can find his way back to Star Rock...."

"Do you think that's where he'll go? You think he won't try to go back to the house?" asked Daniel.

"I doubt it. He's not stupid," Zoë said bluntly. "If he escaped them once it's not like he's going to walk right back to them. He'll go to Star Rock because it's safe and because he'll know we'd look for him there." She sighed heavily. "Assuming he can find it."

Greta was sure they wouldn't be able to sleep, that the excitement of the escape and anxiety over Peter's whereabouts would keep them up. To the contrary, before long, each of the children had found a place on the soft forest floor. Within minutes they surrendered to their fatigue and were fast asleep.

They awoke only a few hours later as dawn began to permeate the forest's canopy. The six children worked out their stiff and sore muscles as they made their way farther up the mountain to Star Rock. Although they were disappointed not to find Peter, they were grateful to see their provisions and camp were still intact. They had a sparse breakfast of trail mix and plums before napping on the rocks outside the cave. All except for Daniel and Dinora who kept watch, both for Peter and for danger. The morning gradually passed as such, each child taking their turn watching while the others recuperated and busied themselves with various improvements to their camp site.

"Do you think we should have left some sort of sign the house wasn't safe?" Greta asked Seymour. It was their turn to keep watch and they were sitting atop a ledge which looked out over the ocean on one side and down the mountain on the other.

"Probably," Seymour responded. "It's hard to say. If it were one of us, it would be easier since we know each other so well. Even if it were you, we could probably figure out how you might approach the problem and where you might go to keep safe. With Peter, it's different. We barely even got to know him. The kitchen guy could be right. He could be lost in the woods or not even have an idea of where to start. He could be trying to find the good guys on his own —"

"Or he could be looking at them right now," came a voice from behind them.

Startled, Greta and Seymour turned around to see the dirty, tired and beaming face of their friend.

"Peter!" they shouted in unison, alerting the others. Greta impulsively ran to hug him and he laughed as he held her.

"No offense," he said, "but the two of you are *not* the best watch keepers in the world. You do, however, make great beacons. I came along the coast and noticed you almost a kilometer back."

Seymour looked down at the bright red tee shirt he wore with his red plaid pajama bottoms. "Like my outfit?" he grinned.

18

❧ The Story ❦

After much excitement and conversation, the children gathered to hear Peter's story.

"I don't know where to start." Peter seemed a little flummoxed.

"At the beginning!" chorused the others.

"Really, Peter," Zoë added. "You've got to be the world's worst storyteller."

"Well," he began, "it started in Tia's kitchen. It's funny — you would think after all that has happened to me lately, I would be more suspicious of people wanting to take me somewhere."

The rest nodded.

"But I was tired, of everything, and I went with him. As we approached the car he opened the door for me so I would sit in the back seat, which isn't itself out of the ordinary. I'm used to that."

"Why?" asked Dinora.

"Because he's a prince, dummy." Zoë's anger with Dinora had simmered down to mere irritation.

"As soon as I got in the car, I smelled cigarettes. Again, this wasn't out of the ordinary — plenty of people smoke — but for some reason it set me on edge. The man got in, immediately locked the doors and drove down to the end of the lane. When the car slowed, I started to feel nervous. There was *something* familiar about the scent of the cigarettes. The car stopped and another man came out of the shadows and got in. That's when it all came together. I recognized the second man — he was the one who came to my dorm room. At the same time I realized the man driving was the one with the chloroform. When he held the rag over my nose, I must have smelled his cigarettes too…before I passed out."

"Then what happened?" Seymour urged.

Peter closed his eyes. He had no difficulty picturing the blackness of the car or the silhouette of the driver. He remembered the man entering the car and turning to face him as the car sped off.

"You've caused us no small amount of trouble, Your Highness," the man said, sneering.

Peter felt a shiver run down his spine. Instantly his mind was tumbling, flooded with random thoughts all at once — flashes of his parents dancing at the German Embassy ball: his mother had looked so happy; his father, so regal. Peter thought of a book he still needed to return to one of his professors. He thought of being with Zoë in the attic and how hard it had been to concentrate. Even her black eye hadn't marred her beauty. Her face was exquisite — the kind that inspires artists to paint. He thought of her jumping into the water and shivering in the cave. He regretted not sitting closer to her. He thought of his newfound friends, Tia's good food and sleeping out at Star Rock. Then one image, stronger than all the rest, cleared his mind. He smiled.

"What have *you* got to smile about?" the man asked indignantly.

Peter didn't answer. He shifted his eyes downwards and tried to stifle his grin. All he could think of was sweet Dinora shouting at them, "This is what separates the men from the boys!"

Now he remembered Mario and his cool logic. Peter took account of the situation, racking his brain for possible means of escape. He thought of a few options but none of them seemed very likely to succeed. As Peter felt the car speeding along the tortuous road, he realized the longer he waited, the harder it would be to escape. *My hands are free but the doors are locked. Or are they?* Peter afforded himself a quick glance and noticed now they weren't. The cigarette guy had unlocked them to let in his friend and hadn't remembered to lock them again. They underestimated him. It was dark outside and there was a sharp corner coming up. *This is it*, he thought, *it's now or never.*

He mustered all his courage and, as the car slowed to take the turn, Peter opened the door. It swung wide and Peter leapt out of the car. His attempt wasn't nearly as graceful as he had pictured or as he had seen in the movies. He tripped and stumbled and fell and rolled. He got up, wincing as pain shot through his ankle. Still, he began to run. But not fast enough. Within moments the two men had caught him and dragged him back to the car.

"We need some rope or something. You got anything like that?" the second man asked.

"I don't know. Check the trunk."

Peter heard the trunk open and the man rifling through its contents. He appeared a moment later with a ball of twine in his hands.

"This is all you got but it'll have to do," he grumbled. "We need to keep moving — there are houses around here and people are still up."

Peter's wrists were tied together behind him before he was thrown roughly back into the car. They drove in silence for what seemed like an eternity, but what in retrospect, Peter figured to be about twenty minutes.

"Damn it!" the driver swore, startling his partner and Peter.

"What now?"

"I need to get some gas."

"Are you kidding me — what kind of idiot are you?"

"Hey, shut up why don't you. It'll just take a minute — we'll still make the boat." The driver pulled over to the road's shoulder, turning the car around in one swift movement.

"Now what're you doing?" his partner demanded.

"Oh, and I'm the idiot? Think about it. We're not exactly in Boston here. It could be forty kilometers before we see another gas station. We passed one a few minutes ago. I'm just hoping it's open."

The other man sat back in his seat, stewing in frustration. Peter had been watching the interplay closely, trying to think of a way to use this to his advantage. At least the car was turning around. If he was able to escape he wouldn't have as far to travel. He moved his ankle around. It hurt a little but he hadn't done too much damage in his earlier fall.

Then as the car swerved, Peter felt his body tilt slightly. He also felt something else — something in his back pocket. He tried to think of what it might be. It dawned on him and he felt his face light up. Unconsciously he tipped his head to the floor so there was no chance for his captors to see the hope in his eyes.

It was the pocketknife Mario had insisted they each take, just in case. There was something else too, something that had been small enough to slip into his back pocket.

Matches.

Peter's hands may have been tied but he had more than enough room to position his arms and fingers. Within a minute he had the knife out, open and sawing at the twine binding him. The men didn't turn around and the hum of the motor masked the steady scratching. He looked ahead and saw the fluorescent lights of the gas station lit up garishly amid the pine trees. As the car slowed, Peter cut the last strand of twine. With this release he felt clarity surge within him and he knew what to do. He shoved the twine partially into the seat. The car slowed and Peter hurried to remove the matches from his pocket. Just as Peter dumped the matches, the car pulled up next to the only pump. The driver cut the engine and all was silent.

A man in his twenties exited the station and walked towards them. He wore a blue jumper spotted with black stains. "Unleaded?" he called as he wiped grease off his hands.

"We got it, thanks," the driver called back. The man shrugged and went back into the shop.

Peter waited as the driver circled the car, unscrewed the gas cap and inserted the nozzle. Slowly, Peter took three matches from his pile and held them, along with the empty box. The doors were unlocked again and he was determined this second attempt would be his last. It *had* to work. He felt certain if this one failed, he'd find himself once again in the trunk of the car.

The nozzle clicked its finish and was returned it to its cradle. *This is it.*

As his partner started to make his way to the clerk, the man shouted, "Hey, Mike. Get me a Coke while you're in there, eh?"

Mike glared back.

Peter recognized the optimal moment. As Mike was turning away from him, he moved quickly from the middle to the edge of the seat. Without hesitation, he turned, struck the three matches at once and threw them onto his kindling. As the lit sulfur met with the shredded twine and twenty or so other matches, they burst into flame. The driver's eyes bulged as he saw the back seat combust instantaneously.

"Then I ran faster than I have ever run before," said Peter, breathless with the excitement of telling his story. "It was getting darker and I could barely see. I was so afraid I would trip again. I figured, though, if it was too dark for me to see then they would have the same problem. I could hear them shouting but their attention was all on the car. They were so focused on putting out the fire, they didn't even come after me at first. Probably by the time they got it out they had no idea even in which direction I had gone." Peter beamed with pride.

"You're having fun!" Zoë accused.

Peter looked down abashedly. "I can't help it. I know it's dangerous, believe me. Those men were terrifying — but something about this — I just never thought I would be able to do something like that. I escaped my captors. I set a car on fire."

"Well, I wouldn't go *that* far," teased Seymour.

"I tracked down my friends and used a knife. By the way, Mario, thank you."

Mario held his head high with satisfaction. "I knew it would come in handy."

Dinora smiled at her brother. "But now what are we going to do?" she asked. "Peter, do you know when the good guys were supposed to have come?"

"I don't know. They never told me. I'm not sure there was even a specific time."

"Look, we're going to make ourselves crazy doing this," Seymour said. "It's better to not think about it and let our minds clear. Let's get some lunch ready and see if we can't get a fresh perspective after we eat."

Seymour and Dinora prepared a meal from their meager supplies. Mario, Peter and Daniel worked on designing an alarm system. Greta and Zoë decided they could at least be useful by gathering wood for the fire. They set out to scavenge for fallen branches, working in contented silence, each girl lost in her own world.

"That's pretty, Greta," said Zoë. "What is it?"

"Hmm?" Greta emerged from her trance.

"The song you're humming. It's pretty."

Greta hadn't even noticed she'd been making any noise at all. She'd been so focused on their problem and her immediate task. "I'm not sure. I just know I can't get it out of my head."

"I know what that's like. It just eats at you." Zoë bent to pick up the end of a tree limb. She dragged it back to the pile she was making at the forest's edge. "It sounds familiar. Now it'll drive me crazy. Hum it again."

"I only know part of it. I only heard a little when —" Greta stopped suddenly, her eyes growing wide.

"When what?" Zoë asked absentmindedly, without looking up.

Greta didn't say anything. Instead she started to cry.

"Greta, what is it? What's wrong?"

Greta began trembling and crying even harder. She couldn't breathe. Zoë ran to her just in time to prevent her from collapsing on the ground. Slowly, she lowered her until Greta was sitting cross-legged on the forest floor, breathing in quick gasps.

"Greta, you need to pull yourself together. You're hyperventilating."

"Oh my...oh my...." Greta felt as if she was going to faint.

"Greta, calm down. Seymour!" Zoë shouted. "Greta, try to slow your breathing." Zoë put her hand on Greta's chest as if she could physically force the girl's lungs to relax.

"What is it?" Seymour called as he ran towards them. Dinora was behind him.

Greta sat, trying desperately not to get hysterical. She was sure the others would soon follow. Then everyone would be here, depending on her. It was too much pressure. What if she couldn't do it? What if she couldn't remember? Then everyone.... And Tia would....

Smack! Greta felt the sting of Zoë's palm hitting her cheek.

"Greta, get a grip. Calm down and tell me. What is going on?"

Greta placed her own palm to her cheek. She could feel the tingling deepen into a slow, painful throb. She gazed at Zoë, as if in a dream. Then the haze cleared and her mind was empty — except for one thing.

"It was the song," she said softly.

"What song?" Zoë asked tentatively, motioning for Seymour to sit down. The rest of the children were behind him and followed suit.

"The song from last night," Greta responded in a barely audible monotone. "The first one — the one Tia played."

"You remember what it was." Zoë wasn't asking. She was helping Greta tell her story.

"Just that part," confirmed Greta. "I was asleep. I was so tired." She looked around at her friends. "Then I heard this playing — this sweet, sad melody. I woke and realized something must be wrong. But then the song ended and a new one began.

"That's when I started to wake you up," she said to Zoë.

"The second song told us we were in immediate danger. The third one meant we had to leave the house." Zoë was trying to keep calm, trying to set the stage for Greta, to help her to remember. Everyone was holding their breath in anxious anticipation as Zoë took Greta's hand in hers. "Greta," she asked intently, "what was the first song?"

"I only remember a little of it." Her voice started to shake. "I don't even know it. I just remember that one part. It's not even long."

"It's okay, Greta. It's okay." Zoë made sure her voice was soothing. "I know every song in the whole entire world." She smiled. "I could recognize a song from just one note," she exaggerated, although more than a few times she had. "And," she waited for Greta's full attention, "Tia would have played a song she knew I would recognize. She wasn't testing me. She wasn't trying to challenge me or stump me. She wanted us to get this message. Right?"

Greta nodded hesitantly. She took a deep breath and began to hum. It wasn't very much — a few measures at most.

"Good." Zoë's voice was calm. She didn't want Greta to panic under the pressure. "Now, one more time," Zoë encouraged.

Greta hummed the tune again. She closed her eyes, trying to forget the people around her, trying to relax and just imagine this was *not* the most important thing in the world.

"Okay. Once more." Zoë's voice seemed far away.

Greta began and this time she remembered a little more. It looped back over the first part before it was interrupted by Seymour's resonant tenor.

"*...rosemary and thyme.*"

"Of course," Zoë whispered.

"But what's the message," Dinora asked excitedly. "That doesn't even make sense."

Suddenly everyone was talking, their spirits and resolve buoyed by the new clue.

Zoë held her face in her hands. "I'm trying to remember the title — it's not *Rosemary and Thyme* — I'm sure of it. Plus it doesn't really have a message, unless it has to do with the market."

"Maybe we're supposed to meet at the farmers market," suggested Dinora.

"But which one?" Mario asked. "It's not like Tia to be vague when something is this important."

"Maybe she just meant the next one. After all, it's not like she had a lot of time," said Daniel.

"I guess." Zoë seemed unconvinced. "Seymour, do you know the rest of it?"

"I don't know the whole thing, but...." He began to sing. "*Are you going to Scarborough Fair? Parsley, sage, rosemary and thyme. Remember me to the one who lives there. For once she was a true love of mine.*"

The children sat in silence.

Then Mario looked up and smiled.

"The bazaar."

19

❧ The Plan ❧

"Brilliant!" shouted Seymour.

"We're sure it's not the market?" asked Dinora.

"It could've been the market if the title was *Parsley, Sage, Rosemary and Thyme*, but it isn't. Tia always goes by the title — that's the fun part. I'm *sure* it's the bazaar," Zoë insisted.

"Great. What's today? Is it Thursday?" Seymour asked.

"No, Friday. The bazaar is tomorrow," said Daniel. "The Fourth of July." He helped Greta up and the children gradually made their way back to their camp site.

"Wasn't there something we were supposed to do — for Mrs. Eaton?" Greta asked Seymour.

"You're right. I completely forgot."

"And we don't even know what it is…." said Dinora. "I wonder if it's really that important. I hope they aren't counting on us too much. I'd feel so bad if we let them down…. But that's ridiculous," Dinora admonished herself. "This is a matter of life and death. With everything else we have to figure out, we certainly don't need any more worries…. Although, I hope it doesn't ruin something terribly."

"I'm sure it's fine," assured Seymour.

"Okay," Zoë said with renewed energy. "So all we have to do is get Peter to the bazaar and keep a look out for the good guy?"

"It almost sounds too simple," said Greta.

"It *is* too simple. These people are professionals," Mario said. "Think of the effort they put into getting Peter here without anyone knowing. It's not likely they'll just walk around the bazaar hoping to run into him."

"He's right." Seymour began passing out the lunch he'd made. It wasn't very appetizing but being ravenous more than compensated for the bland taste and the children quickly devoured the meal.

"We know the date and the place, in general, but we don't know the time and the specific rendezvous spot," Mario said between mouthfuls.

"We also don't know whom we are supposed to meet," Seymour said.

"You think it won't be David?" asked Greta.

"It could be, but we don't know anything for sure," said Seymour.

"Thinking like that will make us crazy," Zoë snapped. "For the time being we need to at least assume some things."

"I think it's worth the risk to go to the bazaar tomorrow." Seymour doled out the remaining soup. "It's not like we really have much of a choice."

"Yeah, what are we supposed to do, stay here indefinitely, hoping the good guys find us?" Zoë challenged the others.

Mario finished his soup. "Tia gave us three clues for a reason. If she only wanted to communicate we were in danger and needed to leave, she would have done that in two songs."

"Exactly," said Zoë. "Tia wants us to take Peter to the bazaar." She collected the tin bowls and placed them in the bucket of water Daniel had brought from the stream.

"Maybe she wants *us* there so *we* can be safe," Dinora countered, finding the dish soap among their supplies.

"Hardly," scoffed Zoë, accepting the soap. "Tia knows we can take care of ourselves." She added a small amount of the lemony liquid to the bucket.

"I agree." Mario's voice was sure and emphatic. "The third clue means either Peter will be met or we'll get some other message."

"Then it's decided," stated Peter. It was the first thing he contributed to the conversation. Up until now his attention had simply ricocheted from one friend to another, as his fate unfolded.

"Maybe just Peter and I should go?" Mario suggested. "We'd attract a lot less attention than all seven of us."

"Ha!" Zoë honked. "The black kid and the Latino kid — sure, you'd fit right in."

"She's right. You'd both stand out and that's the last thing we need." Seymour reprimanded his cousin's sarcasm with an irritated glance. She glowered back at him defiantly and he rolled his eyes in silent response.

"If we're going to stand out anyway, I'd prefer to stay together," said Dinora.

Greta nodded. "I too," she added softly. "It feels safer."

"On the other hand, we always go to the farmers market together so it's not like people aren't used to seeing us. We'll stand out in a sort of 'non-stand-out' way. Does that make sense?" asked Seymour.

"Either way, we need to disguise Peter," Zoë said. "The bad guys might be there too. We don't know how many there are."

"Actually, now that I think about it," Mario began, "the best strategy is to proceed as if nothing out of the ordinary is happening. Not a lot goes on in a small town.

The bazaar's a big deal and people will notice if we're not there."

"What do you mean?" asked Peter.

"For example, when we go to the market, people see us visiting shops and booths —"

"Tia's booth!" shouted Zoë.

Except for Peter and Greta, a look of sudden understanding came over the children's faces.

"I completely forgot," Dinora half-whispered.

"What?" Peter's tone was a mix of curiosity and concern.

Zoë sighed. "Every year, Tia has a booth at the bazaar — lots of people do — to raise money for programs in the community, like the food bank."

"I think it's literacy this year," Greta said.

Zoë was sidetracked. "Huh?" she grunted.

"I noticed a flyer at the library. The money raised at the bazaar will go for more books, homework help and tutoring adults who can't read."

"Oh, that's so nice. What a lovely idea," Dinora said sincerely.

"Yeah, lovely. Lovely but irrelevant!" Zoë's volume increased as her temper flared. "We need to focus here, ladies."

Dinora and Greta looked down, chagrinned.

Zoë released a grumbled "hmph" before continuing. "The point is," her emphasis coincided with another accusatory glare, "people will be expecting a booth. Tia's done this for over thirty years. It will definitely look suspicious if it's not there."

"It'll also look suspicious if *she's* not there but there's not much we can do about that," said Mario.

"And if people start calling her, asking questions, then the men are sure to get nervous and maybe they'd hurt her," said Daniel, protective of the woman who'd taken such good care of him.

"Daniel's right," Mario said as he banked their fire. "We need to keep them thinking everything is fine."

The Plan

"Speaking of which, those men are expecting you sometime today," Seymour reminded Peter solemnly. "When you don't show up, things are going to change anyway."

"What if we got a message to them somehow and told them Peter was going to be coming back tomorrow," suggested Dinora.

"Or Sunday even," Daniel said.

"Yes, Sunday. That way he'd definitely be safe."

"We hope...." Zoë muttered, avoiding Seymour's reproachful eyes.

"She's right, Seymour," Peter defended Zoë's offhanded comment. "This is all a long shot." Zoë rewarded him with a smile and Peter was captivated. He couldn't look away.

"Let's settle one thing at a time." Mario once again served to refocus the group. "Are we agreed people will be suspicious if Tia's not there tomorrow?"

Everyone nodded.

"What if she's sick or too busy?" offered Dinora.

"Not too busy, but sick maybe," agreed Seymour.

"Sure, people get sick all the time," Peter said, trying to be supportive.

"Yeah, but if she were sick, she'd still find a way to make all her pies. She'd just send us down with them." Daniel spoke with the authority of someone who was well accustomed to Tia's habits.

"Pies?" Peter looked confused.

"Tia's pies are famous around here. She sells them every year at the bazaar," Zoë informed him matter-of-factly.

"Not this year though," corrected Dinora.

"What do you mean?" Mario asked.

"She's not selling pies this year, or at least not only pies."

"She always sells just pies," claimed Zoë. "That's what she does."

"I'm not trying to argue about it Zoë," said Dinora, an edge in her voice. "I'm just saying this year she's selling something else. Maybe she just wanted a change."

"Tia hates change. She is the queen of predictability." Zoë was getting worked up.

"What is she selling?" Seymour asked calmly.

"Something weird. At least, I remember it sounding weird when I heard her say it. Are there such things as pickled peppers?"

"*Pickled peppers*? That's ridiculous!" screeched Zoë.

"I agree. It doesn't make sense." Seymour looked pensive. "Dinora, when exactly did she say this? Maybe she was joking."

"I doubt it," Dinora replied. "It was when Greta and I were eavesdropping — when David came and Edith left with him. Before he left he asked Tia if she was going to have any pickled peppers this year and she said, 'yes, at the bazaar'."

"It just sounds so silly — pickled peppers," gibed Zoë.

"*It's Peter!*" shouted Daniel. "He's the pickled peppers!"

"Huh?" the children asked in unison.

"He's right," Greta's face revealed recognition. "Don't you remember the rhyme — from when you were little?" She looked at the blank faces of five children who spent their childhoods in China, Mexico and Lesotho. Then she looked at Daniel.

"How does it go again?" she asked him. "*Peter pecked...*"

"*Peter Piper pecked a pick...*no, *picked a peck of pickled peppers*," Daniel finished slowly.

"You have got to be kidding me," Zoë deadpanned.

"No, that's it!" confirmed Greta.

"That makes sense," rationalized Mario. "If the girls were there, Tia and David wouldn't have been able to finish their conversation —"

"— so they'd have to talk in code," said Seymour.

"If David was asking about me when he said pickled peppers —" began Peter.

"Then David will come to the *booth* for you!" exclaimed Greta.

"Great, now we get to track down a bunch of pies," Zoë said sarcastically.

"And find a way to get Peter down there without anyone noticing," said Mario.

"And how to get the bad guys to wait until Sunday," reminded Seymour.

"And where to meet David…or whomever," Greta added quietly.

"And when," said Daniel.

"And how to free Tia," Peter finished their to-do list.

The children were silent.

"Anything *else*?" asked Mario, letting his frustration show. "Anything at all?" Dinora started to say something but quickly clammed up when she caught her brother's eye. "Okay then, the bazaar is tomorrow but those men are waiting for Peter today. That needs to be our priority."

"Should one of us go to the house?" Greta asked.

"It's too dangerous," insisted Seymour.

"They'd just keep us there," agreed Mario, "or force us to tell them where Peter is."

"And Tia wanted us out. We need to honor that," Daniel said, as he started packing away their supplies.

"And we want to stay together, at least as much as possible," Dinora added as she helped him fold the tarpaulin.

"Well if we don't tell them in person, what are our choices?" asked Zoë.

"We could call," suggested Dinora.

"I think we'll have to," said Mario.

"That means we go into town and call," said Seymour.

"But what are we supposed to say?" Dinora asked anxiously. "The bad guys won't just let Tia answer the phone by herself."

"Well…what if we told her we were in town — like she said we were — and Peter had been in touch with us and he was coming back on Sunday?"

"The men will be listening but they'll assume we are telling the truth," said Mario.

"What if they want to know where I am now?" asked Peter.

"We'll say we don't know. That you just said you'd be here Sunday." Seymour replied.

"Where though?" Mario mulled over the plan.

"I don't know. Church?"

"That might work. There will be a lot of people to distract the bad guys — giving us time to rescue Tia."

Both boys imagined what it would be like to attack a man who surely carried a gun.

"That's it then," finalized Seymour. "Now, who's going to make the call?"

20

❧ The Call ❧

In the end, Seymour and Zoë were the obvious choice. They'd been coming to The Island the longest, and would be the least noticed by the locals. They were also the most familiar with the area and the people. Finally, since none of them had any money and there wasn't a public phone in town, the venture would also mean imposing on someone to use theirs. It was just after eleven o'clock in the morning when they set out down the mountain, casting a wide arc around the house so as not to be seen. Fortunately they had left clothes at Star Rock. Otherwise they would have made quite an impression waltzing into town in dirty, torn pajamas.

The village center was its usual quiet place with only a few tourists wandering down Main Street. The storefronts of the art galleries, ice cream shop and souvenir store were vacant and Maggie's Hair Salon had one lone customer. The post office was open but Walt was taking a late lunch in the gazebo at the center of the town square. He looked up at them to see if he needed to return to his station. Seymour shook his head slightly and the postman returned to his copy of the *Island Ad-Vantages* — their local paper, whose office was kitty corner to the square and also open.

"It's kind of surreal, isn't it?" asked Zoë.

"How so?"

"It's so slow and quiet and relaxed and…quaint really."

"And meanwhile there's this huge case of international intrigue going on?"

She nodded.

"Yup, pretty surreal. Where do you think we should make the call?"

"There's really no place private — people are going to hear no matter what."

"Let's do it from *The Galley*. It'll have the most people and they'll be more interested in getting their groceries than listening to us."

"Good idea," Zoë agreed.

They reached Sunset Street and turned right. A block and a half later, the tin bell on the door jangled and the children entered the store. There were ten or so people inside, including a few locals and the owner, who was manning the till. "Well, look who the cat dragged in," he chortled.

"Hi, Mr. Cranston. Good to see you," Zoë responded politely.

"You too. Hey, Seymour — are you going to play football this year?"

"I don't know. Maybe."

"You should — you're sure built for it. What about you, Miss Zoë? When're you going to start your big modeling career? There's lots of money to be made I hear — as long as you don't go Hollywood like these girls," he said, motioning to the tabloids on the magazine rack which featured young, beautiful women in varying states of disaster and disarray.

"I don't know, Mr. Cranston. I'm thinking about playing football instead," Zoë answered.

He looked at her, confused for a moment before getting the joke. He laughed. "I get it, I get it. Well, it's your life, kids. You can't let people live it for you."

"No, sir," said Seymour.

"As it should be, I say. Old folks are always trying to live their lives over through young folks. I know my father wanted me to run this store of ours."

"And what did you want to do?" Zoë knew she shouldn't be encouraging him, after all, they had important things to do, but she was curious. She couldn't picture William Cranston Junior doing anything other than the work started by William Cranston Senior.

"Now then, I could say I wanted to be a race car driver, or something like that, but to tell you the truth, I wanted to work in the store with him. He was a good man, my father."

"Yes, sir. He was." The senior Mr. Cranston used to pretend to miscount their deposit bottles when they were younger and always tried to give them an extra dime or two to spend on candy. Seymour always corrected him, despite Zoë's frustrated efforts to silence her cousin.

Their conversation ended when a grocery-laden customer approached the counter. Seymour waited before asking, "Mr. Cranston, do you mind if we use your phone for just a minute?"

"Oh, sure. Go ahead and use the one in the back office — door's open."

The children were relieved to have at least some modicum of privacy, although they were sure Marjorie Tuttle would be listening in. That woman never rested nor grew tired of the vicissitudes of her neighbors' lives.

"Are we sure?" Seymour asked, picking up the phone.

"That's why we came," Zoë reminded him.

"Okay, then. Here we go." He dialed the last four digits of Tia's number — the only ones necessary in such a small community. "It's ringing."

After the fifth ring, there was a click followed by the tense voice of Tia. "Yes?" she said.

"Tia, it's Seymour." He tried to sound as casual as he could.

"Yes, dear. So nice to hear from you. Are you well?"

"Oh, sure. We're all fine. There's not much to do in town but it's nice to see folks." Zoë nodded silently and mouthed her approval.

"That's nice, dear."

"So Tia, something kind of strange happened this morning," Seymour continued. Zoë held her breath.

Tia hesitated before answering, "Yes, dear?"

"Peter called us."

There was a slight intake of breath before Tia responded. "Is that so? I suppose that is strange."

"I think something must have happened. He wouldn't say what, but he told us not to worry and he'd be here on Sunday."

"Oh?"

Seymour detected Tia's voice relaxing a little. *She's getting it*, he thought to himself.

"Yeah. He said he was going to meet a friend at church and stay with him."

"I'm glad to hear it. Is he —"

There was a metallic click in the background and Tia's voice halted.

"Oh, he sounded a little tired, I guess, but said he was fine." Seymour fought his own panic and tried to sound casual. "He said he couldn't talk long, just wanted us to know he was okay and said to be sure to tell you."

"That's nice of him."

"So, Tia, the other thing is the bazaar tomorrow."

"Yes, dear?"

"I talked to some folks and everyone is excited about your pies."

"Well…." Tia's voice trailed off.

"I know. I told them you weren't feeling well and wouldn't be able to make them this year."

The Call

"Oh?"

"They didn't like the sound of that. Mrs. Eaton said she waits all year for one of your pies and she's determined to have one, even if she has to come up there and get it herself."

"Is that so?"

"Yes." Seymour forced a laugh. Zoë gave him a *what-in-the-world-are-you-doing-just-get-off-the-stupid-phone* look. He waved her away.

There was a pause on the other end of the line.

"Tia?"

"Yes, just a moment, dear. I need to…. Just a moment." Silence. Then her voice returned. "Well, I think I might feel up to making a few pies. I know how much people enjoy them and it is a worthy cause."

"Oh, that'd be great. If you're feeling up to it."

"I'll manage."

"Do you want us to pick them up or do you want to drive them down here?" Seymour recoiled as Zoë punched him hard in the arm.

"Let me think…." Silence. "Seymour, I'll put them in the truck and Mario can come to drive them into town."

"Are you sure you don't want us to just come in and get them?"

"No, dear," Tia answered too quickly. "I'm still pretty contagious. I wouldn't want you kids to get sick and have to spend a week in bed on your summer vacation."

"Will you be better soon, do you think?" Seymour didn't need to feign his worry.

"Oh, certainly. I'm sure by Sunday, I'll be right as rain."

"Will you be at church?"

Another pause. "No, dear, I shouldn't overdo it. And don't feel like you have to —"

"We want to see Peter, of course — to say goodbye and all."

"Of course, dear. Well, I really must be going. I need to rest and make pies. They'll be ready this time tomorrow."

"You're sure you don't need anything?"

"I have everything I need. Don't you worry. I'll be fine."

"Okay then…. Well…. We love you."

"I love you too, dear. Take care of yourselves."

"We will, Tia. We promise." Seymour hung up the phone.

"Are you *crazy*?" Zoë yelled through clenched teeth.

"Shush — what was I supposed to do? Think about it, how else would a loving nephew behave? Plus, we solved our pie problem."

"Aargh," Zoë groaned. "Okay, let's go."

"Zo, I've got another idea."

"Well, this is just a blue ribbon day for you, then, isn't it?"

"We can buy some food and put it on Tia's account."

"We don't have time for this."

"What are you talking about? We have nothing but time. Do you want to have bean soup *again*?"

"Okay, you're right. But not too much. We're going to have to carry it all the way back."

They spent less than ten minutes debating what their friends would most want to eat.

As Mr. Cranston fit their food into two paper bags they heard a familiar voice. "Oh, Zoë and Seymour — am I glad to see you!" It was Mrs. Eaton. Slowly they turned and smiled at her. "I keep meaning to call but it has been so busy with all the preparations and everything for the big day. You know how it is. No rest for the wicked!" She laughed merrily. "In fact, I was just saying to the Reverend this morning I was going to have to go up to the Witherspoon house today and here I find you. It was meant to be."

She paid for her plums, pasta and laundry detergent before guiding them out of the store. "Is Miss Witherspoon with you? Does she have the truck?"

"Uh, no, ma'am. She's not feeling well," answered Seymour.

"Oh, that's too bad. Is it one of those summer colds? Those really are the worst. One just can't seem to shake them. Well, no matter. Come over to the parsonage and I'll give —"

"I'm sorry to interrupt, Mrs. Eaton," apologized Zoë. "Seymour, I need to run a quick errand. Do you mind? Good. I'll catch up with you."

Seymour obviously wanted to know more but didn't dare ask in front of Mrs. Eaton. "Sure, I'll see you in a little bit," he said warily.

"Just as well, Seymour. This thing is heavy so it'll take a strapping lad like you. Did you say you had the truck with you?" She didn't give him time to answer.

Seymour followed Mrs. Eaton across the town square, stopping at the gazebo to update Walt on the plans for the following day.

"Ah, here we are," she announced, climbing the steps of the parsonage. Mrs. Eaton opened her front door and set down her packages. "The Reverend and I were so delighted you children agreed to help with this. It'll be so much fun, and of course anything we can do to promote literacy...."

She left her thought unfinished as she headed into the parlor, where Reverend Eaton was drinking his afternoon coffee and watching the news. "Ed, do you remember where I put the costume? I can't seem to recall."

Reverend Eaton looked up to see Seymour. "Well, hello there, son — here to get the costume, are you? I hope it won't be too hot for you tomorrow."

"It'll be fine." Mrs. Eaton's assurance seemed more will than certainty. "Besides, they can take turns when it gets to be too stuffy. Dear, do you remember where I put it?"

"I think it's in the snow room, love."

Mrs. Eaton hurried off and her husband started to make small talk. "How's school going?"

"It's fine, sir."

Reverend Eaton proceeded to regale Seymour with stories of his school-day adventures. Seymour attempted to listen but was distracted almost immediately by the television. A newscaster was speaking from his desk. Projected next to him was the picture of someone Seymour had come to know very well in the past week.

Peter.

"Authorities still have been unable to locate Prince Bhekizitha Boipuso Dabulamazi of Lesotho. He was reported missing last Monday after the brutal murder of his parents, King Melisizwe Bohlale II and Queen Nkosazana Nontle, in the military coup d'état on Sunday.

"We now go to Simon Sinclair, who is reporting live from Northfield Academy. Simon, what more do we know about the mysterious abduction of Prince Bhekizitha?"

"Very little, Aaron. I spoke with Headmaster Ryals this morning, who said they still had not received any ransom note —"

"Seymour? Son, are you alright?"

"Huh? Yes, uh, sorry." Seymour forced his eyes from the screen.

"Here we are." It was Mrs. Eaton's voice but she herself could not be seen behind the huge mass of tan foam coming straight at Seymour. He had no choice but to open his arms and receive it.

21

❧ The Bazaar ❧

Normally it would have taken Zoë and Seymour three hours to hike back to Star Rock. Carrying the huge bookworm costume, for that's apparently what it was, increased their burden significantly. When Mrs. Eaton had handed it to him, Seymour tried his best not to look either horrified or surprised. He reminded himself this should have been something he already knew was going to happen.

"Just take turns in the costume," Mrs. Eaton encouraged. "That way it won't get too hot. No need to do anything fancy. Just sort of mingle with the crowd, take pictures with kids, that sort of thing. There'll be a literacy booth near the gazebo so you might want to focus around there. Whatever you like is fine."

"Of course," Seymour tried to smile casually.

"You children are such dears. I thought I wouldn't have any trouble finding somebody to wear this, but I guess not everyone can see how fun it will be."

"Yes, ma'am," Seymour said from behind the mass of beige padding. "I really should be on my way."

"Very well. We'll see you tomorrow around three o'clock or so?"

Seymour bade farewell to Reverend Eaton and headed out.

Zoë was just arriving. "Good Go —" She stopped as she saw Mrs. Eaton emerge from the door. "Hello," she greeted politely.

"Oh! Hello, Zoë. Glad you're here. Your cousin looks like he could use some help."

Zoë stifled a giggle and went to help Seymour.

"Never mind," came his voice from behind the foam. "Get the groceries. I've got this."

"You're not going to walk all the way back to the house, are you?" the minister's wife asked with concern.

"Oh, we'll be fine," Zoë assured.

"Really? It's no bother to run you up there. Ed?" Mrs. Eaton called.

"Really, Mrs. Eaton. We're fine. We need the exercise." Seymour tried to persuade her, but his confident expression was buried beneath the gargantuan costume.

She looked doubtful.

Acting on impulse, Zoë took the initiative and preempted the debate. "Okay then, bye, Mrs. Eaton!" she called cheerfully, walking off at a brisk pace.

"Uh, yeah, bye." Seymour ran after his cousin trying desperately to manage his unwieldy burden.

As they reached the edge of town, they decided to put their food inside the large foam worm and each carry one end. Although it somewhat improved the situation, it still dragged out their journey. As a result, they arrived at the camp much later than anticipated.

"Where were you?" shouted Dinora as she saw them approach. "I was so worr — what is *that*?" She completely forgot what she was going to say as she stared at the bizarre thing her friends were carrying. "It looks like a sleeping bag made out of Band-Aids."

"Long story," Seymour groaned as he dumped his end of the costume on the ground near the cave.

"Hey, be careful!" Zoë reprimanded. "The peaches are in there."

"Peaches?" Dinora asked excitedly.

Zoë unzipped the bookworm and proceeded to unpack the groceries, which were greeted with no small amount of delight. Mario had been about to make dinner but was waiting in case something was wrong and they had to leave in a hurry. This turned out to be quite fortunate as another bean soup would have paled in comparison to the dinner Seymour had selected. He pulled out tinfoil, onions, potatoes, green peppers and ground beef.

"Oh, *these!*" Dinora squealed. "I love tinfoil dinners!"

Greta and Peter looked confused. The others were already beginning to help. Daniel tore off seven large pieces of tinfoil as Mario went to retrieve a knife. Together, they began to slice the onions and peppers that Seymour had produced from his one-of-a-kind shopping bag.

"Hey, Zo. Get the fire ready, will you?" Seymour called as he took the ground beef and began making patties.

After scrubbing the potatoes in stream water, Dinora showed Greta and Peter how to assemble their dinners. She placed a patty on the tinfoil and covered it with sliced potatoes, onions and peppers. She sprinkled the meal with salt and pepper before tightly folding it shut.

Soon the fire was blazing and they each set their uniquely shaped packages around the base. They cleaned as they waited for their dinner to cook.

Earlier in the day, while Seymour and Zoë were in town, the others had scoured the mountain top in search of small boulders. They had found five which suited their purpose and painstakingly rolled them to Star Rock. These now circled the fire and served as excellent chairs. Daniel and Dinora offered to forgo the makeshift furniture. Instead they pulled the bookworm costume over towards the fire. They were careful not to get it too close to the flame as they were fairly certain it would take no more than a small spark to ignite the mystery material.

By the time the children had settled in, the waxing moon was rising and their tinfoil dinners were beginning to sizzle and steam. It was time for the story. Zoë and Seymour told of the day's events from beginning to end. The children gasped aloud when they heard, in Zoë's enhanced and dramatic fashion, that Seymour's phone call to Tia had gone off the agreed-upon script.

"Still," Mario said, "it does solve a number of our problems."

Daniel opened a dinner and tested the potato with his fork. It met with his approval and he passed it to Dinora. Gradually, he did the same with the others and soon they were each relishing their meal.

"Do you think they believed you?" Peter asked hesitantly, before putting another forkful of food in his mouth.

Seymour considered this. "I don't know," he shrugged. "It was hard to pretend they weren't there and I was having a normal conversation with Tia. I guess we'll just have to wait and see."

"So tomorrow afternoon we'll pick up the pies," Mario commenced their planning.

"Thank goodness," Zoë sighed. "Now we won't have to steal some." Seymour took a deep breath and rubbed his temples.

"I hope Tia's not too scared," said Dinora.

"It's not like we have another option." Daniel tried to console himself as well as the others.

"I agree," said Seymour. "It's awful she's in this situation but at least we know she's safe. Honestly, when I talked to her today it sounded as if she were much more worried about us. She picked up on the clues. She knows we're alright."

"I hope so," said Peter.

The children sat together in comfortable silence, before spreading out the sleeping bags on the ledge. They used the bookworm as a pillow. By positioning their heads together on either side of the beige monstrosity, they were all able to benefit from the soft padding.

"What are we going to do with this thing?" Daniel asked, stifling a yawn.

"We have to bring it with us. We promised to wear it," Dinora responded, her eyes closed.

"But we don't *have* to," Mario reminded them. "We need to stick with the plan. Disappointing Mrs. Eaton doesn't mean the end of the world."

"You don't know Mrs. Eaton," Zoë said under her breath.

"We still need to figure out when we're supposed to meet him." Greta too was more asleep than awake.

"And we don't know how we're going to hide Peter so he won't be noticed," Seymour added.

Everyone was quiet.

"Actually," came Peter's voice, "I think there's a way to do two of those things."

"How's that?" Zoë asked drowsily.

"We're resting on it."

By mid-morning they had the whole thing planned. They'd hike down the mountain and, when they got close to town, Peter would don the bookworm costume. At the same time Daniel and Mario would walk back up to Tia's house so it looked as if they were coming from the right direction. Daniel, being the fastest runner, had been chosen to hang back and watch to make sure everything was fine. If it wasn't, he would race to tell the others.

Things worked out easily. Mario approached the truck which was parked in its usual place. True to her word, Tia had filled the back with boxes, each packed with her famous pies. He was tempted to look for a note or secret message from Tia. She would know that even if they had deciphered her clue about the bazaar, they still didn't know what time the rendezvous would take place. It was possible they would be approached or something would simply present itself. Still, if they needed information, then Tia would find a way to get it to them.

Mario resisted the urge to look through the boxes. It was even harder not to look into the house itself. He wasn't sure if Tia was watching but he knew someone would be. He needed to get the truck and get out of there before Tia's captors changed their minds.

He didn't want to seem too anxious and so casually approached the old Chevy, opened the driver's side door and got inside. The keys were in the ignition. He started the motor, backed out onto the lawn and then made his way down the gravel driveway at a *nothing-wrong* speed of twenty-five kilometers per hour. He was well out of sight when he stopped to pick up Daniel.

"Everything go okay?" his friend asked as he climbed into the truck.

"Fine," Mario replied. "A little eerie though." He took an audible breath and released it. "Well, we have the truck and the pies. So far, so good."

It was turning out to be a very hot Fourth of July. Peter, who had now been in the costume for over an hour, was drenched in sweat. Zoë and Dinora tried to keep him hydrated but it wasn't easy with the only opening being at the base.

The costume itself was made for an adult so Peter had room to breathe. The downside was that it dragged on the ground, making it difficult to walk without tripping.

"At least you'd land on something soft," Dinora pointed out the bright side.

"At least you look like a real worm," Zoë commented dryly.

Peter tried to stay in the shady areas but found people would strike up conversations. In the end, they decided the reprieve from the heat wasn't worth the risk of being discovered, leaving Peter unbearably hot and uncomfortable. He tried to keep his nerves from getting so frayed that he wouldn't be able to act when the time came; but as the afternoon stretched on, this became increasingly difficult.

Another consequence of his hour-upon-hour entombment was a bizarre mood swing, alternating between irritability on one end and outright goofiness on the other. At one point he found himself in a fit of uncontrollable giggles. The more Zoë scolded him, the more he laughed.

He was becoming delirious when Zoë muttered forcefully, "Stop that! What in the world do you think you're doing?"

Between bursts of laughter, Peter forced out his answer. "Pro…moting…literacy?"

This earned him a swift kick in his shin, the force of which both rid him of his good humor and nearly tipped him over.

Zoë happened to be the one guarding him at the moment, although "guarding" was somewhat of an overstatement. The children accepted that it would look suspicious if they all manned the booth, so even though it made them nervous, they separated into teams. Mario had established checkpoints. Every half hour they would meet up with each other and switch roles. A new person would accompany Peter, technically to make sure he wasn't abducted, but more realistically to keep him from heatstroke or boredom. *And now hysteria, as the case would seem*, Zoë thought to herself.

Grudgingly, afternoon gave way to evening and the absence of the broiling sun was the only noteworthy event. It was peculiar. There were thrilling rides and interesting booths. People were feasting on funnel cake, caramel apples and cotton candy. There were games and contests and performances everywhere. The whole town seemed to be there, along with every tourist in a hundred-kilometer radius. Still, for the seven children waiting desperately, the day was no fun at all and the longer it went, the more worried they became.

Finally the monotony was broken. Unfortunately, it wasn't so much an unfolding of their plan as it was an unraveling. Seymour discovered it as he was taking his turn walking around the bazaar with Peter. They ran into the church secretary whom Seymour had known since he was a toddler crawling under pews. During the course of their inevitable conversation, Mrs. Damon mentioned how disappointed she was about not getting one of Tia's pies.

"Are they sold out already?" asked a nonplussed Seymour. This was strange since there had been so many of them, over twenty from his count.

"No, there are a whole pile of them there," the elderly woman complained. "They're just refusing to sell them."

22

❧ The Message ❧

About an hour earlier, Dinora, Zoë and Greta were
minding the stall.

"You know what's strange?" asked Dinora.

"*Everything*," came Zoë's terse reply.

Dinora gave her friend a saucy stare. "The pies," she
said flatly. "The pies are strange." She waited for some
encouragement.

"What do you mean?" asked Greta graciously.

Dinora smiled and continued, her natural enthusiasm
returning. "Well, Tia usually makes different kinds."

"These aren't different?"

"I guess they are, I mean sure, there are different
kinds but this just *feels* strange."

"Blueberry," Zoë commented dryly. She was standing
at the back of the stall where she could survey the crowd
without being noticed herself. She didn't even look at her
friends when she spoke. She was determined to find
whomever it was they needed to meet, and while she
would have much preferred being free to roam, she had
consented to stay with the two younger girls at the stall
for the next hour. She knew she shouldn't feel resentful

but the excitement and adventure were outside the stall. That's where she wanted to be. That's where she could be useful. *Nothing interesting is going to happen trapped in here*, she thought. Further, it was bad enough to be stuck in the stall with the little kids. Now Dinora was making it worse by prattling on about the pies not *feeling* right.

"Huh?" Dinora asked.

"Blueberry, Dinora," Zoë patronized, making no effort to hide her irritation. "Normally she makes pies with Maine blueberries and today there aren't any. It's not a great mystery. They're just pies."

Dinora gave Greta a questioning look to which the younger girl shrugged her shoulders in silent response. Then Dinora, never one to hold a grudge, continued her conversation, trying to be a little quieter out of honest consideration for her friend.

"They are wonderful pies," she whispered to Greta, "my favorite. Well maybe not my absolute favorite. I adore the apple — and the strawberry-rhubarb too. It's so tart. But the blueberry ones are so beautiful because Tia does this fancy crust thing where she weaves it together. These are all just the regular —"

Dinora stopped in mid-sentence and stared at the pies before her. At the same time, a woman approached to purchase one. Seeing that Dinora was ignoring her responsibilities, Zoë stepped forward and accepted the woman's money. The purchaser picked up her pie and began to walk away.

"No!" Dinora shouted, snatching the pie away.

"Dinora!" Zoë yelled, before giving the woman an apologetic smile.

"I'm so sorry, lady, but you can't have that pie." Dinora grabbed the money out of Zoë's hand and thrust it at the woman.

"Why in heaven not?" the woman asked indignantly.

"Yeah, why not?" Zoë echoed with a tenor in her voice bordering on malevolence.

"Because…because…" Dinora faltered.

Greta saved her. "Because I just remembered I lost my retainer in one of them and I don't know which one."

The woman looked disgusted. She grabbed her money and walked away haughtily.

"Dinora, you little...." Zoë looked at the girl as if she were about to strangle her.

"Zoë," Dinora whispered urgently, "look at the pies." For a moment Greta wasn't sure what Zoë was going to do. Then Dinora added a distinct and heartfelt, "Please."

Zoë's ire de-escalated slightly. She rolled her eyes and grudgingly did as she was asked. "What? They're pies. Just pies," she stated, her tone softer than before.

Greta too was looking at the pies. "It's a message," she murmured.

"Where?" Zoë asked, her mood catapulting instantly to one of sincere interest.

"Here, look," Dinora instructed, pointing to the crusts in each of the pies. She had been wondering why there was so little variety. Now she realized Tia had done it for a reason. The slits Tia made in the crust in order to let the steam out were not arranged randomly or even in a pretty pattern as usual. The slits formed letters.

"How many have we sold?" demanded Zoë.

"What?" Dinora looked confused.

"How — many — have — we — sold?" Zoë enunciated each word and tried not to shout.

"I don't know. Mario and Seymour were here first. They didn't say. I think we sold two though, maybe." Dinora was starting to panic. "I don't remember."

"There were twenty-three total," Greta said simply.

Zoë and Dinora looked at her.

"Are you sure?" Zoë asked.

"Yes," Greta said with confidence. "I remember because there were six boxes, each with four, except the last one only had three. I thought it seemed odd and figured maybe Tia had just run out of time."

"Okay," Zoë started. "There are twenty-three. That means" she paused to count, "five have been sold."

"I think one had a circle. That'd be an 'O' right?" Dinora said, hoping to get back on Zoë's good side.

"Could be," Zoë was still staring at the pies. "Or a zero," she said absentmindedly. "There are eighteen here. How are we supposed to unscramble them?"

Greta began moving them so they were lined up in three rows of six. She looked at them carefully, and then started to switch them around.

"Can you figure it out?" asked Dinora.

"Sorry — none of these are for sale," Zoë said rudely to a newly arrived customer. He looked confused and Zoë explained the retainer.

"I don't know," Greta said, keeping focused on her work. "I'm just moving them around to see if something clicks." She did this for another few minutes but came up with nothing.

"We need help," Zoë announced. She grabbed a pen from the truck and ripped off a corner of one of the cardboard boxes. Carefully she copied down the letters.

O P b P L T E R C C O D P R O S I P

"Add another circle," Dinora insisted. "I swear I remember it."

Zoë did so and then she wrote: missing four letters. She copied it again onto another piece of cardboard and handed them to the girls.

"It might attract attention if we are all here staring at the pies. Go and give these to the others and explain what's going on. I'll stay here and guard the pies. Make sure no one hears you and go together. I don't want you two separated, got it?"

The girls nodded solemnly and darted off to relay the message. Zoë stared at the pies. She rearranged the letters in her head. She closed her eyes to picture them in various configurations. Nothing.

It wasn't long after Seymour heard of the refusal to sell the pies that Greta and Dinora found him.

Surreptitiously they handed him the piece of cardboard and explained what was going on. Now Seymour was walking slowly with Peter, trying to keep one eye on him, one on the crowd and another on the coded message.

"I wish I had three eyes," he said to Peter.

"I wish I could help," came the muffled response.

Daniel and Mario were in slightly better shape. They bought food with some of the pie money and sat down at a picnic bench. To any passerby it would have looked like two friends huddled over junk food and teenage conversation. After half an hour they had four possibilities, none of which made any sense. When they brought these back to the girls, they heard the other results had been just as unlikely.

"She wouldn't have made it this hard," Mario insisted.

"I agree. She knew we'd be in a hurry. Who can unscramble twenty-three letters?" said Seymour.

"Especially with five of them missing," Daniel added.

They were now at the stall with Greta. Dinora had gone with Zoë to keep Peter company, and safe.

"Maybe there's something else, something we're not seeing, but that is just as obvious," Mario suggested, looking again at the pies. "We need to ask ourselves: what's different and what's the same?" he continued his methodic approach.

"The crust," Daniel blurted.

"Right, but what else?" Mario was lost in thought.

"No," Daniel clarified. "The edge of the crust — the patterns are different."

He was right. Some pies were rimmed simply with fork imprints. Others were more elaborate and twisted. The last ones had braided edges which must have taken Tia a considerable amount of time and effort. They were each distinct.

"Let's group them by edges," ordered Mario. They did so rapidly and got:

POCCOD SLTER RIPPPb

They stared at this awhile.

"What's 'ripppb' supposed to be?" Daniel asked the group.

Greta stepped up to the counter and began rearranging them to no avail.

"Maybe there's something else," Seymour wondered aloud.

Mario used his finger to break through the crust of pie "D". He withdrew it and tasted the amber filling. "Apple," he announced.

Seymour repeated the action for pie "C" of the same crust group. "Raspberry."

The others proceeded to taste the rest of the pies and group them thusly before stepping back to survey their handiwork:

COD Pb SLTER POC PIPR

"We're missing four letters," Mario reminded them. "It's not likely they'd all come from the same word. We should assume each word is missing one letter. Statistically, that's the most probable."

"But we're missing five *pies*, remember?" Greta said. "I wonder if Dinora remembers the flavor or crust."

"I'll go ask her." Daniel started to leave the stall.

"Hurry," Mario instructed. "Tell them what we know so far and not to leave Peter."

"Piper!" exclaimed Seymour.

"Huh?" the rest responded.

"Maybe the first word is 'piper' — like the peppers."

"Perhaps." Mario was reluctant. "But we're looking for a place and a time. That's neither."

"Well, we don't even have a time. There aren't any numbers here," Seymour pointed out.

"I hope the five missing ones aren't the time," Greta said. "That circle could have been for something like 7:05 or 8:10."

Seymour was still rearranging the letters within the words when Daniel returned, breathless. "She says she's almost certain it was the braided one."

"Did you give her the choices or did you just ask her?" Mario demanded.

"I just asked her. She's the one who said it."

"In that case, it'd be here with the 'poc'."

"So now it's 'pooc'?" Seymour couldn't help but giggle. Mario glared at him. "What?" Seymour defended. "It sounds funny."

"It could be pooch if there was an 'H' missing," Daniel said, although he didn't believe it was.

"Or *poco* — maybe she wrote it in Spanish?" Seymour suggested.

"That is unlikely," Mario said. "If there is a code, she'd want all of us to be able to decipher it."

"Code!" Daniel said excitedly. "I bet 'cod' is supposed to be code."

"Then maybe it is 'piper'. Like, that's the code," reiterated Seymour.

"Let's try that. We use two 'E's' and get 'code piper'." Mario switched the pies and they read their new message:

CODE PIPER Pb SLTER POOC

Then Greta began rearranging the pies again.

"What are you thinking, Greta?" Seymour asked, uncertain as to whether or not he should interrupt her concentration. Apparently, she was undisturbed. She didn't stop her movements as she answered him.

"I think we should put the pies in order of their crusts, from simplest to most complex. Tia had the time to do all of this and so far every choice she's made has been for some purpose." She finished her work. The pies now read:

Pb SLTER POOC CODE PIPER

"'Pooc' could be 'coop'," Seymour exclaimed.

"It's the lobster co-op," said Mario. He was looking at the third word. "If we added a 'B' this would be lobster."

They rearranged pies, leaving spaces for where the missing letters would be.

Pb LOBSTER COOP CODE PIPER

"We've used four letters. There's one more." Mario deduced. "It must go with 'pb'."

"'Pub'?" Daniel asked.

"'Bip'?" offered Seymour.

"What's a 'bip'?" giggled Greta.

"I don't know, I'm just saying, it could be 'bip'."

"How's it going?" Dinora asked, startling the rest of them.

Seymour took a deep breath and tried to calm his heart's palpitations. "We have it all — we're just missing the time." He pointed at the two coded pies.

"Pb?" Dinora raised her eyebrows.

"No," said Greta. "It's not. It can't be. Look, all of the other letters are capitalized. See? Except for the 'b'."

"She's right. I can't believe I didn't see it all along." Mario ran his hands through his hair.

"It's not a 'b'," Greta declared. "It's a six."

"Or a nine," Mario put in.

"Then the missing letter must be an 'M', as in 'P.M.'"

Dinora shifted her body to look at the number from a new perspective. "Do you think it looks more like a six or a nine?" she asked.

"It better be a nine," said Mario.

"Why?"

Mario showed them his watch. "Because it's 8:50."

23

☙ The Bookworm ❧

Just as Mario spoke, Mrs. Eaton approached the booth. "Splendid! Just the brawn I hoped to find," she crowed giddily. "Boys, do you mind terribly helping us set up the stage? We're getting ready to start the fireworks. What a night!

"Now, let's see here. Who's missing? It's our Zoë, right? I bet she doesn't much care for being in that costume. Still, it's for a good cause. Literacy, you can't read without it. Oh!" She was surprised by her unintended joke and began to titter. Greta wondered if Mrs. Eaton's elation might not be a little bit *inebriation*.

Mario interrupted before the minister's wife had a chance to catch her breath. "I'm sorry, ma'am, but we can't," he apologized.

"Why ever not?" Mrs. Eaton looked as if she had never been turned down before and didn't quite know what to make of a refusal to serve.

"Well, we…uh…" Mario couldn't think of a reasonable explanation and was beginning to realize that a minister's wife had a lot more experience getting people to help out than he had avoiding it. He was also beginning to worry about the dwindling time and how much attention they'd attract if they all went to the co-op together.

Seymour had been thinking the same thing. "We'd be happy to help, Mrs. Eaton," he said. "We're right behind you."

"That'll be lovely. Thank you, boys." She turned away from the stall and progressed towards the bandstand.

As soon as she was out of earshot, Mario grabbed Greta with an intensity that scared her. "Quickly, go tell Zoë. And don't forget to give her the password. You and my sister need to come right back to the booth and stay here. Go!"

Greta raced off to find Zoë, making her own plans as she ran. She knew this would be her last chance to see David. Greta scanned the crowd and easily spotted the worm's golden head. She ran towards it, darting around klatches of people, roving carts and activity booths.

"We — solved — the —" Greta began, as soon as she reached them. "You need to —"

"Not so loudly," Zoë shushed, dragging Greta closer. Greta whispered the information in Zoë's ear.

"Got it. Let's go," she said decidedly. "Dinora — you and Greta go back and tell the others to meet me at the truck. Tell Mario I saw a man who looked like he didn't belong. Tell him the man is lanky with brown hair and a dark blue jacket. Tell him the guy's shoes were too nice."

"Okay," Dinora agreed, dread coating her voice.

"No," Greta blurted. "I'm coming with you."

"Greta, we don't have time for this. It's too dangerous. I'm sorry." Zoë rushed towards the harbor with the still-encased Peter.

"Dinora," Greta said intently, turning to look directly into her friend's eyes. "I need to do this."

"Greta, he might not even be the one who comes." Dinora gazed at the girl she had known for just a few weeks. Already Greta seemed so different — like an entirely new person. Dinora took a deep breath and clasped Greta's hands tightly. "Be careful, okay?"

Greta hugged her fiercely. "Thank you, Dinora. I will. I promise. I'll be fine." She released her friend and gave her a broad, grateful smile before racing after Zoë whom she could barely distinguish in the emerging twilight. She caught up with them just as they reached the co-op. It was a red building with faded white lettering that read: *Deer Isle Lobster Cooperative, est. 1820.*

Zoë turned as she heard Greta approaching. "I knew you wouldn't listen," Zoë muttered under her breath. "Will you at least do me a favor and stay out of my way?"

Greta was expecting a worse reprimand. She nodded affably as Zoë tried to open the front door. It was locked.

"What is happening?" came Peter's voice from inside the costume.

"It's locked," Zoë replied. "Greta, give me your sweater."

The night air was cold but Greta didn't hesitate to remove the lavender cardigan she'd found so many days earlier from the basket labeled *sweaters* in the girls' closet.

Zoë quickly wrapped the sweater around her fist and smashed the small window closest to the door knob. She wiped the large pieces away and reached inside. Within moments the door was unlocked and they were in. It was dark and the strange shapes of lobstering equipment loomed eerily above them.

"Hello?" Zoë called softly.

There was no answer.

"Stay here," she whispered to Peter and Greta.

Slowly Zoë moved through the room, using her hands to feel the way. She found the back door and opened it onto the dock where lobster boats unloaded their hauls. She peeked outside. There were boats moored in the harbor, looking collectively like a murky graveyard. One seemed different.

She squinted and could barely distinguish the gray outline of a figure in a motorboat. It almost looked like he was raising his arm, as if to check the time. She heard a motor start and the boat came towards her. In less than a minute, it sidled up to the dock. Zoë looked down at the drop, five meters below, recognizing the driver at once.

"Zoë?" The scratchy voice that rose from the small boat was like music to her ears.

"Edith?"

"Yeah. Keep it down. I think there might be someone else nearby. Wait, I'll come up." She cut the engine, tied the boat to the piling and climbed the rickety ladder. She patted Zoë heartily on the shoulder. "You're the last person I expected to see. Is Dot okay?" Edith used her pet name for Tia.

Zoë wasn't sure whether or not to tell her.

Edith detected something in Zoë's hesitation and clutched her arms. "What? What is it?" she demanded.

"They've got her Edith — the bad guys. They're holding her hostage up at the house." Even in the dim light Zoë could see the effect this had on Tia's oldest friend.

"Did you talk to her? Did she sound alright? Damn!"

Zoë knew what Edith wanted to do and they both knew what Tia would want. "Edith, Tia is depending on you. You know that. Peter's safety is more important. We can't do that part — only you can. We can take care of Tia. We'll save her, I promise. We've got it all worked out. We just wanted to wait until he got away."

Edith wasn't listening, but her own reasoning coincided and arrived at the same conclusion. "I hate this!" She clenched her fists, swallowed her frustration and readied herself to do what needed to be done. "Okay, let's get him out of here. Once he's safe, I'll be back. Don't do anything stupid. You got it?"

"I know," Zoë assured. Her attention was drawn towards the door.

Peter had freed himself from the costume and stood next to a hopeful Greta. "Edith, is it just you?" she asked.

Edith looked perplexed. Then realization dawned. "I'm sorry, Greta. He couldn't come."

"Oh." The crestfallen expression made the tiny girl look even smaller.

"Tell you what, I'll tell him you were here, that you came to see him."

"Edith, who is he?"

"Honey, that's a big question needing a long answer and I'm not the one to give it. Besides, we don't have the time. Your Highness?" Edith directed Peter's attention to the ladder.

Peter hesitated. "What is the code word?" he asked coldly.

Edith smiled. "Good boy," she said. "It's 'piper'. Now let's get you somewhere that's really safe."

Peter smiled back at her before turning to face the two girls. "Goodbye, Greta. Thank you for everything. Tell everyone that, okay?"

"Yes, Peter." Greta tried not to cry as she embraced him. "Take care of yourself. I'm so sorry about your parents and…well, just everything."

"I know," Peter said. "Thank you, Greta."

He turned to face the older girl. "Zoë, I…." He'd been thinking all evening of what he could say to her. Now that the time had come, it all seemed pointless. He'd be living in hiding indefinitely. After that, hopefully he'd be home, but what did that even mean anymore? He was a king in exile. He couldn't just ask her out on a date.

He sighed resignedly, smiled and took her hand in his. "Zoë, it was very nice to meet you."

She looked at him with her head slightly tilted in curiosity, oblivious to the effect she was having on him. To Peter it made her look even more breathtaking.

"It was nice meeting you too, Peter," she beamed.

Peter held her gaze for as long as he dared. He bowed his head slightly, turned and descended the ladder. A moment later, Edith was also in the boat. She started the motor and they were off. Within another minute, there was no sign they'd even been there.

"Well, Greta. I guess that's it. It's finally over."

Greta was lost in her own sorrow, distracted so much by her disappointment that she didn't notice the four shadows which stretched subtly out from the doorway.

"Not exactly over." It was the voice of Jake Sewall who blocked their way back, his friends looming on either side of him. "In fact, I'd say it's just beginning." He grinned slowly and Greta felt her blood run cold.

24

❧ The Predicament ❧

"Go ahead and try screaming," Jake taunted them. "Everyone's back at the bazaar and they're just about to start the fireworks." As if to punctuate his words there was a sharp blast followed seconds later by a shower of red and blue lights blazing above them. Greta looked at Zoë, trying to gauge her fear. Zoë stared blankly at Jake, her face implacable.

"I'm not sure if you have the same rules where you come from…" Jake started to walk towards them but his eyes were focused solely on Zoë. "…but around here, it's illegal to break into a building. Did you not know that?"

Zoë said nothing.

"I asked you a question!" he screamed at her.

Greta jumped. Zoë still said nothing. Someone who didn't know her might have thought she was scared senseless or frozen with fear. Greta couldn't imagine it was either. She wasn't sure what was going on in Zoë's mind but she knew it must be something. Zoë was smart and brave — and gutsy. Greta was confident this girl she'd come to idolize was taking this all in, strategically assessing their situation and evaluating their options. Greta decided she was safe in Zoë's hands.

"Get some rope," Jake said under his breath.

"Rope?" one of his friends replied — the stocky one with red hair.

"Yeah, stupid. Rope. We don't want our criminals to get away do we?" The boys found some rope and tossed it to Jake.

"Hey, I'm not sure this —" the red-haired boy started.

"Shut up, Ben," Jake bit back.

It all happened so quickly. Greta didn't know what to do. She kept waiting for Zoë to yell at them or try to intimidate them with her fake karate. Zoë did neither, just stared blankly. She didn't even struggle when Jake roughly pulled her arms and tied them behind her.

He forced both girls back into the store before gently lowering Zoë to a sitting position. The care he showed was discordant and gave Greta goose bumps along her arms. It reminded her of a book she had once read, in which this character, Lenny, doesn't know his own strength. At the end of the story he tries to be gentle with a puppy but ends up killing it instead. Greta looked at the way Jake was holding Zoë as he knelt down next to her. *Definitely a Lenny.*

Before he got up, Jake moved closer to Zoë and whispered something in her ear. Greta shuddered to think of what it might be. Zoë gave no indication she was listening at all.

"You guys go get Officer Maddox."

"Listen, Sewall, is this really necessary? I mean, they just —"

"What did I tell you?" Jake shouted at his friend, a few droplets of spittle flying out of his mouth.

"Sewall?" Greta asked softly. "Is that your surname?"

"What?" Jake looked at her incredulously, as if shocked both that she *could* speak and that she'd dare speak to *him*.

"I was wondering if you might be related to Captain Ignatius Sewall."

Jake's entire demeanor shifted. "Yeah," he said calmly. "He was my dad's great grandfather."

"And one of the town founders," boasted one of the two boys who hadn't yet spoken. He had the nasal, ingratiating voice Greta expected from a sycophant.

"Shut up, Evan," Jake ordered. The boy obeyed instantly. "What, you've been studying our local history, huh?" he asked Greta snidely.

She didn't know what to say. She kept waiting for Zoë to do something but was afraid it might be up to her. Greta began to worry that getting in trouble for breaking into the Lobster Co-op was not the worst thing that could happen to them tonight.

"He ate people," she blurted, thus casting her die.

"What did you say?" Jake's temper raged instantaneously. The word "volatile" occurred to her.

"He...ate...people," she repeated slowly.

"Who told you that?" he demanded, grabbing her face with his hand, his nails sinking into her cheeks.

"He did." Greta didn't know why she felt so calm. She should be terrified but instead she felt a rush, knowing her words had put him in the palm of her hand. She felt powerful.

"What?" Jake was visibly irritated by her impudence. He pushed her back as he said this and Greta's head hit the wall. It was a very physical reminder of her power's limited jurisdiction.

She swallowed and steeled herself in case he hit her again. "He did," she repeated. "I read it in his book."

"What book?"

Greta could see Jake did not want this story to continue, that he wanted this conversation to be over but couldn't help it. All he had to do was ignore her, let this eleven-year-old girl have the last word and that would be it. They both knew this. They also knew his pride wouldn't let him.

"*The Sea Maiden: a Captain's Tribute.* You should read it. It's very good." Greta's tone was precocious. Again, she felt the surge of influence within her. *Knowledge is power*, she privately mused.

"You're lying." Jake's voice betrayed his uncertainty.

"No. I'm not," she said coolly, looking right at him. He began to tremble with rage. Greta continued in the same vein. "He was stranded in the Atlantic without food for seventeen days. He and his crew ate the first mate."

"You're lying!" he screamed at her.

"Actually, I heard the same thing," the fourth boy said, not registering the full effect this topic was having on his friend. "Remember, Ben, in Mr. Pelletier's class — about the crew who —"

"He — did — not!" Jake turned rabidly on his friends. "Now shut up, Howie, and get the cop."

They stared at Jake. Greta could tell they were beginning to realize their prank had the very real potential for turning sour.

The one he had called "Howie" approached him. "Hey, Sewall," his tone pacifying, "maybe one of us should stay behind —"

"What? You think I'm in danger?"

Howie cast an intentional glance at the girls tied up on the floor. Greta knew that was *not* what Howie feared at all. He thought it was she who was in danger — she and Zoë.

"You think I can't handle two girls? Even tied up?" Jake was indignant and only getting more furious.

He's not thinking straight, Greta started to panic. *He's too angry.*

"No, it's not that…." Howie again tried to placate his friend.

"Just go!" he screamed.

The boys looked at each other. Greta pleaded silently for them to stay. Maybe it would make a difference if she begged them aloud. But it was too late. The boys left and

The Predicament

Jake was alone with them in the darkness and the immediate quiet.

Finally, Jake spoke, his voice hoarse from screaming. "You know…I watch you every summer. It's 'Zoë', right, your name?" She didn't answer. "You and your friends, with your fancy boat and horses. I guess you think you're too good for us locals, huh?"

There was nastiness in his tone that made Greta even more nervous. She wished the boys would hurry up. At this moment, she would love nothing more than to see the bigoted face of Officer Maddox.

Jake approached Zoë, squatting down next to her. He had a look in his eye which petrified Greta — like he was in a dream and nothing was real…so nothing counted.

"Not going to say anything?" Jake asked, almost sweetly. He reached out and caressed Zoë's cheek.

Greta could see Zoë's jaw clench. At that slight flexing of muscle, something occurred to Greta. As much as she admired Zoë, there was no question the girl had one of the worst tempers she'd ever seen. She could fly off the handle at the drop of a hat, this girl. Considering that, Greta was amazed Zoë was able to keep her rage in check. *This was no small feat*, she thought. *She must be practically volcanic inside.*

Jake's hand was still on Zoë's cheek and the girl's stoic façade was cracking. "Oh, you don't like that, do you?" Jake cooed. "Well then, you're probably going to hate this." He brought his face to hers.

Suddenly, Zoë recoiled and slammed her forehead hard into Jake's. He reeled back and toppled to the floor. The volcano had erupted and Jake was out. Cold.

"Oh…my…oh…my…." Greta felt herself succumbing to hysterics.

"Keep it together, Greta. We don't have time for it." Zoë wriggled out of the ropes which had bound her. Greta saw they were shredded and noticed a rusty nail protruding from the wall. She smiled. Zoë's bravery had now reached epic proportions in Greta's eyes. She should have known better than to underestimate her friend.

Quickly, Zoë untied her and they used the ropes to tie Jake's wrists together. Zoë stood, staggering as she clutched her head. She steadied herself against the wall for a second before moving to the window. "Someone's coming," she hissed.

"Is it the police officer?" Greta asked. "Are the boys with him?"

Zoë peered closer. Then her eyes went wide. "It's the man," her voice wavered, "the one from the bazaar, with the nice shoes. I knew there was something suspicious about him," she admonished herself.

She looked around the room. The only entrance was the one he would use in just over a minute. The back entrance was a five meter drop into the Atlantic Ocean.

"Think, think…." she commanded herself.

"The costume!" Greta cried. "We can pretend it's Peter."

Zoë let the concept filter through her brain. Greta could almost see the wheels turning as the idea was analyzed. "Perfect."

They rushed to put the costume over Jake's body. He started to regain consciousness and Zoë looked around for something to use as a gag. She noticed a red neckerchief in his back pocket and tied it over his mouth.

They had just finished pulling the costume over his body when the front door opened. The girls looked at each other.

"Don't worry, Peter," Greta said, flashing Zoë a grin. "They'll be here soon."

"Yeah, Peter. It'll be okay. You'll be safe in a few —"

"Okay, girls. Keep calm and stay where you are. Let's do this right and no one gets hurt." The man pulled a walkie-talkie out of his jacket and spoke into it. "Ron, I have 'em; bring the boat around. We're at the Lobster Co-op."

"That the red one?"

"Yeah."

"Got it."

The man returned the device to his pocket. "I bet you kids thought you were pretty clever, huh?" He smiled at them in genuine admiration. "It was good. I have to admit. I wandered that fair for hours — must have seen our prince here a hundred times." He motioned to the figure on the floor. "Can't see what's right in front of you, I guess."

The girls said nothing.

"Good thing I was born under a lucky star."

He cocked his head. A boat's motor sounded in the distance.

The man laughed to himself. "Funny, really. I just happened to be near your town police officer when those boys showed up to rat you out. Everything I needed to know, right there on a silver platter. At first, I thought I was going to have to do this whole song and dance to convince the cop not to check it out. But he didn't even believe those kids — thought they were trying to trick him or something."

This is just like in the movies, Greta thought, *when the bad guy confesses at the end and tells you all the details.* Then she remembered why the bad guy would tell all. He wasn't planning to let them go.

"Then those boys," he chuckled. The motor boat was louder now. "They were only too happy to let me take care of it. Gave 'em five bucks and they were off on some ride. This really is a small town you have here." He seemed almost friendly and so casual. But he would hurt them if they tried to leave.

The boat pulled up level with the dock. In an instant, another man, presumably Ron, had entered the building in long, heavy strides. Greta noted that neither of these men was the "library man" which meant he must still be with Tia.

"Is this him?" asked Ron, looking at the crumpled costume on the dirty, wooden floor.

"Yeah, can you believe it?"

"Whatever," Ron replied dryly. He knelt down and tried to remove the costume. Jake stirred and kicked out. "How in hell is this thing supposed to come off?"

"Forget about it. Just put him in the boat."

Ron shrugged, kicked Jake sharply and shouted for him to get up.

"Hey, keep it down. We're not supposed to attract any attention."

"Who can hear us? The fish?" Ron laughed at his own joke and forced Jake out on the dock. Greta heard scuffling sounds as the man struggled to get the cumbersome bulk onto the boat.

"What are we going to do with the girls?"

"We should bring 'em with us, just in case," Ron called back.

"Just in case of what? I say leave 'em here."

Greta breathed a sigh of relief and bowed her head in soundless prayer. *It's almost over.* Soon she'd be safe with her friends and they could find a way to rescue Tia. But this time, Greta wouldn't rush blindly into danger. She'd had enough danger to last a lifetime.

"The boss may want to —" Ron started.

"Fine, we'll take 'em." He reached under his jacket, retrieved a gun and pointed it at Greta. "Okay, girls, we'd best be going," the man said grandly.

As they walked, Zoë noticed the large, square hole in the middle of the platform. *For unloading,* she thought, deducing its purpose. She hazarded a quick glance at Greta and directed her eyes to the hole, easily big enough for both of them. Greta looked at Zoë. She knew what her friend was asking. She also knew she could barely swim. Most importantly, she knew they could not get on that boat. It would not be long before these men realized they had the wrong boy. When that happened, she and Zoë had to be as far away as possible. She gave Zoë a slight nod. The gesture was not as subtle as she had intended.

The Predicament

"Nothing funny, okay girls? You'll be fine. We'll just go for a short ride and then I'll let you go." His voice got harder at the end, his casual manner from earlier gone entirely.

Zoë took Greta's hand and led her to the edge of the opening. The fireworks were still going and as they lit up the sky, Greta could see the promise in Zoë's eyes. *She won't let me die*, she thought.

"Stop!" the man shouted. "Hey! Get back from there!" He re-trained the gun on Zoë. At the same moment, each girl took the last step backward, plunging noiselessly into the water below.

The blast of cold water and the force of the fall nearly knocked Greta's breath right out of her. She tightened her grip on Zoë's hand but every other part of her went limp. She wasn't kicking, which forced Zoë's legs to work even harder to return to the surface. The girls stretched away from each other in slow motion. Greta felt Zoë's hand slip away as she sank deeper. As the first of the salt water entered her lungs she felt them convulse. Then everything went black.

25

∼ The Doctor ∼

Her body lay, half-conscious, on an outcrop of rocks. The waves tugged at her feet. Some part of her brain seemed to be clamoring for her to move but she was simply too weary to respond. Diving into the darkness for Greta, with her heart racing, had taken every ounce of strength she possessed. When she finally reached her, Greta was unconscious. Against the tumult of the waves, the fireworks and the shouts of the men above her, she had tried desperately to save the tiny girl, praying it wasn't too late.

Zoë dragged Greta's weightless body upward, her left arm hooked tightly underneath one of Greta's and over the opposite shoulder — like a seat belt. As they broke through the surface, she brought Greta's face up hard. She had hoped to hear a gasping or choking — some sign the girl still had air left in her lungs…and life in her body. Greta's head sagged silently forward onto her chest.

Zoë wasted no more time. She slammed her hand down on Greta's back. It slipped on the wet fabric of Greta's summer frock. She tried again. This time her flattened palm made its mark with a sound *thump*, followed by a slight cough. "Attagirl, Greta," Zoë coaxed. She didn't dare make any other noise.

The current was taking them in an easterly direction and as they were moved farther away from the dock, she could still see the blurry form of the boat, but not the men. Although Zoë was grateful the water was pulling them away from danger, she also couldn't help but notice it was taking them farther out to sea. She'd need to begin fighting her way back as soon as she could.

She tried checking for a pulse but it was impossible to do anything more than tread water and keep both of their heads above the waves. She hit Greta again, and again the girl coughed. The third cough coincided with the roar of the boat's engine. Zoë could barely make it out as it left the dock. It came closer. She feared it was coming for them, but it turned and wound its way through the harbor, following the general path Peter had gone less than an hour before.

For a moment she hesitated, thinking it might be best to return to the co-op. She tried to make her mind work. It wouldn't. She thought of what Mario would say and she could almost hear his voice. *When they realize they don't have Peter, they will come back.*

"You're right," she whispered to her absent friend.

Zoë allowed herself one wistful hope that Peter would be safe soon before redirecting her effort on getting Greta to shore. "You — will — not — die!" Zoë ordered, pounding Greta's back to punctuate each word. The last stroke did it and Greta began to vomit sea water. Zoë felt the girl's body heaving, then coughing and then gasping beautifully. "Thank you, Greta," Zoë began to cry. "Thank you."

As Greta inhaled tenuously, Zoë assessed their situation. They were less than ten meters from shore but there was no easy way to get to land. Maine's renowned rocky coast was no misnomer. She'd have to swim farther and try to find an area with enough of an incline to support their bodies. She repositioned her left arm solidly around Greta's torso, grateful her friend was so small. Zoë then used her legs and one free arm to swim on her side.

With excruciating slowness, she made her way along the coast, keeping as close to shore as she dared. It was a calm night but she could still feel the pull of the tide beneath her. It wouldn't take much for the two of them to be picked up and thrown against the jagged surface. *Like Mario.* She grimaced the thought away.

She distinguished the shadowy shape of a large outcrop sloping into the sea. Up until then she had tried not to exert too much energy. She knew she'd need it for this final stretch. It had been agonizing to restrict herself like this. She longed to make a mad dash for safety, but if she had given in, she would have nothing left for this moment — and this would be the hardest yet.

Zoë was utterly depleted. Even the buoyancy of the water did little to alleviate the burden of carrying another person — no matter how small. She mustered her reserves and set a gradual course towards shore. Painstakingly, she swam against the current, watching the rocks creep closer, stroke by stroke. At last her feet met ground and she was able to use them to push herself along. As she emerged from the water, Zoë felt the shock of the night air.

The full weight of Greta's body set in, and for a moment, Zoë thought she wouldn't make it — that she'd slip under and that would be it. Zoë struggled to pull Greta out of the water. She crawled and dragged and eventually collapsed. Closing her eyes brought the immediate comfort of losing consciousness.

There was still something she was supposed to do. It nagged at her. *What was it?* She heard a slight coughing. *Am I coughing?* she asked her subconscious. *No — someone*

else — girl. The new girl. Gracie? Gretchen? Greta? Greta. Greta — Greta!

Zoë's eyes flashed open. She reached for her friend and listened carefully for breathing. It was faint but definitely there. "It's okay, Greta." It sounded to Zoë as though the words were coming from someone else's mouth. "We're safe now. We got away. Peter got away. Everything is fine."

She turned the girl on her side and hit her back again, hoping to force out any more of the water she still detected in Greta's breathing. Some came as harsh coughs racked through the small lungs. She vomited again, muttered something incoherent and slipped back into oblivion.

Zoë wished she could do the same. She longed for sleep. Every muscle in her body ached; every nerve had been frayed to the breaking point. She let herself shut her eyes and rest for just a moment, just a…. It felt heavenly. *I can't go to sleep. Greta needs help. I need to get her help.*

"Zoë?"

She jerked herself awake. How long had she been sleeping? Surely just a minute. *Please let it be a minute.* She felt for Greta's body. It was still there. She felt for a pulse. It too was there but much weaker than before. Something was different. What was it? The fireworks — they had finished. Something else….

"Zoë!" It was Daniel's voice. She looked up and saw him coming towards her. "Are you alright? What happened? We've been looking everywhere for you. What's wrong with Greta? Zoë?"

She just stared up at him, dumbfounded. It was all too much. She started to cry.

"Hey, it's okay," he soothed. "It's over. It's going to be fine. Did Peter get away?"

She nodded.

Daniel leaned down and easily picked up Greta. "Good, then all we need to do is take care of you two. It's going to be okay, I promise."

Zoë knew this wasn't entirely true. It wasn't over. There was something else. She was sure of it but her mind was muddled from the barrage of emotional and physical strains. She had been threatened and scared and hurt. She had almost let her friend die. It was too much.

"Zoë, I need you to stand up. Here." He held out his hand. She took it and he hauled her to her feet. "Careful — the rocks are slippery. Follow me."

She concentrated on placing her feet where Daniel told her. When they got past the rocks he set Greta down on a lookout bench. Zoë sat next to her.

"We need to get Greta help," Daniel said decisively.

She couldn't stop sobbing.

"We'll take her to Doc Ingraham."

"But what if —"

"We'll take her to Doc Ingraham," he repeated forcefully.

She looked at him, grateful someone else was taking charge. She felt the relief of not having to decide anything. For better or for worse, she was off the hook and no one was relying on her. She just needed to take care of herself. Her sobs subsided into tearful whimpers.

Zoë nodded at Daniel, sighed heavily and rose from the bench. He picked up Greta and they made their way to a large house on the edge of the town green.

The lights were off and for a moment Zoë feared the doctor and his wife were still at the bazaar. Daniel wasted no time. He rang the bell and proceeded to bang loudly on the door. Soon they heard scuffling sounds from inside and the door opened.

"Come in, come in. What seems to be the — Danny, is that you? And Zoë? And who's this?" The elderly man looked as if he'd been asleep but not for long. His untamed white hair skewed to one side as he coiled a pair of wire-rim spectacles around his ears.

"Yes, sir." Daniel rushed through the front door. "A friend — she's hurt."

"She nearly drowned. I tried my best. I tried.... I didn't.... I —" Zoë blurted, tears streaming down her face. She couldn't stop crying, couldn't stop imagining all the horrible things which might have happened. *It's all my fault.*

"Quickly, bring her into the office." The doctor motioned towards a door off of the foyer while shouting upstairs, "Meribah!"

Moments later a white-haired woman, looking more like a sister than a wife, descended. She joined them in the small, sparse room; assessed the situation with an expert glance; determined what was needed and left silently.

Daniel laid Greta down on the examination table while Dr. Ingraham turned on the lights and reached for his stethoscope. "Help me sit her up, Danny," he said with the authority of a man who had seen everything and lived to tell the tale.

Soon Mrs. Ingraham returned and handed Zoë a large Turkish towel.

The girl stared at her, bordering on a catatonic state. Why was this woman passing her a towel?

Mrs. Ingraham noticed the hesitation and pointed to Zoë's clothes. "You're wet, dear." The information didn't register. She looked at Zoë more intently and said something to her husband.

He nodded succinctly.

"Come with me, dear. We'll get you out of those clothes," Mrs. Ingraham said kindly. Zoë followed obediently, grateful again not to have the pressure of making any decisions.

"Will she be okay?" Daniel asked anxiously. He could barely tell if Greta was breathing and she still hadn't regained consciousness.

"Where's her family?" Dr. Ingraham replied.

"I don't know. She's with Miss Witherspoon for the summer. I just met her two weeks ago."

"And what happened? Did she fall in?"

Daniel hesitated. "I'm not entirely sure, sir. I found her and Zoë on the rocks. At first I thought they were both unconscious but then Zoë woke up. She seemed kind of out of it. And Greta…. I didn't try to wake her up. I didn't know what I was supposed to do."

"It's alright, son. You did just fine. I'll go ahead and keep both girls here for the night."

Daniel must have shown his confusion.

"Zoë's in shock," the doctor elaborated. "Mrs. Ingraham is taking care of her. It's this little one who concerns me." He was opening Greta's eyelids and shining a light on her dilated pupils. "What's Miss Witherspoon's number?"

Daniel didn't say anything. He didn't want to lie to the doctor. "I'm sorry, sir. You can't call her."

"Is she not home? Are you kids on your own up there?"

"Not exactly…."

"Well, then what?"

"I'm sorry, sir. I don't know what to tell you. I don't want to lie to you but you can't call her. Not yet, please."

The doctor looked at Daniel and seemed to consider this. There was a long silence as he did so. "I'll call first thing in the morning."

"Thank you, sir." Daniel didn't know what else to say. At least this bought them some time. "May I see Zoë before I go?"

The doctor nodded towards the direction in which Mrs. Ingraham had taken her patient.

"Thank you, sir. I'll be back in the morning."

Daniel found Zoë lying on a sofa in the parlor. Mrs. Ingraham sat next to her, holding a steaming cup of tea.

"Daniel, I…." Zoë began to cry again.

"Try to keep calm, dear," Mrs. Ingraham consoled. "You've had a terrible shock, that's all. Your friend will be fine. You just need to rest and keep warm. Here, try another sip of tea."

Zoë looked at her and then back at Daniel. "She said I'm to stay here tonight. I told her I can't, that I need to…but she…. Why can't I stop crying?" Zoë started to panic.

Mrs. Ingraham looked troubled. "I'll be back in just a minute, dear." As she passed Daniel she added, "She needs sleep Danny and she needs to stay here. Don't excite her."

"Yes, ma'am."

He waited for her to leave before sitting on the couch next to Zoë's feet. "Zo, everything's going to be fine. You did great."

This seemed to agitate her more. "I didn't. It's all my fault. We should have gone on the boat. I should've made her go back." She clawed at his hand. "Daniel, what if I killed her? What if I —"

"Zoë, you can't do this to yourself. You did the best you could. What's important now is that you're safe. I need to go tell the others. I'll be back —"

He turned as he heard Mrs. Ingraham re-enter the room. She had a syringe in her hand. When she saw that Zoë was even more frantic, the woman reprimanded Daniel with a glare.

"Here, dear." Mrs. Ingraham knelt next to Zoë. "This will help calm your nerves and let you sleep. Sleep is the best medicine for a scare like this."

"No!" Zoë shouted, sitting upright and trying to stand.

Mrs. Ingraham was up just as fast, uncapping the needle with her teeth. "Hold her, Danny!" she ordered.

Zoë screamed incoherently. "No! Please, no! I can't! I have to — Daniel!" She was trying to tell him something but he couldn't understand her.

Newspaper? Daniel thought. *Is that what she said?*

Mrs. Ingraham deftly raised the sleeve of Zoë's oversized pajama top and inserted the needle into her arm. Instantly Zoë stopped screaming, stopped crying, stopped everything.

Slowly she turned to look pathetically at Mrs. Ingraham, then at Daniel. "No...." Her voice was barely audible. Despondent, she began to tremor.

Mrs. Ingraham supported her back onto the couch.

"Daniel, I...." Zoë said distantly.

"It's okay Zo — we'll take care of everything."

"Daniel, I...." Her eyelids drooped heavily.

"Don't worry. It'll be fine. I promise."

"Daniel?"

"Yeah?"

"Daniel?" she slurred.

"Yes, Zoë. I'm here."

"I...placed...an ad...." Her head rolled to one side. She was asleep.

26

❧ The Advertisement ☙

"She said *what?*" Seymour asked for the third time.

"I told you — that she placed an ad."

"But what does that mean? Are you sure you heard her right. If she was sedated, she could have —"

"I know what she said," insisted Daniel.

Seymour started pacing again, muttering to himself. He had been gradually going mad with worry over the past few hours. First, Dinora reported that Greta had gone with Zoë. He, Daniel and Mario were setting up the stage. It was infuriating not being able to go to them. With help from Dinora, they rushed through the stage construction until Mrs. Eaton finally nodded her approval.

When they arrived at the Lobster Co-op it was too late. They hoped Peter had gotten away safely — but where were the girls? Seymour ran back to the truck in case they'd gone to meet them there. Mario and Dinora headed back to the bazaar and searched frantically for their friends. Daniel followed the coastline. They agreed to meet at the truck in half an hour.

He didn't know why he felt called to search along the shore but Daniel didn't question it. His mind was calculating possible scenarios, each of which compelled him to trace and retrace his steps. Then he saw their bodies. The half hour was almost up but Daniel only cared about getting the girls to Dr. Ingraham. Subsequently, Seymour and Mario had been all the more worried when Daniel too had gone missing. Dinora was not worried — she was hysterical. It was all the older boys could do to keep her from losing her wits entirely.

"We'll stay here," her brother assured her, opening up the passenger side door of the truck and helping her inside. He took off his sweatshirt and draped it over her quivering shoulders. "We'll stay here and we'll stay together. Right, Seymour?"

His friend's face was panic-stricken, but he managed to stay relatively calm. He looked at Mario and nodded.

The celebration was winding down. The boys passed the time by dismantling the booth and disposing the ruins of eighteen pies.

"Oh!" Dinora looked dismayed at such a waste. "Well...I suppose I can have a little bit...of the apple," she answered their unarticulated offer. Mario brought his sister a pie and she smiled wanly. She broke off pieces of crust with her fingers and daintily dipped them into the filling.

The boys smiled.

Just when Seymour thought he was going to have to tear out on a rampage looking for his friends, Mario yelled, "Look!"

Daniel was running towards them. They darted off to meet him. Breathless, he tried to update the others on all that had taken place. Making their way back to the truck, the children inundated Daniel with questions. He haltingly conveyed the little he knew, which only seemed more because it took him so long to say it.

"I want to see them," said Seymour.

The Advertisement

"She's sleeping," said Daniel. "We can see her in the morning."

"He's right," Mario agreed. "There's nothing we can do now for either of them. They're in the safest place they can be and we have work to do."

"Why would she place an ad?" Seymour groaned.

"We need to find a paper," Mario reasoned. "It has to be the *Island Ad-Vantages*. It's the only —"

"Yes!" Seymour exclaimed. "When we were in town yesterday…. Zoë went somewhere while I went back to the parsonage. She wasn't gone long but I suppose it could have been enough time to put in an advertisement."

"It must have been in today's paper then. Why didn't she tell us?" Daniel wondered aloud.

"Who knows why Zoë does anything," said Seymour. "Maybe she got distracted with everything else going on."

"Let's find out." Mario shut the door to the truck and began to walk towards *The Galley*. The others followed. It was past midnight and the town was empty. The only signs of the earlier festivities were the streets littered with firework remnants, bits of food and an assortment of wrappers which flitted past them in the cool summer breeze.

As they approached the newspaper bin outside the grocery store, Mario could tell it was empty.

"They're all gone," Dinora said.

"There are others though — the post office has one, I think," said Seymour.

"Yes, and outside the souvenir shop," added Daniel.

"Does the diner?" asked Mario.

"I can't remember…." replied Dinora, absentmindedly chewing on her fingernails. Her brother, just as absentmindedly, slapped her hand out of her mouth.

"I think they don't," Daniel said, "but we should check just in case."

"What was she thinking? Why didn't she tell me? We had the whole hike back. She had plenty of time." Seymour's brow furrowed. "She's up to something," he said. "She wasn't distracted, she was mad."

"About what?" Mario asked.

"About the phone call — about me taking matters into my own hands and not following the plan. She *hates* it when someone thinks for themselves, without her approval. This is just like her. She's such a baby."

"Well, it's done now," Mario said, "and we need to find the paper."

"Fine." Seymour frowned. "But prepare yourself. 'Hell hath no fury like *Zoë* scorned'," Seymour adapted the Congreve quote.

They divided up and scoured the town for a newspaper. At one o'clock they gathered back at the *Island Ad-Vantages* office to share their mutual failure.

"I can't imagine where else we could look," whined Dinora.

"We could go to someone's house," Daniel suggested, "or wait until morning."

"No," Seymour said with finality. "We need to find it. Whatever half-baked plan that daft cousin of mine concocted, we need to know about it *now*. I just hope it's not too late to fix it."

"Seymour!" Dinora approached the storefront window of the one-room office.

"What?"

"I found one." She pointed at the window and the others crowded around her. They shielded their eyes to remove the window's glare and pressed their faces against the glass. There they lay on the counter — a whole stack of the paper's most recent edition.

"I hope one of you can pick a lock," said Mario.

It didn't take long for them to conclude that the only way they were going to get the paper would be to break into the office.

"We might as well get it over with," said Seymour.

The Advertisement

For the second time that night, the children were responsible for breaking into and entering a local business.

"This isn't going to do much for community relations." Daniel's attempt at levity did little to lift Seymour's mood.

"Just do it," he growled.

Daniel held up the large rock he had found. This time it was not the small pane next to the doorknob they had to break but the entire glass door. It shattered instantly, spewing glass inward and loud clanging outward. The children jumped back. They hadn't anticipated how much noise it would make. A dog started barking, followed by a light coming on.

"Quickly!" Mario ordered.

But Seymour did not need to be told. He kicked glass out of the way, barreled through the door and grabbed a newspaper off the stack. He glanced down to make sure it was the right date before racing out. He didn't bother to stop, just kept running down the street. "Let's go!" he roared back but the others were already right behind him.

Panting, Daniel reached the truck first. He tore open the driver's side door and jumped in. The keys were still in the ignition. He was revving the engine when Mario showed up.

"Seymour's coming with Dinora," he wheezed, hurrying into the vehicle. Daniel didn't wait for his friend to shut the door. He shifted into reverse, hit the gas, then the brakes, shifted into first and spun the truck around to pick up the other two. They were a block away and Seymour looked up as the truck screeched to a halt. Seymour leapt into the truck bed and reached for Dinora. As soon as they were in, Daniel peeled out. Dinora grabbed hold of Seymour so as not to be thrown completely back onto the street.

Daniel drove in silence. He didn't have a particular destination in mind. He just wanted to get out of town before anyone recognized them or the old Chevy. As they approached the outskirts, Daniel swerved onto an old logging road. He stopped about twenty meters in, cut the engine and hopped out of the cab. Mario followed. They found Dinora staring expectantly at Seymour as he rummaged through pages. He stopped, shifted the newspaper to catch the light and began to scan the classified section.

Mario and Dinora had picked up a little Mandarin over the summers they had spent with Zoë and Seymour so they understood a few of the words which proceeded to stream out of Seymour's mouth in a rush of anger and frustration. Dinora was glad for two things — that she didn't get all of it — and more importantly, that Zoë was far away, unconscious and couldn't hear *any* of it.

Finally, Seymour finished his ranting, placed one hand on his forehead and used the other to pass the paper to his friends. They huddled together to read the advertisements. It didn't take long to find the large one Zoë had placed the day before.

Priceless antiques at rock-bottom prices.
Witherspoon Estate on High Clearing Lane
Sunday, July 5th 8am

"What was she planning? How did she think it would help?" Dinora was almost afraid to ask — afraid the question would spark another tirade of four-character sentences.

"Oh, I know *exactly* what she was thinking," Seymour scoffed. "It's simple. Simple and stupid and rash and —"

"Just tell us," Mario instructed calmly.

Seymour took a deep breath and tried to regain his composure. "She's thinking," he began, his voice still rife with annoyance and disapproval, "that at around seven o'clock tomorrow morning — because these people always come an hour early — Tia's house will be flanked on all sides by a horde of antique-crazed tourists on the hunt for a good deal."

"And in the commotion, we can rush in and save Tia! That's a great plan!" Dinora's expression and tone clearly demonstrated her unbridled enthusiasm.

"It's *not* a great plan, Dinora!" Seymour admonished the younger girl.

"Sorry. It just seemed like —"

"It certainly has a lot of variables," said Mario.

"That's it!" Seymour shouted. "Too many things could go wrong. There are too many unknowns. This is just like her. She never thinks anything through. She has always been like this. Act now — think later. It's the most asinine plan. It's ridiculous. It's —"

"It's the one we've got," Mario concluded.

Seymour looked up. There was something in his defeated expression which made Dinora wonder if Seymour's fury was over something more than the advertisement. *He must be going crazy with worry*, she thought.

All four children were quiet.

Finally, Seymour's sigh broke the silence. "I know...I know," he said resolutely, looking into the weary and moonlit faces of his fellow adventurers. "Well, as Tia would say, 'in for a penny, in for a pound'." He put his hand out and the other three grasped it.

27

❧ The Rescue ❧

At that exact moment, Miss Dorothea Witherspoon was making her famous raspberry strudel. Although her captors had first balked at her request, they had gradually given in as they tasted the mouth-watering fruits of her labor. Over the past two days, she had shuffled — the bonds on her feet allowed for only discreet movements — back and forth in her spacious kitchen. Her only sleep had been short naps in her large armchair as pies baked, soups simmered and dough rose. The men holding her hostage, whom she had secretly named Grumpy and Sweet Tooth, had taken shifts sitting idly on the kitchen counter, sipping tea and following her with their gun.

It was Sweet Tooth who was currently keeping her company. Unlike his counterpart, he didn't seem to mind her incessant chatter. This was a great relief to her as talking helped calm her, almost as much as cooking did. But this solace was not her intended purpose. Dorothea was lulling her captors.

She had started from the very beginning — when they were still pretending to be David's colleagues. "That's simply dreadful," she feigned worry when they had first returned to tell of the prince's inexplicable absence. "Well, no need to fret. I'm sure he'll find his way back. He must be so scared, poor thing." She paused before asking, "Tea, gentlemen?"

They had accepted, along with the proffered plate of pastries. By the time she went to play the piano — "it calms my nerves and passes the time" she had said — they had both succumbed to the notion that she was a sweet, doddering old woman with a penchant for cooking and altogether harmless. Their guards thus lowered, they'd been completely unaware of the children escaping right above their heads.

When Peter didn't return by the next afternoon, Grumpy had lost his patience and revealed their true allegiances. To this too, Dorothea had responded with shock and fear worthy of the most accomplished actress. She was in the process of developing even more strategies to delay the inevitable when the phone rang. *What a smart boy my Seymour is.* She knew they'd figure out something. She smiled proudly. Fortunately, she did so as she tasted her consommé.

"Is it done?" Sweet Tooth asked eagerly.

"Mmm hmm." Her smile embodied kindness and warmth.

Sweet Tooth really was a very nice man, Dorothea decided, although he certainly hadn't made the best of career choices. Grumpy, on the other hand, appeared to have found his ideal vocation, in her humble opinion. He was a mean man. Regretfully, he did seem to be the one in charge. He had stayed with her last night which meant she got to spend the day with Sweet Tooth, whose company she much preferred. Throughout the day she had gotten to know him better and saw the potential in him for a good man. She told him as much. He had thanked him politely but didn't seem terribly interested in pursuing that line of conversation.

She looked at him now and almost felt sorry for what she must soon do. "Let me get you a bowl. Do you think your friend would like one?" she continued without giving him a chance to respond. "I'm sure he would. It's very good. I've actually won awards with it, if I do have to say so myself." She let out a small laugh, precariously close to a giggle. "And what about sandwiches? Roast beef again?"

Sweet Tooth nodded with enthusiasm. Earlier, for lunch, both of the men had devoured one of her thick roast beef sandwiches with homemade French bread, Gruyère cheese and horseradish aioli. Her mother had taught her that a hungry man was an angry man. On her own she had discovered that a well-fed man, or better yet, an overfed man, was more docile. This is what she needed: two overfed men.

Of course, she could have disposed of them anytime — that wasn't difficult. The problem was information. While they were here, she had firsthand access to their side of things. Already she had figured out — whether through seemingly innocuous questions or good, old-fashioned eavesdropping — any number of things which Edith and David would be sure to find useful. Now she was waiting for the last radio transmission — the one which would confirm their mission had failed. Then it would be time to act.

Her mind held no doubt that the children had deciphered her message in plenty of time to make the rendezvous. Assuming all went well, the meeting should have gone off without a hitch and Peter was well on his way to safety. At least this is what she hoped. Around ten o'clock, the radio alerted them with an off-key twang. She prepared herself for what might come: good news, bad news, mixed news, no news. Those were the options and she had a subsequent plan for each of them.

They had Peter! How was this possible? And now something about the two girls getting away. She wondered if it was Dinora or Greta who accompanied Zoë. She had no question her niece had been involved. She was fearless, that girl, and always had to be where the action was. *I really must speak to her about that*, Dorothea thought to herself and made a mental note of it. The thrill of adventure, as she could attest, would prove both dangerous and addictive. But for now she had bigger concerns. After all their work and precaution, Peter was in the hands of his enemies.

Something puzzled her. The rendezvous was scheduled for nine o'clock and the call came at ten. *Had the children been late? Had David? Or....* Dorothea let her mind trail off.

"So I guess we just leave now then?" Sweet Tooth turned off the radio as he asked his partner.

They were in the living room but Dorothea, standing next to the kitchen door, was able to hear them — at least she could hear Sweet Tooth well enough. Grumpy spoke with an indistinct mumble. She doubted if she'd have any better luck understanding him even if they were in the same room.

Grumpy murmured something.

"Is that really necessary? We have what we came to get," said Sweet Tooth, followed by another garbled response.

This time Grumpy's voice was raised slightly and Dorothea was able to hear the last of it: "— not to leave any loose ends."

That would be me, she thought. *Very well, I suppose the time has come.* She scanned the list of options she had generated and chose the one least likely to cause permanent injury. It was a little more complicated but getting to know Sweet Tooth had softened her heart and she didn't want to hurt him.

The radio sang again, and again Dorothea prepared herself for any news which might necessitate altering her plan.

"This is Red Dog, over," came Sweet Tooth's voice, followed quickly by, "What? Please repeat. Over."

Grumpy asked something incoherent.

"I don't know," replied Sweet Tooth. "He says they don't have him, they've got some other — hold on…. Yes, Eagle. We're here, over…. Affirmative. Over." A long pause. "Affirmative. Any further instructions? Over…. Got it — Red Dog out." Sweet Tooth hung up and updated his partner. "Sounds like Blake and Ron got the wrong kid — something about a costume. Turns out it was some kid from town. They ended up dumping him at the ferry dock — scared him out of his wits, I'll bet."

Grumpy mumbled.

"Nah, Eagle said he thinks the kids were trying some sort of decoy and that the boy really is due tomorrow morning."

Another mumble.

"Yeah, but what can we do? Hey, there's some food the lady made in the kitchen —"

This was interrupted with an angry grunt.

"What, because I'm hungry? Listen, man. You do what you want — I'm getting something to eat."

Dorothea moved away from the door and returned to her soup. An hour later, Sweet Tooth was just finishing his second helping of strudel.

"Ma'am, you really are the best cook I've ever met. This was good. Really good. Fantastic."

"Oh, you're sweet to flatter an old woman. Well, I wouldn't want you to go hungry — not while I'm here and happy to cook for you. I'm glad you enjoyed it."

"You ladies having a nice time?" Grumpy interrupted.

Dorothea knew Grumpy had been loitering just outside her kitchen. Still, she made herself jump and put her hand to her chest. "Oh, my! You startled me," she lied easily.

"I thought I told you to keep your mouth shut."

"Mike, relax. It's not like —"

"No! You relax — I'll take my shift now. You look like you could use some sleep — straighten your mind out a little."

"You're the boss." Sweet Tooth raised his hands in mock surrender, nodded politely to Dorothea and left the room. "Thank you again, ma'am."

"Oh, you're quite welcome," Dorothea called after him. She turned back to face Grumpy — Michael was too nice a name — and offered him some dessert.

"No. I've had plenty, lady. I've had plenty of your damn food; plenty of your big, fancy house; plenty of your Suzie-sunshine attitude...." He moved in closer to her, pointing his finger in her face. "And plenty of your lies."

"My lies?"

"Don't act so innocent. You know something — I can smell it."

"I don't know —"

"Shut up, you old cow! Just shut up and get in the chair." He took the rope he'd used earlier and proceeded to bind her tightly.

"Is this really necessary," she asked, recalculating her plan.

"I'll tell you what's *not* necessary, lady. A gag. A gag isn't necessary because, know this — if so much as one more word pops out of your mouth..." He raised his pistol, pressed it against her temple and whispered, "...it's over."

Making sure she was secured, he went to the other end of the kitchen, sat down on the floor and simply stared at her.

Dorothea saw no need to antagonize the man. She shut her eyes, slowed her breathing and pretended to fall asleep. The warmth of the kitchen and the sound of her deep breaths, combined with his exhaustion, created the perfect recipe for sleep. Soon he was snoring and Dorothea opened her eyes. She let the knife slide from sleeve to palm. Patiently, she cut the ropes. Dorothea decided then and there she'd had quite enough of this man and his negative attitude.

Once freed, she peered out the window. The sun had risen and she hadn't even noticed. How long had it been since she'd slept more than twenty minutes? Two days? Three days? Whatever it was, it certainly wasn't the worst thing she had ever experienced. She glanced at the clock. Seven. She could not afford to give the children any more time.

A loud rumbling came from the end of her driveway. *Cars*, she thought, *and a lot of them*. Her captor was still asleep but he wouldn't be for long and she readied herself. Whatever was about to happen, she knew would have to happen quickly or not at all.

Dorothea grasped her knife with her left hand and waited. Moments later car doors began slamming and Grumpy's eyes shot open. She looked around with an expression she hoped portrayed that she too had no idea of what was occurring.

The man moved to the window. "What in hell?" He turned just in time to see Dorothea standing directly behind him. He looked down to see the knife she held in her right hand as she deftly hit him in the back of the head with what she held in her left hand — her favorite cast iron frying pan.

Her opponent slumped to the floor just as the throng of strangers flooded into her home. Gracefully, she stepped over the body and smiled as people rushed past her. They were too focused on something else to notice the unconscious man at her feet.

Then the children were there.

"Tia!" They ran to embrace her.

"Oh my, oh my." she laughed, hugging and kissing and counting them. "Where are —" she began, then changed course. "That'll have to wait for a minute. This is no time to talk. No time to talk. Now, my darlings, would you mind taking care of this for me." Her eyes indicated the floor. "I have one more guest to whom I simply must attend."

They looked down and for the first time saw the body.

"Tia, did you —" Dinora began.

"Did I what? Oh, kill him? Well, certainly not. Certainly not. No need for that kind of nonsense. No need, no need. It will make things a little easier though if he and his companion are out of the way for the moment. The cellar might do. Yes. It might do quite nicely. Quite nicely."

Daniel, Mario and Seymour picked up the man's limp body and carried it downstairs.

"And Dinora?" Tia continued.

Startled, Dinora looked up from where the unconscious man had lain. "Y-y-yes, T-Tia?" she stammered.

"I need you to start making sandwiches and not stop." Tia reached out and stroked Dinora's hair, which was showing the full effects of the past few days. The girl wore a dazed expression. "Darling, it's over." Tia said softly.

Dinora refocused her eyes from the wall to Tia's face. "*¿Verdad?*" she asked.

"*Claro*," confirmed Tia. "But, my darling, neither men nor children can live on bread alone and Rome was not built in a day. I need you to start making sandwiches. Do you understand?"

The hint of a smile touched Dinora's lips. "Idle hands are the devil's workshop?"

"Exactly!" Tia enveloped her in a full embrace.

"We need to make hay while the sun shines?" Dinora added when Tia released her.

"Indubitably. Now get to work," Tia ordered.

"Yes, ma'am," answered Dinora.

As an invigorated Dinora rolled up her sleeves and washed her hands, Tia placed some freshly ground coffee in the percolator before heading to her study. She emerged ten minutes later with a packet and a determined expression. She set the former on the counter, opened a drawer and retrieved a large paper bag. She smiled her approval at Dinora's work and took the two sandwiches the girl had finished. She wrapped them, placed them in the bag and added a large piece of raspberry strudel. To this she added some oranges from the overflowing fruit bowl and a thermos filled with the hot coffee that had just finished brewing. Finally, she slid the packet inside and folded the top of the bag to form a handle.

"You stay here, dear. I'll be right back."

"But Tia —" began Dinora, panic returning easily to her.

"I'll be fine." Tia paused for a moment as more antique lovers entered her kitchen. "Actually, Dinora, it would be most helpful if you could begin ridding my home of these hooligans. Goodness knows how much havoc they've wrought already."

Dinora rallied to the call of service. "Of course! I'm on it, Tia."

"Good girl." Tia patted the girl's head, nodded congenially to the soon-to-be-evicted shoppers and marched out of the kitchen.

Dinora began to clear out the tourists in her best military voice. "I'm sorry, folks. It was a prank. There's nothing for sale here. Let's take it outside." She noticed an elderly man who had removed a priceless painting from the wall. "Put that down, sir, and don't try anything fancy."

Dorothea found Sweet Tooth in the downstairs linen closet. He had the radio with him and pointed his gun nervously at the opening door.

"Put the gun down, dear. You've no need for it now." He lowered the weapon, reminding her of a stray dog — scared, wary and all the more dangerous because of it.

"It's over, dear. Your partner is unconscious and tied up in my cellar. My friends will be here soon to..." she chose the words carefully, "...tidy up."

Sweet Tooth's face blanched.

Dorothea smiled maternally in response. "It's probably best if you are not here when they arrive." She held out the large paper bag, forcing Sweet Tooth to choose between setting down the gun or the radio.

He chose the radio.

Dorothea smiled again. "There's some food for you and something else, but you mayn't open it until you are on the ferry. Please, do not misunderstand me." Her voice hardened. "These are not words of advice but ones of instruction. Do what the letter says and everything will turn out just fine. Just fine, dear."

Sweet Tooth didn't say anything, only stared at this strange woman in disbelief and wonder. He went to tuck his gun back into his pants and Dorothea stopped him. "No, dear. That will have to stay with me." She held out her hand for the pistol.

He seemed reluctant.

"I promise," she assured solemnly. "If you follow the instructions in the letter, you'll not require it again and your little girl will have her father for a very long time."

Sweet Tooth placed the weapon in Dorothea's outstretched palm and used his freed hand to pick up the radio.

"That too, dear..." she nodded towards the communication device, "...will have to stay. My friends will have need of it. You will not."

This time, Sweet Tooth didn't hesitate as long. He drew back his shoulders, lifted his chin slightly and made to leave the small room. Dorothea stepped aside for him and he exited into the fray of giddy customers. "Thank you, ma'am," he muttered.

"It is my pleasure, dear." She reached her hand up and lightly touched the back of his head. *If things had been different*, she thought, *this would have been where I hit him with my frying pan.* But this was too whimsical a thought to reside long in the pragmatic mind of Miss Dorothea Witherspoon. *It was providence,* she decided. *It couldn't possibly have turned out any other way.* She continued, "And tell your daughter I look forward to meeting her someday." She smiled warmly as she took his arm and led him to the rarely used front door.

"Goodbye, ma'am."

"Goodbye, dear." Dorothea watched him run down the drive with a bagful of food and hopefully, a future. She prayed he was smart enough to heed her instructions.

Taking deep breaths, she turned to face the mass of people rummaging through her home. *I know they wanted to rescue me,* she shook her head and smiled resolvedly, *but did it really have to be so messy?*

28

❧ The Lesson ❧

Greta lurched awake with a gasp. The vestiges of her nightmare still clung to her. It had been cold and she didn't know where she was. She was scared and couldn't breathe. No matter how hard she tried, she couldn't get any air. It was the same nightmare that had continued to plague her, ever since...

"Tia!" Dinora yelled recklessly. "She's awake!"

Greta winced at the volume, prompting Dinora to turn and ask softy, "Are you alright, Greta?" She didn't wait for a response. "We've all been so worried about you. All of us. We thought you might die — you almost did. At least that's what I heard Dr. Ingraham say to Tia. He told her it was a good thing Daniel got you to him so quickly because if not...if not.... Oh, it's just too awful.... And then for days and days with your fever and being unconscious, and then you had these convulsion things and —"

"*Déjala*, Dinora," Mario's voice interrupted reproachfully. "Give her a chance to get her bearings."

"Oh! Was I talking too much, Greta? I'm so sorry. It's just I'm so happy to see you alive and awake and....

Okay, I'll shut up now. I will. I won't say another word — well, not like ever — but for a long time — unless of course you want me to." She looked at her brother indignantly. "Some people find it comforting."

He mimed the zipping of lips. "I believe Tia needs help downstairs."

Dinora let out a small huff. "I'll be right back, Greta. Don't worry."

She left and Mario took her place on the chair positioned next to Greta's bed. He picked up her hand, pressing two of his fingers against her wrist while watching the small clock on her bedside table. To Greta, everything seemed surreal, like this itself was a dream — and not her own. She felt detached, as if she were a character in someone else's imaginings. She closed her eyes and withdrew.

The next time she awoke, it was dark. Greta vaguely remembered the room being filled with sunlight when Mario had been here, checking her pulse. Now the only light was from a small lamp perched on top of a mahogany dresser nearby. She furrowed her brow in concentration.

"You're up." This time it was Seymour's comforting voice which greeted her.

She smiled wanly. "I'm not in the girls' room," she said, her voice weak from lack of use.

"No. You're on the third floor — in the room next to Tia's."

"How long...." she started to ask, wondering why it was taking so much energy to speak.

"Have you been here?" confirmed Seymour.

Greta nodded.

"You've been back at Tia's for five days. Before that, you were with Dr. Ingraham for two."

Greta let this information filter through.

"Here, you should try to drink something." Seymour helped her sit up, propping pillows behind her back. He poured some water into a glass and passed it to her. She tried to lift her hand but it was too heavy.

"It's okay," he said. "I've got it." He held the glass up to her lips.

She took a small sip and swallowed. "Did Peter —" she began.

Seymour nodded, helping her take a longer drink. "He's fine. Your David came himself and told us."

Greta's eyes brightened. "I'm glad," she said softly. "And Tia?"

"Tia's fine. Everyone is. They're all worried about you, though. I keep telling them they don't need to be." He smiled. "You're going to be fine too. It's just going to take a little longer."

She returned his smile half-heartedly. "I'm tired," she said and he helped her lie back down.

Greta was wakened by a jab of pain in her arm. She opened her eyes to see a small, white-haired man removing a needle from her. It was attached to a tube which led to a plastic bag hanging from a thin metal pole. The bag was filled with water — or what looked like water.

"Greta, dear?" She turned to the other side. It was Tia.

Instantly she felt a wave of happiness wash over her. She smiled broadly and then announced, "I'm hungry."

Tia beamed, clearly delighted at the pronouncement. "You just wait two minutes, dear. Just two minutes. I've got the perfect thing. Reginald, that's fine, right?" she asked the man.

He too smiled. "Just don't overdo it, Dorothea. Start her slow and see how she does."

"Certainly," Tia assured him. "Now, Greta, I'll be right back with something delicious for you."

Greta nodded, pulling herself into an upright position. Imagining all sorts of delectable morsels made her mouth water and her stomach grumble.

"You gave everyone quite a scare, young lady," the old man said as he looped the plastic tubing, "but it looks like you're out of the woods. You'll be on your feet in no time."

It was at that moment the door opened. Greta wondered how Tia could have been so fast, but it was Daniel who entered.

"Hi, Greta."

She could tell he was trying to control his exuberance. She vaguely remembered Dinora being quite animated and wondered if the rest of them too had been warned not to overwhelm her with their excitement. She was still exhausted, yet at the same time felt as if her life was finally returning to her — as if it were spring and her body was coming out of hibernation.

"Hi, Daniel." She gave him the smile she'd given Tia earlier and it seemed to have the same heartening effect on him.

"Tia wanted someone to keep you company and I hadn't seen you awake, so...." He hesitated before asking, "How are you doing?"

Greta's feelings now seemed to be cascading towards her, as if her emotional dam were overflowing. "Bemused..." she said, feeling the click and the rightness of the word, "...and ravenous...and grateful and curious...and *ravenous*."

"You already mentioned 'ravenous'," he teased.

"I'm very hungry, Daniel," she replied with mock gravity.

"I bet you are. You've had quite a run of it."

Greta reached out her arm and beckoned for him to sit down. "Tell me," she said. "Tell me everything."

Daniel commenced with all the stories she had missed. He told her of Tia's rescue and the fake estate sale. He told her of the unique strategies Dinora had utilized to get all of the antique addicts out of Tia's house. She laughed softly when Daniel told of one tourist who had remained undetected for the better part of the day, only to emerge at last with her arms full of the doorknobs she'd unscrewed from practically every door in the house.

"You should have seen the look on Tia's face when the lady asked, 'How much for the lot?'. It was unbelievable. I've never seen Tia so mad. It took us forever to put them all back."

The door opened and Tia entered with a tray of small dishes. Following her was a gaggle of familiar and friendly faces.

"Now, don't crowd her. Don't crowd her and don't jostle the tray, my darlings. Really, you'd think she was the Queen of England the way you bunch carry on," she chortled as she set the tray down over Greta's lap so the legs extended on either side.

There was a small pot of tea from which Tia poured a fragrant liquid. She set it down and passed the small teacup to Greta. This time she had no difficulty raising her hand to accept the cup. She blew softly against the surface before taking a small, preliminary sip. It burned slightly and tasted heavenly. She smiled her gratitude and everyone laughed. She gazed at them with sheer contentment before noticing that Dinora looked as if she was about to burst from restraint.

"Yes, Dinora?" Greta feigned obliviousness.

Dinora sought silent permission from Tia who responded with a combined look of both consent and caution. Dinora took a deep breath and everyone prepared themselves for the onslaught of chatter.

But she was silent.

It was as if there were so many things she wanted to say that they clogged her mouth, rendering her mute. Dinora, for the first time in her life, was speechless.

Mario laughed. "I believe what my sister wants to say is how happy she is that you're alright. We all are."

Dinora nodded vigorously.

Greta accepted the small beignet Tia offered and took a bite. She swallowed and felt some of her energy returning. "I'm happy too —" she stopped, puzzled. Someone was missing. "Where's Zoë?" she asked.

Tia and the children averted their eyes and looked at each other. *She's mad at me*, Greta thought. *She thinks it's my fault — that I slowed her down, that I endangered her. And she's right. It was a selfish thing for me to do.*

"Oh," she said dejectedly, remorsefully.

"Never mind about that." Dinora and her voice were reunited. "Did Daniel tell you we broke into the *Island Ad-Vantages* office, and Tia nearly killed a guy with her frying pan, and that when David heard you were sick he practically —"

"That's enough, Dinora," Tia silenced. "There is plenty of time to inform Greta of your shenanigans. Really, children," she admonished. "Now the whole town is talking about the 'crime spree' and the need to start a community watch program — and all over a few broken windows."

"Tia paid anonymously to have them fixed," Dinora piped in, earning another disapproving glance. "It was very sneaky," she added quickly.

"Well, it's a lot of fuss and bother over nothing really. Fuss and bother."

"The costume wasn't 'nothing'," Seymour added in good humor. "Mrs. Eaton was none too pleased to hear it was gone, that's for sure. Plus, she sounded like she didn't even believe me."

"You did give her a pretty far-fetched reason," Mario teased.

Dinora could hardly contain herself. "He said he'd been mugged," she blurted.

"I couldn't think of anything else," Seymour defended himself with an untroubled shrug.

Greta laughed weakly and closed her eyes. Her energy had waned and now she could barely concentrate.

"We'll let you get some sleep, dear." Tia said definitively. "Mario, will you take the tray?"

"Sure, Tia. Bye, Greta. Sleep well."

The rest wished her sweet dreams and quietly exited her room.

Tia pressed the back of her hand to Greta's cheek and smiled in satisfaction. "You'll be just fine, dear. You get your rest." She sat back on the chair and took some knitting from a basket on the floor.

Then Greta was asleep.

She heard Zoë's voice but from a distance, garbled and dulled. Then it was clearer and Greta remembered it had sounded strange because she'd been underwater. She had been drowning. She had been drowning but Zoë had saved her. She heard Zoë screaming and felt a hand pounding on her back. Greta heard crying and pleading. Now, Zoë seemed closer. She was still crying but it was different now, softer somehow. They weren't outside. It was quiet.

Greta's eyes fluttered open.

"— so very sorry, Greta." Zoë's voice was hardly more than a whisper and Greta could tell from its direction that Zoë wasn't looking at her but downward instead, as if praying. "I can't say it enough. I don't know what else to say. I'm so sorry. I know you can probably never forgive me." She sniffled. "It's unforgivable — what I did."

Greta reached out her hand and touched Zoë's long black hair. Normally in a thick braid, it now hung free, curtaining her beautiful but tear-stained face. The older girl looked up and stared at Greta.

"Will you turn on the lamp?" asked Greta. She needed more than moonlight to be certain.

Zoë nodded and pulled the brass chain on the small bedside lamp. The soft click coincided with an amber burst, illuminating a face fraught with guilt and sorrow. Greta also noted the faded remnants of a large bruise on Zoë's forehead.

"What time is it?" Greta asked, sitting up.

Zoë looked at the clock. "Almost four." She wiped her eyes with her sleeves.

Greta thought about this and about what she had gleaned from Zoë's earlier ramblings. She sought clarification. "You're not mad at me?" she asked.

Zoë looked dumbstruck. "What?" she asked incredulously.

"I thought you were mad at me," Greta repeated. "I thought that's why you didn't want to see me."

Zoë let out a heavy sigh. "Greta, you're the one who should be mad at me."

Now Greta looked confused. "Why?"

Zoë couldn't help but laugh at the simplicity of the question. "Oh, I don't know. Maybe because you nearly died and it was all my fault."

"You saved me."

"Yeah, after I practically killed you."

Greta thought about this a moment. "That's not true." She held Zoë's gaze in hers and reiterated more firmly. "You know that's not true."

Zoë looked as if she couldn't decide whether or not to believe her. Then the tension left her face. She reached over and embraced her friend who was even frailer now. Zoë was afraid to hold her too tightly, afraid she'd hurt her. But Greta returned the hug with unabashed fierceness and the two girls held each other for a long time.

At last Zoë pulled back, wiping tears of relief from her face. "Thank you," she said.

"Thank *you*," Greta replied.

The Lesson

Greta and Zoë sat on the porch swing together. The others had gone off. They hadn't said where but it was probably to do something thrilling, something to do with water, something Zoë would have relished.

Greta studied her friend, who hadn't left her side since the moment Greta had been released from her sickbed. At first, all of the children spent their days with Greta, playing cards in the parlor, singing in the music room, reading in the library. But after a few days, Greta could see how restless they were becoming, how much they longed to be outdoors. "Go," she insisted, and they had gratefully accepted.

All but Zoë.

When another day had passed, the girls extended their realm to include the fresh air of the wrap-around porch. Greta thought her friend would surely be stir-crazy by now, with so little to do, but Zoë seemed content to convalesce alongside her for as long as it took.

Greta wondered how long it would be before she felt up for adventure again. The doctor said there was nothing wrong with her, that her body had fully healed and it was ready whenever she was. *It's my heart*, she thought. *I'm scared.*

She put down her book and gazed out onto the orchard. Through the fruit trees she could see the ocean glistening brightly in the afternoon sun. Greta remembered how excited she was when they first arrived. The others had joyously filled their days with plans of horseback riding, sailing, hiking, exploring, camping, kayaking and, of course, swimming. Was this how she was going to spend the rest of her summer? Reading? She still had six weeks left. Would she be wasting them all on the back-porch swing?

Greta considered how much she had changed in just the first week of being here — how much she liked the person she was becoming. *Now I'm even more timid than when I first arrived.* She imagined leaving the house —

maybe climbing up to Star Rock. What's the worst that could happen? Certainly nothing more than had happened already. Peter was safe. Tia was safe. The danger had abated and now all that was left was a summer which stretched out before her, begging to be enjoyed.

"Zoë?" Greta rose from the swing and extended her hand to the girl who had saved her life.

"Hmm?" Zoë glanced up from the book she was reading, a quizzical expression on her otherwise serene countenance. She set down her book and accepted Greta's hand up.

"Let's go to the pond and you can teach me how to swim."

❧ Epilogue ❧

Each of the children was in a different place when they heard the news. Dinora was studying with a friend. They had a physics exam the next day and she couldn't wrap her head around the concepts, no matter how hard she tried. Her father had helped her first. She'd frustrated him almost as much as she had herself. Even Mario, undeterred by distance, had offered to explain it. Dinora was smart enough to decline. She knew how persistent he was — that he wouldn't stop until she understood the foundations behind the fundamentals, backward and forward. She had no interest in any of that. She wanted to memorize the notes, regurgitate them on the exam and move on to something infinitely more interesting. She and her classmate Dulce Maria had taken a break to fix some lunch in the kitchen. The television was on. Dinora was in the middle of describing her latest failed memorization technique when she saw him.

Seymour heard it on the radio. He was in the car with his father, who had recently purchased a tract of land in the Cascade Mountains. They had decided to build a log cabin by hand and were heading over to survey the property. As they talked, the news had been on. Ascending the mountain, they were getting out of range. Seymour heard something that caught his attention. He turned up the volume.

"There's too much interference," said his father. "Is it important?"

Seymour nodded, fiddling with the dial to see if it helped.

"Then we'll head back down a ways." His father swung the jeep around and drove until the signal was clear again. They pulled over to the side of the road and listened.

Zoë was in the middle of a photo shoot in Nanjing. She hated modeling. It was ridiculous and pointless. All of the people were shallow and obsequious. It was a profession completely void of any redeeming value *but* it did pay a lot of money. It wasn't always lucrative — and certainly not at first — but her grandmother was relentless. Now, Zoë would make enough in this one day to pay the exorbitant fees associated with leaving China next summer. She sat in the makeup chair as the bossy stylist argued with her *nai nai*. In a desperate attempt to keep her composure, Zoë put her head in her hands. The man screeched at her blatant disregard for his craftsmanship and she jumped out of her chair.

"Zoë Qingyue —" Her grandmother's tone held whole volumes of previous lectures, most of which boiled down to family honor and ladylike behavior.

Zoë apologized to the haughty man and her grandmother. "Just give me a minute, please," she added, in her perfectly-accented Mandarin. She knew it was rude not to wait for permission. She also knew neither would give it to her and she didn't want to risk the punishment of disobeying them.

As she left, she heard her grandmother explaining that her granddaughter's behavior was a direct result of being half-American and spending too much time in that garish and undisciplined country.

Zoë's temper flared even as she tried to remind herself that this was the kind of thing which could put her summers of freedom in jeopardy. She tried to calm herself using the meditation techniques Tia had taught her, but ended up laughing instead, as she remembered how the others had mimicked them.

She opened her eyes to see his eyes, projected on the television screen in front of her.

Daniel was sitting with Edith and Tia in the parlor. Tia had known it would be airing ever since a mysterious phone call the night before. After dinner she had asked Daniel to set up the television. He looked nonplussed but she offered no further explanation. He'd lugged the ancient machine out of the closet, dusted it off and placed it on the sturdiest table he could find. He then proceeded to spend nearly an hour trying to get some reception. When it finally came on, the three had to view it through lines and static scratches, making it seem even farther away than it must have been.

Mario was staring at his hands. More specifically, he was staring at the ring he had just placed on his index finger. It was the one Tia had given him on the day he had left The Island, nearly a month earlier. He hadn't had the courage to put it on until now. It seemed so light — a simple, handcrafted silver band, not at all suggestive of what it represented. He took it off to read the inscription he'd already read countless times.

He had been sad when Tia told him he wouldn't be joining the others next summer. He had known it of course — not just because he was starting college and would be busy during the breaks. This is how it had always been. He had spent his summers on The Island ever since he was eleven. Over those seven years, he had seen four friends not return after they also had turned eighteen. He hadn't thought too much about it — until recently — and it made him wonder what they were doing now.

Then Tia had called with her intriguing invitation. This, combined with the vague conversation they'd had when she'd given him the ring, had made him even more curious. She'd asked him to spend Thanksgiving weekend with her. He had accepted eagerly, delighted he wasn't to be banned altogether. He had commenced his studies at MIT, home to one of the best chemistry programs in the world. Being in Boston situated him within a four-hour drive of The Island.

"I'm looking forward to seeing a lot of you," she had told him earlier on the phone. "I know you'll be busy with school but I'm hoping you'll still make time for us." She paused then. "So you're definitely coming?"

"Absolutely."

"Wonderful, wonderful. There are some people I'd think you'd enjoy seeing."

Mario wanted to ask her more but she continued quickly, "Darling, you should turn on your television — Channel Four."

Greta was making the salad for dinner. Her mother would be home soon and she wanted to have everything ready so they could eat right away. This had become their routine. Greta, who was daily discovering new things she could do, had started cooking a few nights a week. This saved her mother time and meant they could begin their evening ritual earlier. First, they would eat and tell each other about their respective days. After cleaning up, they would study — each of them entering her own private world. Later, they would go for a walk or play a game or just visit on the couch. On the weekends, they had started being more adventurous. Often this meant diving into the deep end of the pool at their YMCA.

Greta had turned on the television to keep her company. She was slicing carrots when she heard the anchorman say the name.

"King Bhekizitha Boipuso Dabulamazi of Lesotho came out of his forced exile last week to address the world. King Bhekizitha succeeded his father, King Melisizwe Bohlale II, after his parents were assassinated at the hands of the military, nearly four months ago. We turn now to Robert Monroe, reporting from Lesotho's capital city, Maseru."

"Thank you, Kevin. The world was shocked earlier this week when King Bhekizitha, who also goes by the English name Peter Dabulamazi, came out of hiding to interview with an unnamed reporter in an undisclosed location. King Bhekizitha's need for secrecy is widely known. His life would be forfeit if his whereabouts were to be discovered by those currently controlling his country. In the message, King Bhekizitha shared little of his mysterious abduction and rescue, choosing to speak primarily on issues of his country's welfare."

A video clip replaced the reporter who had been dressed in a light cotton shirt in front of an ancient and formidable palace. Greta stared at Peter's face. He looked so different — burdened, older — not the same boy who had gushed over his escape on Star Rock.

Peter looked directly into the camera. "The men who murdered my parents are cowards. They are afraid of what will happen if my people are given the power to govern themselves."

The reporter returned. "The current government has encouraged their king to return to them and take his rightful place on the throne. King Bhekizitha had this to say in response."

"I recognize no government but one freely elected by the great people of Lesotho. The ones holding my country captive are not leaders. They are usurpers."

Greta grimaced as the camera switched to show scenes of soldiers beating students.

"The people seem to agree with their king." The reporter announced. "Protests are erupting throughout the country — calling for free elections and the return of their monarch. Hundreds of protesters have been arrested and are being held without charges. There are also regular reports of torture. The government has issued a statement saying King Bhekizitha is the one responsible for these unfortunate events. They say if he were only to return, the people wouldn't need to protest and the government wouldn't be forced to keep the peace."

Peter's face reappeared. "It saddens me to be apart from my country. However, if there is anything I have learned through this ordeal, it is not to underestimate people — no matter how powerless they might appear. Until I am reunited with my home, I must hope someday soon we shall be free and know peace."

"Wise words from a fifteen-year-old king, who will most likely have to live in hiding for many years to come. This is Robert Monroe reporting live from Maseru. Kevin, back to you."

Greta clicked off the television and sat down on the couch. She stared at the blank screen, trying to process all she had seen and heard and felt.

The phone rang. She reached for the receiver.

"Greta, is that you?" She didn't say anything. All she could see were those students — they looked to be not much older than Mario.

"Greta? Are you there?"

"Mama?"

"Yes, baby. Are you alright? Is everything okay?"

"It's fine. I'm fine. I was just distracted, that's all."

"Oh." Mrs. Washington didn't sound convinced. "I let the phone ring five or six times, Greta. Weren't you in the house?"

"I was here, Mama. I was just —"

"Distracted," her mother finished.

"Yes."

"Well, you better not get so 'distracted' you burn down the building."

Greta smiled. "No, ma'am."

"Good girl. Now, I'm on my way but I missed the 5:50 so I'll have to catch the 6:05. I just wanted to let you know so you wouldn't worry."

"Okay, Mama."

"What delicious meal are we having for dinner tonight?"

"*Enchiladas de mole.*" Of all the things Tia had taught Greta to make, it was her mother's favorite.

"Yum. I may just have to run home."

Greta laughed.

"Okay, baby. I'll let you get back to your magic. I'll be home soon. I love you."

"I love you too, Mama."

Greta replaced the receiver and returned to the kitchen. She fried the rest of the tortillas, shredded the chicken and stirred the sauce.

A thought occurred to Greta and she went to her mother's bedroom. She wasn't sure why she was doing this or what made her think of it now, at *this* moment. She was often alone at their apartment. Perhaps it was something about seeing Peter, fearing for him, remembering where she had been a month ago. She opened the door and stepped inside. Her pulse began to quicken. If her mother came home and saw her, Greta wouldn't know *what* to tell her.

She went right to the bedside table. Greta was certain this is where it would be. She opened each of the drawers, rifling through their contents. Nothing. She thought about it, thought about how Mario and Dinora, Seymour and Zoë would have found something. She closed her eyes and imagined them with her, helping her. She pulled out the first drawer again but this time felt underneath. There was something taped to the underside of the drawer. She smiled and gently pulled it off.

In the photograph, a younger version of her mother was posing with a handsome young man. They both seemed so happy — carefree and innocent. Greta had never seen her mother look like this. She wondered if that young woman even existed anymore. Greta's gaze lingered on every detail, memorizing it in her heart. It looked as if her mother was laughing at something the man had just said.

Greta allowed herself to scrutinize his face more closely. The eyes didn't look quite as sad, but they were the same — she was sure of it. She turned the picture over, recognizing Tia's elegant handwriting immediately.

Susan and David, Summer 1954

Greta still struggled to think of the word to perfectly describe David's eyes. They were sad and hopeful and something else. They seemed oddly familiar. Then it struck her and she felt her heart leap. Slowly, she walked over to the mirror above her mother's bureau. She stood before it and cleared her mind of all expectations. She tried to imagine what it would be like to see her face for the first time, impartially, like a stranger would. When she felt ready, she looked up decidedly and stared at the image in front of her. The chin was sharp, making the girl's face heart-shaped. Her lips were full, her cheeks thin. Her nose was cute, turning up ever so slightly at the tip. And her eyes were…sad and hopeful and something else. Greta's mind swarmed with questions.

Epilogue

She heard the key in the lock. Quickly, she taped the picture back underneath the drawer and rushed to turn off the bedroom light. She re-entered the living room just as her mother came through the front door.

"Hi, baby. Mmm — that smells good. Here, help me with these, will you?" Mrs. Washington passed grocery bags to her daughter. "Thank you!" She sighed with exhaustion and leaned down to unzip her boots. Once discarded, she flopped dramatically onto the couch. "Greta, honey, remind me never to wear those things again. They're cute — but not that cute. My feet are killing me."

Greta smiled at her beautiful mother.

"What?" asked Susan Washington.

Greta set down the groceries and climbed onto her mother's lap. She laid her head on her shoulder and felt her mother's arms wrap tightly around her. She was so happy.

"You're lovely," she said.